A

1

Dedicated to Washington Irving who put our town on the map, and to my son

Malcolm who walked these woods with me.

Table of Contents

Prolog

1. Another Day, Another Debt

2. Bounty in Hand

3. Richard No More

4. All Downhill

5. A Few Oohs and Aahs

6. These Streets

7. The Book of Damen Willem

8. Damen Howls Like the Wind

9. Most Haunted

10. Sick in the Soul

11. Brimstone, Mama, Brimstone

12. The Heart of the Matter

13. Trapped

14. Under the Spell

15. A Midnight Visitor

16. God's Many Mansions

17. The Hayride

18. It's All Over

19. Prayers and Rest

20. Footsteps in the Pink Snow

Epilog

Call me Richard, please. Don't call me Rich because I'm not. Don't call me Dick because I don't act like one, though I guess you should be the judge of that. I insist on being called Richard though I know this may indicate a neurosis or mental defect. Worst of all is the sobriquet, "Poor Richard," which some people still say, if only behind my back. What is left when life comes to a stop? Memories. Memories, which I put up on a shelf, to be dusted off once in a blue moon. Memories which I didn't want to remember because they hurt too much. Does that make any sense? There isn't any mystery. My fiancée died. I wanted to cry out, Am I not the same Richard that I was before? But, mostly I didn't say anything at all.

I just wanted to go to work and come home again. I certainly didn't want to be "Poor Richard." Didn't Michael J. Fox say, "Pity is a form of benign abuse?" Where did I read that? *People?*

I didn't go whale hunting, or even out to sea. All I did was take the Hudson Line up to Sleepy Hollow to collect a debt. That's what I am, a bill collector. You may not like me very much after hearing this, but, someone has to balance the grand checkbook of the world. All I wanted was business as usual. Or, should I say, I only came about my cough? Isn't that what you declare when you expect something ordinary like a prescription for cough syrup, and the Kraken gets released? For that one brief shining moment, as I strode across Tarrytown, before the ambiance of the streets changed in Sleepy Hollow, I held a slice of America in my hands, and that the country I came of age in, had come back again. Time didn't shift, but something did, and I felt compelled to go back up to visit again. And again. There was no need to tell anyone about my weekend excursions, except for the cat.

Was I bewitched, bothered and bewildered by the legendary region? No, but I did get my money's worth. I was bemused by the quirky, local people, bothered by Halloween events and spooky settings, and possibly bewitched by a post-Revolutionary War journal which purported to contain "rare doings," and "odd usage of local vegetation," which I bought in a second-hand store as a souvenir. I only purchased it because I wanted to remember my day. A schoolteacher I befriended up there likes to say, not without humor that I am the guy from New York City who went up to Sleepy Hollow one man but came back another.

Maybe this journal didn't unravel an age-old, storied mystery as much as it unlocked a rocky heart. At first, my Hudson Valley excursions did me some good by getting me out of the house on the weekends. That was miracle enough. What did I find that kept me coming back, you ask? Of course, you will want to know about the Headless Horseman. There was a man up there without a head who was quite dead, though he didn't get it. How could he, brainless as he was? I suppose that even before the Headless Horseman arrived upon the scene, the chase was on. Already adept at chasing myself up hill and down, all about the town, I would soon learn to stand outside myself watching myself. That was all rational enough.

But, from where did this strange urge to dig, to literally dig up the ground beneath my feet, come? Something up there unearthed that compulsion. One thing just leads to another. You do have to step out of yourself to find yourself. And, others. Truth is, if I hadn't gone to

Sleepy Hollow I wouldn't have a story to tell at all. I'm no Washington Irving. Who is? I wish I were a better man with a story to tell. Or, a worse man with a better story. I can say for myself that I did manage to keep my head. Even if you do not believe the half of what follows, it will still be true.

Chapter One

Another Day, Another Debt

There, in Sleepy Hollow, where Beekman Avenue meets Broadway, two imposing fire trucks stood on opposite sides of the street. Their ladders bent and raised at right angles to meet in the middle, draped a slab of an American flag over the scorched tar. Tarrytown boasted an impressive blue rescue truck, and a yellow, hook and ladder, but these were splendidly red. That blue and yellow color combination reminded me of someone's high school jacket, but the image did a quick fade. Nothing can beat tradition. Toys from childhood came to mind. The heat was red too. Red hot that is. On this sweltering day in late August, the only refuge from the sun was the flag's shadow.

To a city slicker like myself, the vehicles seemed too large for the – well; I hate to use the overused word- "quaint" towns. Sweating there in the sun, the drama of it took me. Reality and expectation often don't meet in the middle, even if fire truck ladders do. Then it hit me that though much of the setting was quaint, the heart of Sleepy Hollow was not. I didn't get what was going on. What was I expecting? Ducks in a pond? Up tails all? A farm with pigs in the mud? Women in long dresses with flouncy bonnets and men in straw hats, knee breeches, and broadcloth shirts? What was it with these bodegas? Shouldn't there be a souvenir store over there? Stores offering money order deals to Ecuador? Where's the tourist office? Where did all these dark-skinned people, who lined the street with sad faces, come from? All that was needed was a grave. Did all these people live in the apartments over the stores or the few freestanding houses at the top of the steep street?

It was too late for Independence Day and too early for Labor Day, so a parade would not be in order. Judging by the looks on their faces, these folks were not exactly in a festive mood. A white-haired woman wearing a fast food uniform, stood outside the laundromat with her muscular arms folded tightly across her chest. A young girl, a writer, might say, a slip of a girl, slumped against her. An overweight, but cute, middle-aged woman sitting on a bench outside the Adirondack Bank, looked at her watch, then quickly disappeared inside. I knew I was out of the city when the bank's logo included an acorn. That bank was my destination. I had come up to collect a mechanic's lien at the closing of a condo at the heart of Tarrytown. My line of work made me about as popular as rain on the Fourth of July, but someone had to collect outstanding debts and make things meet in the middle. Maybe that explains why those two fire trucks were so satisfying.

People talk about Karma. Sometimes they even call it a bitch. Such people show a lack of understanding. A bitch is malicious and spiteful. Look it up. Karma seeks to put things back into balance. It's as simple as making tepid water by adding cold to hot. Karma is mandatory, dispassionate, and deserved. For every deadbeat, cheater, and flimflammer, a day of reckoning will come. We may hope to see it in our lifetimes, but probably won't. When I thought about it, which wasn't very often anymore, I took satisfaction in being part of this balancing act. Like most, I was only a cog in the wheel.

The streets had changed. Crossing over from Tarrytown, which ended at the north end of Patriot's Park, I saw an ornate, wooden sign announcing Sleepy Hollow. Some tourists were posing in front of it. A man was trying to take his girlfriend's picture though she kept dissolving into laughter. "Make a horror face!" he asked so loudly I could hear him on my side of the street. They must be from New York City. The sign gave atmosphere to the open expanse, but the backdrop was the local high school. There was a row of professional buildings on the other side of the street and middle and elementary schools next to the high school. Set back from those buildings there was a much older looking administration building with some satisfying architectural details, and a small, red, modern schoolhouse tucked into a corner. An impressive town clock and signposts indicating historical sites beckoned me from up the street, but Beekman, the main artery in Sleepy Hollow, took a turn for the worse. The main drag seemed a throwback to 1950's. Time, or the economy, had faltered here.

I may have been all about business, but something in the street scene kept its hold on me. An oddly shaped cupola topped off a mobile phone store. A Medicaid mill was housed in a building that had probably been a movie theater back in the 50's and 60's. *The Strand* was embossed on the side. The squat but pleasing, red brick bank had a aroused a feeling of nostalgia. Blocks, mismatched in color, chipped, dark green window boxes sprouting tilted geraniums, and a hand-painted, wooden sign, were genuine. This was the stuff of my childhood on Long Island. Unreliable materials require far too much testing. How far down do I have to dig? I thought the world owed me surfaces firm enough to keep me from falling through the cracks. Too many faux exteriors, attempting to pass themselves off as the real thing, have us surrounded. Columns and fronts of even major structures like supermarkets and box stores, dribble Styrofoam out onto the sidewalks. Ripped canvas over Styrofoam, masquerades as stone on all too many building facades or even as iron on street lamps. Doesn't take too long for material like that to reveal its true nature. I need to be grounded in a reality that won't slip out from under my feet. How did we let this happen?

Just as I started to enter the bank, the shrill shriek of bagpipes shot right up my spine. The hot air, which seemed incapable of stirring, wavered. A funeral procession began making its way up to the corner from the bottom of the hill. Death would explain those grim faces. Reality enough for any man. Dark expressions and clothing contrasted with the sparklingly blue water of the Hudson which flashed between the distant trees in the full green leaf of summer at the bottom of the hill. Things were going sour, and I had the feeling that maybe I didn't want to be there anymore.

Suddenly the flag-draped casket appeared. I blinked. It had been placed in a caisson which was being pulled up the street by two, powerfully built, dark horses. Black and white montages of the Kennedy funeral flashed before my eyes, images from newsreels which had been with me as far back as I could remember. Someone important must have died. When the small, slumped, Hispanic woman's eyes caught mine; I asked, "Can you tell me who passed away? Please?" I should have said, "Por favor? She might not know a word of English. Any attempt at Spanish on my part would be ludicrous. Why can't they speak English? We could attend church together. No need for a separate service. Why can't I let things go? I worried about everything. I was never going to be good with people. If I am to banter on, give me a good topic to banter. Make me a proper introduction. Let's not go too deep. How do you get close to people? Caught between being either overly polite or too blunt, I rarely got my approach right.

Now I had done it. Why did I have to be curious? I could have gone into the bank to bide my time before the closing began. My simple question released the sluice gate. Tears, tears I had no idea how to handle, spilled out along with a stream of words: "The marine, he died. His name, Ricardo Abarca. He shot himself. He shot himself in the head. His mother. His poor mother," she replied. She struggled to breathe. At 6'3, I must have stood a foot over her head. Suddenly I became self-conscious about my height. My hand reached out, fumbling about the air more like a paw. I didn't know what to say or do. No tears. Please. Good thing I am a stranger in town. Not much would be expected of a daytripper. Seeing the young woman break down, the heavy set woman uncrossed her arms and drew her to her breasts. In Spanish, they found words to express their grief. Good thing women are so much better at this in any language. As her sobs quieted down to sniffles, I felt like someone had taken me down from a meat hook. A better man would have done more.

The piping stopped. The street went silent. The hush served as an acknowledgment that words in any language would fail. No cry could be loud enough for the dead man to hear them now. Any flares he may have sent up before placing a gun to his head had gone unnoticed. Judging by his funeral, somebody loved him. Or, maybe this was the love that comes too late, more remorse than care. Must have been this insane war with Iraq. A phalanx of images marched into my imagination: weapons of mass destruction no one could ever find, the execution of a dictator who no one cared about anyway, veterans who blew up, not in armored, but transport vehicles, our tedious presence in Afghanistan, the World Trade Center, greedy corporations.

Once these processions started up, there would be no stopping them. Why not throw in the Crusades for Christ sake? Of course, it might be that no one knew what drove this guy over the edge. He sure must have been proud to show off that uniform on the first day he tried it on. A United States Marine. He was probably 5'7 or so. Though I would have towered over him, I would have never measured up. What me, fight? No one would take that much care in arranging my funeral.

This heat was just unbearable. What was the old expression? It was something about mad dogs and Englishman in the noonday sun. Taking off my sweaty glasses, I wiped my brow, then pushed my hair back off my forehead. Across the street, a slim, blond boy stood over a fallen purple bike. Was he watching me? A roly-poly Spanish boy mindlessly spun the front wheel by kicking it. The blond boy put his fingers to his temple to form a revolver. "Pow! Pow! Pow!" he shouted, crumpling to the sidewalk. What a lousy thing to do. He shot himself in the head but clutched his stomach as he fell. Of course, he was just a kid. Why aren't these boys in school? Someone call the attendance officer. His fat friend pulled him back to his feet which were covered in white Converses. Some things never go out of style.

Things started wavering before my eyes. Even the early morning sun had shown no mercy. What could it do now but boil the tar off the streets at midday? There was more than the heat troubling my head, but it would take me a while to get it. Something inside might have started stirring. All I knew then was it was time to get this all over with, so I went inside the bank.

The day had begun ordinarily enough. I got out of bed with my usual refrain, "Another day, another debt to collect." Business as usual. The closing for the Tarrytown condominium was being held at the Adirondack Bank in Sleepy Hollow. The Bronx contractor, who had worked hard to make it saleable, would finally get paid. Last minute deals had been worked out to avoid a short sale. Simple as that.

From my apartment in the Flat Iron district in Manhattan, I made my way through the littered streets to the subway on East Twenty-Third Street. I was lucky enough to catch the express to Grand Central. I don't know why I was in such a hurry because the ticket lines were endless. All these people buying tickets! Don't they hold monthly passes or something? Let them buy their tickets on the train at higher rates. They're rich enough if they can afford Metro North. Eight million people on the island of Manhattan, and they're all here on my queue buying tickets for the Hudson, Harlem, or New Haven lines.

Grand Central. Some things about it were eternal though much restoration was needed to bring back its faded glory. With the Kodak billboards removed, the sun streamed down through massive iron windows, not unlike the lighting found in the great cathedrals of this world; people were compelled to look up. Well, not everyone. Marble walls and floors, constellations frescoed on ceilings, ticket sellers sitting in fancy cages, all recalled the days when train travel was the only way to go. And the sounds were equal to the sights, from the screeching of the trains to the cacophony of multicultural New Yorkers, who no matter what language they spoke, were guaranteed to be loud. A young woman, with a wavering, sweet, soprano, Joan Baez like voice sang Judy Collins songs on the lower level, while above, a classically trained cellist played the Elgar concerto. Someone said that the Philharmonic wanted him, but he was too unstable mentally. He did have a nasty habit of jumping out at people. Such talent! Wonders never cease. With its landmark status, Grand Central would retain its glory, though, whether time or terrorists would bring it down, only time will tell.

"Only forty-five minutes from Broadway," George M. Cohan sang of Yonkers. I think it was Yonkers. The reader can Google it. I can only do so much. Anyway, this could almost be said of Tarrytown as well. The express does it in less. It was worlds away. On a few occasions, I had taken this train past the Bear Mountain Bridge all the way to Poughkeepsie, the end of the line. The views of the Hudson alone were worth the trip. You go through the dark, dirty tunnel to emerge at Ninety-Sixth Street, that great divide between the rich and poor. On the one side the affluent neighborhoods of Lenox Hill, Carnegie Hill, and Yorkville. On the other, El Barrio or East Harlem. The great divide had not been written in stone. Though most of the Clinton Foundation had moved downtown, Bill Clinton still kept an office near the famed Apollo Theater. Instead of coming up to see performances, then scurrying back to the safety of midtown, lower Manhattan, the outer boroughs or suburbs, before they turned into pumpkins or something, middle and upperclass people were buying homes in Harlem. Some people cried whitewashing! Gentrification! New York was not a city to stop and listen. New York was the city that didn't sleep.

The first grand sight that used to greet Metro-North riders emerging from the tunnel was the crumbling Corn Exchange. An eye-catcher even in its dilapidated state, it gave an "Abandon all hope ye who enter here" message. What a broken down ruin of classic, terracotta brick. Not too long ago, you could see junkyards complete with junkyard dogs below the tracks. All this had been cleaned up. Since the nineteenth-century brick base of the Corn Exchange had achieved landmark status, a modern steel structure was designed to rise above it. If you think this is impressive, go downtown and see the modernized Bellevue.

The Bronx was looking better too. Now riders can glide past the old and new Yankee Stadiums. Subway series that night. Yanks versus Mets. I hoped to be home in time to see the game on TV. Soon came Riverdale which many people believed was in Westchester since it was much too upscale to be part of the Bronx. Yonkers, which some wag had called, "The sewer of Westchester," brought a return to reality with its Industrial library complex, McCondos on the riverfront. After that, the towns started spreading out and becoming greener. Ah! Westchester, where your taxes and property values rival New York City.

I was that rare thing, a native New Yorker. Wedged between a stone and a brick structure, my apartment building on East Twenty-First Street, now lay some fifteen miles down the track. The dark blue, light-filtering drapes and barred fire escape window, kept the drug addicts and vagrants at bay, allowing me to take refuge in books, movies, sports, and the Internet so I could live with my lone wolf, sour psyche. Or that's at least that's what my brother Stanley said. He lived in Philadelphia with his wife and child. New York had soured him. Stan left for Philly, and mom, sans dad, went to Florida. Not much I could do about it. Just get on with it. I couldn't step outside my front door without stepping over people who were strewn about like broken glass, but I wasn't going anywhere.

Except to Tarrytown and Sleepy Hollow for the day, that is. I might have heard the announcements of Ludlow, Yonkers, Glenwood, but then zoned out. Not until I heard, "Tarrytown!" did I tune back into reality. It felt good to get out into the relatively fresh air and stretch my legs. Cabs were lined up just north of the station, but who needs unnecessary expenses? If only it hadn't been so damn hot. As I started walking about, I could see why the town made the Forbes list of the ten prettiest towns in America. Striding up Main Street, I turned left to Broadway and headed for Sleepy Hollow. A huge, blue rescue truck was sitting in its berth at the firehouse. Flower baskets were hung on the lampposts. The earth rose up in natural tiers. From the top of the hill, I could look down the winding main street to get a grand view of the Hudson. Topping this all off was a golden dome. Or was the gleaming color just the glint of the sun. The foothills of the Adirondacks wavered blue in the distance. On any other day, the air at this height would have been bracing. I felt an almost imperceptible stirring in the air. That was the last breeze I would feel that day.

The fact that this village, and the neighboring town, had formed the setting for *The Legend of Sleepy Hollow,* was evident in the iconic images. Depictions of the awkward, schoolmaster Ichabod Crane, with the rearing Headless Horseman, flaming pumpkin in hand, in hot pursuit, were ubiquitous. The local restaurant was called *The Headless Hessian*. The real estate office was *Legendary*. On the shields of police cars and police uniforms, fire trucks, and ambulances, the pair kept up the chase. They reappeared, in different colors and styles, on official vehicles in Sleepy Hollow. Look out! One came galloping up on the front of a squad car as I turned onto Beekman. Here they come again on the grimy windows of a corner bike shop. Look up! The Horseman loomed overhead, in bright contrast, on the stain glass windows of the Sleepy Hollow Village Hall. An artist had depicted the characters in such rich detail on the side of a volunteer ambulance; the panel would not have been out of place in a museum. The pair chased each other all over town, or I should say towns.

But even a region steeped in such dreamy fantasy as this could not keep the daylight out. I had a debt to collect. The locals had a funeral to attend. That schmo of a seller who had stiffed so many people was about to get his comeuppance. All that hammering, sawing, and painting was about to be paid in full There would be nothing for the seller. The devil was coming for his due. The looks on sellers who saw their profits slipping out between their grubby fingers like crumbling grains of sand were satisfying. I enjoy seeing faces sorrier than my own. I never thought that I would be in for a reckoning of my own.

Chapter Two

Bounty in Hand

Inside the bank, an attractive receptionist directed me to a back office. The closing was scheduled to begin at three. I was right on time. The woman I had seen sitting outside now sat at a large, oval, French-polished, table along with three men in dark suits. She gave me a sweet smile. A portly man, with upturned lips, got up to greet me. "Richard Post? Thomas Connelly here. I represent the mortgage company." He must have been about seventy. Don't people retire these days? After I had answered him in the affirmative, he introduced in turn, Brooke Deering, the buyer, Leon Lazzari, her curly haired attorney, and Nathan Roth, the seller's attorney, a tall, elegant man with a trim mustache. Except for the banker, everyone was about thirty-five. I too was pushing forty. All the men wore dark, pinstriped suits on the hot, hazy day. Miss Deering, was refreshing in polka dot blouse, and pink, pleated skirt. I congratulated myself on my wardrobe choice, a lightweight, tan suit. My dad would have worn seersucker. Does anyone wear seersucker anymore? We shook hands all around.

"Richard has come to collect some liens," Connelly declared. Oh, Oh! Scanning the room, I realized the seller was not present. With his curled lips, frozen in a smile, Connelly acknowledges, "There are problems in paradise. Our seller has yet to arrive." Brooke frowned. The attorneys looked bored. "Tsk, tsk," I added. There goes any hope of having time to poke about the historic districts of the two towns. Better to go straight home to catch the Yankees.

"Have you seen the property, *The Milepost* condominium, Richard?" Connelly inquired. I shook my head. "You really should see it. You will be impressed." The lawyers didn't care.

"No, I came up from New York City. 'Strolled through Tarrytown a little. I am not familiar with the area though I believe my parents brought me up here when I was a kid. Years and years ago."

"Well, Brooke here is buying into a grand building situated at the heart of 'old and storied Tarrytown.' A stately, red brick edifice near Hamilton Place and Route 9. It dominates the town center. Back in history, a tavern stood on the spot. In more recent times a school occupied the block, which, after extensive renovation became *The Milepost.* There are still some folks about who attended school there. Recently, I saw a woman standing outside slack-jawed and pop-eyed. She was hoping to revisit her alma mater. Brooke teaches elementary school in a New York City public school."

"You are the rightful owner, Ms. Deering. Not only will you reside in a former schoolhouse, but you will carry on the noble profession of America's most legendary schoolmaster, Ichabod Crane," I said to keep the conversation going. I sounded stilted. Brooke gave another sweet smile. Compared to the vacuous orbs of the others seated at the table, her eyes were positively glowing.

"Not sure I could sleep nights there with all those, tortured children haunting the premises. I would hear their groans. Must be my memories of Catholic school in Yonkers. Those nuns in black habits! 'Looked like giant bats flapping around my befuddled head." Connelly guffawed at his joke while the attorneys bowed their heads as if in prayer, to study their cell phones.

"Were you naughty in school, Mr. Connelly?" asked Brooke.

"Well, now. Way back then, the good sisters didn't hesitate to smack their students' hands with wooden rulers. Even small infractions had to be punished. On most days, my palms were good and red. The shillelagh stood in the corner at the ready." Connelly glanced around the table to see if he could draw the lawyers into the conversation. Apparently, their cellphones had sucked up their souls.

"Ichabod Crane would have approved. One of his favorite adages was 'Spare the rod, spoil the child.' He would have been secure in the belief that the little-chastised urchin would be grateful for the discipline for the rest of their lives," Brooke added.

"Now we're back to religion because that saying can be found in the Bible, *Book of Proverbs*. Don't you ever believe that Catholics don't read their Bibles. You have to see *The Milepost*, Richard. Nothing like it. All the architectural bells and whistles. Terracotta brick, stone wall, arches, and skylights. Set back from the street, it has a stately front lawn with a WW I monument," said the banker. I nodded.

We all fell silent. Truly waiting is the hardest part. I studied the room. Like the town, it spoke of the past. Local history in understated tones all around us. The wellpreserved, ornately carved crown molding, the stately secretary behind whose glass panels a Grecian urn rested while a phalanx of metal, British toy soldiers marched around it, and a large painting of the Hudson in a gilded frame on the back wall, set the tone. Roth finally surrendered his phone to his breast pocket. His now restless fingers started to beat a steady tattoo on the shiny table top. Lazzari dozed off in the chapped leather chair. Pulling out a paperback edition of *The Poems of Emily Dickinson*, Brooke buried her nose in the book. I turned my head sideways to read the spine. Tilting her head at the same angle, Brook beamed me a smile. "Yes, 'a certain slant of light.'"

I was not thinking about poetry, but the line did sound vaguely familiar.

The sad, brown eyes of that dead marine transfixed mine from the front page of a local newspaper which someone had thrown on a vacant chair. No death in the afternoon for me please, I wanted to shout. I'm sure no one would have minded, I thought as I averted my gaze. They wouldn't bother to pay attention. To break the unnerving silence, I asked Brooke: "How did you come to choose Tarrytown? Will you continue to work in the city?"

"I came up here with my parents when I was about ten. My mother insisted on weekend excursions to historical or educational places. I suppose it was just one of her phases. My first encounter with *The Legend of Sleepy Hollow* was the Disney cartoon version. It cast a spell. I went down under the spell. I just fell in love with the story, the spookiness as well as the fun of it, and the entire Hudson Valley region. The condo is pricey for me. I will have to learn to do the commute. Some days it takes me over an hour to travel from Middle Village, Queens, where I now reside, to my school on East Twenty-Third Street. So it won't be that bad. Of course, I will still have to take the subway downtown. The building has no amenities. No sauna, or tennis court. No private patios, or terraces. I will have a seasonal view of the Hudson if I stand tippy-toe in the corner of the living room. The less expensive *The Hamilton,* a co-op building across the way next to the Croton Trail, has better views."

I could have, should have, spoken up about the coincidences: my childhood visit to the region, the proximity of my apartment building to Brooke's school, but I didn't. Sizing her up as a dreamy, romantic, the literary type, I both admired and pitied her. She was throwing years of scrimping and saving at a grand, but overpriced location. Location, location, location. She would get revitalizing nights away from the fray of the big, bad New York City schools. You could never pay me enough even to set foot in one of those public zoos. Not the glassy, modern ones who aged so prematurely, or the older, more gothic ones that sank upon the foundations, or even the more familiar yellow, brick ones. Growing tired of cataloging school architecture, I put my hands behind my head, and sat back. Not much to do. I checked the cell phone. Not much happening.

Dust particles hovered in the high afternoon sun. The soldiers still marched around the urn in the cabinet, and the marine still stared at me from the newspaper. Nathan Roth's fingers kept tap, tap, tapping. The pendulum on the wall clock swung hypnotically back and forth. As it began to chime, the door swung open, and into the room blustered the long anticipated seller. Out of breath, overweight, and most likely overdrawn at the bank, the man plumped himself down next to Brooke. In a cold, dry tone, Roth introduced his client as Joseph Goggins. Raising a chubby hand to swipe at his straggly, bright red hair, Goggins accidentally popped open the buttons on both his light blue shirt and his seersucker jacket. Ah, so some men still do wear seersucker. With his exposed stomach grazing the table's edge, he reached out to shake hands with all parties. Judging by the look of Roth's face, the man's attorney couldn't stomach him. Moving a large stack of papers to the center of the table, Connelly announced, "Let the signing begin."

The left-handed Ms. Brooke repositioned the papers so she could put her John Hancock/initials on each and every page of the impressive stack. The usual. As she signed her savings away, the men took turns congratulating her on the wisdom of her purchase. Brief explanations of clauses, followed by a pointing finger, kept the action going. Papers were shuffled. The ballpoint pen scratched. A check was about to be cut for me. Nods of approval abounded, though Goggins kept shaking his blubbery face.

Then we hit a snag. As Brooke positioned her hand to sign yet another document, Goggins abruptly announced, "Uh. Oh. I forgot to bring the keys to the unit. Not to worry, Brooke. Just give me a ring in a few days, and I'll take care of it. I promise." He put his hand up to indicate "Call me." He just made me sick. Why did such people exist? Just when you thought everything was in order, you get blindsided. Maybe it was my imagination, but Brooke suddenly seemed older. I had been thinking thirty-five, thirty-six, but now forty seemed moré accurate. Young men might have seen her as their mother. In a few years, they will call her grandma. Her wide, childlike eyes narrowed to slits. All the sense of wonder went out like a light. Turning to her lawyer, Brooke protested, "He hardly returns my calls as it is. . . "

The Italian raised his hand with the large palm facing out. Pushing back in his chair, and folding his solid arms across his chest, he proclaimed, "We're not closing until we get the keys. Without the keys, the deal is off."

Ha. Ha. Ball in your court, you Goggins had. Of course, he wasn't giving in without a fight. Shaking his head, he gave it the old college try. Evidently, he was used to getting his way. Roth was having none of it. "Go back. Go back, Mickey Mouse, and get the damn keys." What a pathetic excuse of a client. Was Roth even getting his fee? Faltering back up to his feet, Goggins headed for the door. His entire body deflated with each step. Since Nathan Roth assured us that his client only lived a few blocks away, I figured he'd be back soon. He needs to get every cent he can into his hot little hands. The wait was on again. Again, the silence returned. The pendulum swung. The fingers tapped. That dead face grabbed at me again too. Don't look at me I silently pleaded. I started calculating. Ten minutes to his house, ten minutes to locate the keys, another ten to return. I told myself just to hold on until Goggins got back. I started engaging in a compulsive habit, scanning the corners of the room for dust. Then I ran my fingers through my hair to see if I needed a haircut. I examined my tie for lint.

The clock chimed four. As if on cue, Goggins stumbled back in. You wouldn't think him exactly swift on his feet, but at least he came back. The keys jangled across the slick table. Wooden heads came back up at the startling sound. Connelly and Lazzari reached for the keys simultaneously. Lazzari won. Passing the keys to Brooke as if they were a holy relic, he declared, "Back in business." A few more signatures and I would be able to secret my bounty, the check, in my satchel. Patting it for dramatic effect, I stood up to go. "Brooke Deering, the rightful owner of unit 3B of the Milestone Condominium, 28 North Broadway, Tarrytown, Lower Hudson Valley, the state of New York," the banker, declared with a flourish of his hand. Oh please don't add America, Earth, Milky Way, the Universe.

"Everything will be uphill from here; I'm sure of it," prophesized Goggins. I figured he was addressing himself. An attempt at humor or did he just get it backward? Around the table, hands started knocking on wood. Not mine. Not even in jest would I give in to superstition. Now it seemed there couldn't be enough handshaking. Wonderful to see people taking their lives in new directions. My mounting up a sense of faith that quickly collapsed. New beginnings work for the people you see in church. I didn't see them because I didn't go to church. Another day. Another debt. Bounty in hand, I headed for the door.

Chapter Three

Richard No More

I woke up the next morning drowning in sleep. Images that were holding on even as they were letting go stuffed my head. Pink lipstick, red hair, loud laughter from a wide mouth, spiraling away, along with cowboys and trumpets. One thing was missing, and that was my hacking cough. I didn't miss that at all. Three weeks sans alcohol cleared up my lungs. The Scotch says a good whiskey will clean out your lungs. I guess it went the other way with me. That's the yin and yang of it. Not that I drank that much. A few shots in the evening to put my lights out. My lame cat, Chester, a good old boy, jumped up on the bed to nuzzle my face. Yes, I named him after the character in the old TV Western, *Gunsmoke.* His right leg was stiff. Not sure why, but it was like that since he was a kitten. It didn't seem to bother him much. Good thing he didn't run around calling out, "Mr. Dillon! Mr. Dillon!" That would spoil a perfect peace. He circled all around my legs to the kitchen.

It was 7:45 on a Saturday, but since I was up, I stayed up. I put some whole grain bread in the toaster and made instant coffee. Chester got salmon cat food and a fresh bowl of water. Placing the butter and marmalade on my multipurpose card table, I flicked on the TV. The center of the table had a checkerboard that flipped over to reveal a Mahjong board. I had to be careful not to flip it with the coffee resting on it. Or Chester for that matter. For a moment, I experienced sadness in thinking no one would ever play games on the table. The Olympics were over but the presidential race on, full speed ahead. Since I didn't care much for the candidates, I tuned much of it out.

Going over to the window, I looked through the bars down to the street. The junkies were up and about. Did they care about the president? The only issue they cared about was their benefits. They were heading for McDonald's on Twenty-Third Street for breakfast. The one with the yellowish-gray hair and beard looked up. Could he sense my presence three flights above the street? I held my ground for the principle of it. Ground? What ground? I was defending a space that hovered in the air. Sky space. Apartment living. You don't know your neighbors. You don't even see them half the time. You don't care to see them. Those derelicts would fill themselves up with cheap food and cigarettes now, drugs later. They would beg for money all afternoon. Filled with brotherly love, they would hug each other. Good comrades. Then, at the drop of a hat, they would go for the jugular. The snarling, cursing and shoving would start. I suppose I should feel a deep sense of gratitude for all I have. There but for the grace of God, my mother would say. I really should give her a call.

I sat back down to finish my coffee. The remains of yesterday came tumbling back into my mind. The flag-draped coffin coming up the hill, the astonishing horses, and all those people lining the streets. Where did they come from? I found myself humming

"Eleanor Rigby."

I saw them now through the wrong end of a telescope, distant and fuzzy. Then, the mourners zoomed into my face. I wished I could forget the day. It should have been just another closing. There it was playing with my head. British soldiers marching around an urn, the dead marine, Brooke Deering and her new condo, not to mention that dirty little rat of a seller. What was his name? Bobbin Head? Noggin Head? Chester started nibbling at my toast. He loved the butter. Not too sure about that marmalade, huh Chet? He licked a little, then screwed up his little, pink nose. He took his time preening his thick fur. Sirens sounded off in the distance. A pigeon landed on the window sill. Chester made the chirping sounds felines make when they see a bird.

That's about the size of it. Not much happening. Is that all there is? Was I going to have an old Peggy Lee song playing in my head now? Please. I stretched my long leg across the other kitchen chair. It wasn't as if anyone else was going to sit there. I looked out across the room. You could take the whole place in at a glance. I was interested in practicality, not décor. No traces of history here. No marching soldiers, or urns, or impressive paintings here. A functional space. Not much to look at except for Chester, with his muscular body and bold, orange tabby stripes. Having eaten, he was already circling to nestle in for a good rest. He had been up for twenty minutes or so. Maybe I should perk up the place a little. Chester should have something impressive to contemplate.

I started rummaging through the closet near the door for the still life painting my mother had given me as a house-warming present years ago. There it was behind the LL Bean snow boots. After removing the plastic covering, I held it out at arm's length. Not exactly a Rembrandt. A milky glass vase with a blue flower, a white table cloth, and a few fallen petals were all depicted in light, feathery brushstrokes. Not bad. It was my mother's taste. I could just see her leaning back to give it her consideration, with her ash blond hair swept back in a fancy chignon, in some gallery uptown. A little masculine, a little feminine. A flower, a blue flower. Scrounging up a nail from the kitchen drawer, I got out the hammer and hung it up on the wall across from the table. It looked okay, but the beige wall didn't. It could use a fresh coat of paint in a new color. That was the trouble. Changing one aspect of the décor led to another. I would resist.

Pfffffft! The day stretched out before me. It seemed even longer than my legs. I didn't know how I could bear staying inside all day on this blessed cooler, though bright, summer Saturday. We all agree it's the humidity that makes us uncomfortable, not the heat. Right? Well, the humidity it was gone. How about a trip up to Sleepy Hollow? I turned to the cat. What cha thinks Chet? Scarecrow schoolteacher? Headless Horseman? Flaming Pumpkin? A bit early for fall foliage. I know. Pre-Revolutionary graves. Now I got you, Chester. Chet rolled over on his back revealing the lighter buff color of his belly. Had I ever spoken to him in some many words before? Probably not. His legs were splayed out.

His mouth was making a snorting, snoring sounds. His sleep was good for another twenty years if he had that many. A regular Rip Van Winkle cat. It is just too quiet here. Neighbors bound to start up an argument any minute now. I swung my legs around. I would return to the Hudson Valley as a tourist to take in the sights.

After gulping down the dregs of the coffee, swallowing the last piece of toast, I started cleaning up. I placed the marmalade back up on the top shelf. Not much in the pantry here. I'll have to do some shopping. I washed the dishes in the sink. Though I gave myself a nice, close shave, I didn't want to peer into my face too closely. Not sure who I would find. Finally, an opportunity to wear those slightly busy, plaid pants. The problem was finding a solid shirt that wouldn't clash. I started scrummaging in the drawers for a white, golf shirt. OK, I look good. After putting down some more fresh water for Chester, I bent down to pet his furry, round head. Sweet dreams old boy. I got the first two locks on the door open, but the third one was so stuck that my hand slipped off it, throwing me back a step. That needs some work. It will take my hand off next time.

It was too quiet. Won't last. After agreeing with myself, I stepped out the door. Someone was lying there. Bending down, I turned the body over. I was tempted to use my foot kick his body over, but I wanted to keep some decent bones in mine. Looked pretty dicey, but you never know with these young people. Coming to with a start, he demanded, "Who the hell are you?" I began to grab on to his jacket to stand him up on his feet but then stopped my foolishness. "Just someone who pays rent to live here, that's all." I couldn't tell if he was a derelict or a scruffy, hung-over, Friday night partygoer. These grubby young people can be mistaken for homeless people. Leaving him to sleep it off, I ran down the stairs, and out onto the street. There was an elevator, but I never felt taking it. I was only on the third floor. Stepping carefully around the vomit at the curb and the broken bottles all over the sidewalk, I headed over to Twenty-Third Street. When some kids went up to climb inside the plastic tube outside McDonald's, three homeless men came scurrying out. Apparently, not every vagrant makes it to Mickey D's for breakfast. The subway steps were cracked, filled with hardened dirt that clung like barnacles. It seems like they never get swept anymore. Maybe they do. It could be that the moment they are cleared of debris, piles of litter blow right back on. A blast of unbearable heat hit my face as I skirted two derelicts fighting over money on the stairs. A woman couldn't get the Metro Card machine to accept her credit card. I was glad I had one in my wallet.

After ten minutes of tedious waiting, the faint but growing slash of light appeared on the grimy tiled, tunnel walls, the first sign that a train was coming. As it pulled in, most people stayed behind the yellow, safety line but one fool almost slammed himself into the train before it came to a stop. There is always one in every crowd. As long as it wasn't "a pusher." Didn't relish the sight of blood on the tracks. I got on in the middle of the train near the conductor. Safety first. The subway car was freezing. Where else in the world can you experience such extremes of temperature? Platforms tropical, trains, icy. Maybe exiting the overheated Macy's in Herald Square, then hitting an arctic blast of air on ThirtyFourth Street at Christmas is comparable. A man in a wheelchair pushed his way through the car to scrounge up a few bucks. A street preacher with a Caribbean accent, waited for someone to start laughing at him. He relished ending his sermon with a warning, "You may be laughing now, but God will have the last laugh!" To those who dared to mock him, he held his worn, black leather Bible up in the air, angled like an ax.

I was so glad to get off the subway; I resolved to walk next time. That is if there was a next time. Here we go again. "Only forty-five minutes from Broadway . . ." Maybe this will become my new refrain. I muscled my way through Grand Central. Guy with gold dust on the back pockets of his jeans, silver sneakers, red and white underwear exposed by his falling pants, and a price tag still attached to his flat-brimmed cap, bobbing, was weaving his way to the ticket booth. Couple with a kid with impossibly blond hair and pink skin were standing near the clock mouths agape at the wonder of New York. Two juvenile prostitutes were not so much out of place, but time. They were way too young. They looked all of fifteen. Shouldn't they turn to dust by morning? And the homeless people that Michael Bloomberg had kept at bay were creeping back in under De Blasio's weaker reign.

Things changed at the station after 9/11. My business partner had been there that day. One day after the tragedy, Stars, and Stripes started appearing all over the city. Grand Central did it up right. Enormous American flags were hung vertically from the ceiling.
Tourists posing by the clock made sure to fit Old Glory into the frame. Police, National Guardsman, military dogs were everywhere. Most arresting, though, were the posters which displayed photos of the missing. It wasn't only Grand Central which displayed these. They were all over the city. Mostly they were put up near Ground Zero. Families, writing in ink, magic marker, paint, even crayon, pleaded for information regarding the whereabouts of their missing loved ones. One poster near St. Paul's church, a structure which should have fallen given its proximity to the Towers, was blank. A cup of markers sat on the sidewalk below it. People could write their personal messages. One person wrote, "Came to pray. There is nothing else."

Grand Central had a whole wall of posters which became known as "The Wall of Mourning." It went up right after the towers fell, but it couldn't come down. The tragedy was too overwhelming: the quick change from search and rescue to search and recover was mind numbing. To take down cries for help when the city was still bleeding would be seen as an insensitive act. Families were desperate for information. People knew, even in the first few days, that individuals who don't return within twenty-four to forty-eight hours aren't coming home at all. They knew, but like parents of missing children, they didn't want to know. The fate of many victims would not be revealed until physicians sorted through body parts in refrigerated tractor trailers on site, and a decade later, in Fresh Kills landfill, in Staten Island. How many people were vaporized into the dust that about the city, block after block? I didn't see much that day. Just a few dust covered folks making their way home. I thought them lucky then. Reports of fatal cancers sucked that confidence right out.

We felt a whole lot safer when I was a kid. When had we gone up to Sleepy Hollow? I must have been ten or so. My brother Stanley and I drew an imaginary line at the dead center point of the back seat of Dad's old Buick. I told Stanley, "You don't want to know what will happen to you if you cross over this line." He would say the same to me.

Dad only complained if we got out of control. He was pretty tolerant. If Mom drove on the way back, we had to *be* quiet so we could hear the sixties music on the radio. Our parents apparently remembered far too much about that era to have been there. Songs of love and peace. Dad preferred an open window so he could lean his arm out; mom, fretting that the wind would muss up her hair, wanted the windows down. They were not always at peace. Mom usually won. "Age of Aquarius," "Good Morning Stars Shine," "Get Together" by The Youngbloods. There was Bubble Gum music too. "Build Me Up Buttercup." That sappy song. We protested against, "I am the Walrus," but any Beatles song by Ringo pleased us.

If you wanted to please us, just give us, "Octopus Garden," or "A Little Help from My Friends."

We were innocent back then. We loved, "Do You Think I'm Sexy," because it sounded dirty. It seemed we were always visiting relatives. Bay Ridge, or maybe it was Bayside. Maybe even The San Francisco Bay for all I know. Nah. I would have remembered that. So many songs and memories come back to me. "I Will Survive" brought on our hysterical laughter, but *YMCA* brought us up out of our seats. "Sit down!" mom would command. She was woman.

All these memories were now locked up in songs. I couldn't name you one song in the top one hundred today. But dad with his bushy sideburns, fat tie, narrow trousers, is right before my eyes. I didn't come up out of my reminiscences until Marble Hill. The towns started growing greener and more refreshing again. College Kid got on at Yonkers, plonked his backpack down on the middle seat, to take the aisle seat across from me. Though he studied a book for a while, he soon stopped to consult his phone. Soon he abandoned his accounting textbook to play *Angry Birds*. Accounting: good subject. Concrete. There were no such distractions like that in my college days. I didn't read too many books these days, though.

The train stopped at Hastings-On-Hudson. When the train on the opposite side pulled out, I experienced that sense of traveling backward. Soon I took out my phone to scope out the main historical sites. There was Washington Irving's home, Sunnyside, Lyndhurst Castle, and Philipsburg Manor to the north. We had an Irving monument in my neck of the woods. On Eighteenth Street and Irving Place, there was a zoo of a high school named after him. A huge bust of the author stood near the front door. The great man, depicted with a grossly bulbous forehead looked ugly, to put it bluntly. You want to hear something scary? Forget the Headless Horseman. A Washington Irving student threw a chair out the window of an upper floor, striking a pregnant woman who was walking on the sidewalk below. I was leaving all that down the tracks for the day. Good riddance. Suddenly Irving's home, Sunnyside, snug on the river bank, surrounded by trees, covered in ivy, came into view. It's sure looked historical if not haunted. Then the announcement came, "Tarrytown."

Not too many people got off the train. The station smelled of sandalwood. I was not sure if I noticed that the day before. I wasn't used to air. Without the ubiquitous skyscrapers of Manhattan, space seemed to open into inviting vistas. Crossing the parking lot, I headed for Main Street. This time I was prepared for the steep climb to Broadway. Some kids were kicking a soccer ball around down a side street in front of what looked like public housing. An old black man walked next to me for a few steps, then fell behind me. "Cardiac Hill. Cardiac Hill. You won't need an electrocardiogram if you can make it up this hill," he quipped. I gave him a nervous laugh.

With energy, if not vigor, I pushed up Main Street to the top of the hill at Neperan and Broadway. Yes, just as I expected. The air is bracing here. Looking down, I was rewarded with a grand view back down Main, a winding street of shops and cafes. I could see silver and blue glimmers of the Hudson River. The foothills of the Adirondacks, were more defined today in the cooler, crisper air. Main Street had a coffee shop, which was luckily not a Starbucks, a toy shop, a liquor store but mostly it had funky restaurants and antique shops. It was nice but not upscale like Rye or Cooperstown. This town was the real thing, a slice of Americana. Even without the ghosts and goblins, Tarrytown was a special place. How did that old NY Lottery commercial go? Charlie Weir of Tarrytown, a kind of Jimmy Stewart type, bought a lottery ticket. The rest was history.

Touch of fall was in the air. Not too many people were going about town. Small flow of locals and tourists. At the corner of Hamilton Place and Broadway, I found Brooke Deering's condo, *The Milepost*. It was impressive. Decorative orange-red brick, wide, stately lawn with the World War I monument depicting a soldier holding a rifle, bowing his head. A metal plaque indicated the presence of a time capsule dated 1989. I wonder what they had in there. A Nintendo Gameboy? Someone seemed to be watching from a window of a taller building across the Croton Trail. I thought I had left all prying eyes back in the city. They quickly withdrew.

I still had the rhythms of the city jangling in me. I had to pull in my stride to keep myself from riding up the backs of people. I was tailgating. Then it hit me that other people weren't too slow. I was too fast. This realization was not exactly an epiphany, but I made, there-and-then, a conscientious decision to slow down. When I saw people taking their coffee and pastries outside to the plastic tables at The Golden Harvester deli, I was tempted to stop for a second cup. Nah. Waste of time. I had places to see. No time for that. Resolutions sure don't last.

Heading across the town to Beekman Avenue in Sleepy Hollow, I fell into my steps from yesterday. The fire trucks were safely moored in the fire house. It was growing a little warmer. The streets here were deserted. The town did feel sleepy. It wasn't like all those European cities I had visited in my twenties during my off-to-see-the-world phase. Then, the air had always been bracing as I blazed my way from site to site. All those delightful town centers with wooden signs pointing in multiple directions. This way for the castle. That way for the cathedral. Go to the left for the museum! Go to the right for the restrooms. You won't see that last sign in New York. I dare you to find a public restroom. Some wag in Nottingham had twisted the signs so that the cathedral sign pointed to the castle. Nottingham didn't even have a castle, just a few, remaining stones. Pranks on tourists might have amused me back then. Now I think I would deeply resent each and every step it would take me to find my way back.

I soon found myself at the top of Beekman where I had to shake off the bitter memories of the funeral, the sad faces of the crowd, and, above all, the haunting eyes of the dead marine. Didn't want my spirit to sink. A better glimpse of the Hudson through the trees might have helped. Onwards and upwards Richard! Soon it will be fall. Sleepy Hollow High School had an electronic sign announcing the first day of school. It was less than a week away. There was even a touch of color in the trees, here and there. Then I saw a sign showing the way to Philipsburg Manor, a colonial restoration funded by the Rockefellers back in the 1950's. According to my map, it was on Route Nine. The Old Dutch Burying Ground and Sleepy Hollow Cemetery were just down the road from it. They buried Irving near the church, but on the other side, the Queen of Mean, Leona Helmsley and her husband Harry had a mausoleum. Oh boy. Not sure if I will have time and energy to reverse direction, and take in Sunnyside. Irving was one our first men of letters. He created lasting American characters. Everyone from Walter Huston to Johnny Depp to Tom Mison had taken on the role of Ichabod Crane. I should pay attention. Reading brochures and websites was one thing. Someday I should read the story itself.

Pausing to read the inscription of the large town clock which dominated the intersection, I was surprised. "Thanks to the people who raised funds to erect it for embodying the spirit of the legend." Shouldn't this be the other way around? The short story embodied the spirit of the people who lived in the town. All those folks are just ghosts and legends now. A police car came roaring around the corner with the Horseman rearing up on his mount of the door shield. Déjà vu all over again. Was this some warning? Had I disturbed a ghost or something? These New Yorkers.

I fell into my stride. Bending down to pick up a candy wrapper, I appreciated how much cleaner Westchester was than New York City. Let's keep it that way. Across the way, an old mansion, fit for the Addams Family, stood. Odd mixture of classic American and Gothic style. A white, picket fence lost its way, morphing into a corroded iron gate which virtually ran into a brick wall. Were they keeping us out or secreting some monstrous freak? Twin turrets rose up into a beautiful blue sky. The white, generic, energy-saving windows with their grained, plastic frames were a big let-down. Dreadful to be imprisoned there on this bright day. Small puffs of dust hovered in the air the gables. Nah. That was just my imagination.

Street names morphed. Nature calling. Pine, followed by Maple, then Spruce, where a huge pine tree, still covered in chunky, fifties style Christmas light bulbs, stood. Though such street names could be found back in the city, especially in the outer boroughs, they added to the sense of rusticity here. The city was light years away. Then the street names brought in the legend. Crane Street followed by Van Ripper. Gory Brooke Lane? Ghastly. Whose spilled blood was here? Then, I got this queasy feeling in the pit of my stomach. I swear I smelled blood. Something was wrong. I was still on Broadway, and Broadway was Route Nine. There was no colonial farm in sight. Just private houses. Sinking feeling. Glimpses of the Hudson River shimmering with the foothills of the Adirondacks in the background down every side street. Too residential. Too many dead ends. I must have taken a wrong turn. No one around to ask. I started to check the location of my phone, but there was no service. I could take it all in stride and just wander aimlessly. I could tarry. Ha. Ha. I could just dissolve into the air. Whatever happened to Richard Post, late of New York City? Dreamy Richard, who was Richard no more.

Chapter Four

All Downhill

A tall, iron gate loomed down the road. Maybe I wasn't lost. Thinking that might be the way to Phillipsburg, I forged ahead. Behind the gate was an enticing woodland. But, just putting a foot through the gate, brought on a feeling of foreboding.   Something had happened here, something odious. Where did the raw smell originate? A strange compulsion to dig up the ground right under my feet came over me. Could I find something to dig with here? Wait, I didn't even have to dig. There were bones strewn around. In broad daylight? I rubbed my eyes to look again. It was only the broken, sun-bleached branches of trees. I took the long, sturdy branch that resembled a thigh bone and started dragging it across the soil. It was slow going. I should go down on bended knees to throw the dirt between my legs like a dog, I thought.

I dug deeper and deeper in the same spot. A piece of black cloth, faded to sepia, came up. It seemed quite large. I came to my senses. I didn't need to know what was down there. I started pushing it back down and throwing the dirt over it in haste. Soon I was smoothing the ground over it, hoping no one would catch me in the act. I wouldn't have a clue what to say.

How foolish. It took a whole pack of wipes to get the dirt off my hands. What was I thinking? I don't know what I was thinking. No need to tear up the ground beneath my feet. Good thing too because if I couldn't plant my feet, I couldn't stay grounded. Did I think I might fly away? As the foreboding subsided, a sense of peace descended.   Being all alone in nature was alien to me. I didn't even try to find peace in the city. The only place of solitude in the city was my apartment. Isolated areas of Central Park held this much charm, but only for those who wanted to risk bashed-in heads.

Just when I thought I was alone, there was a startling rustling in the bushes. A huge creature reared up its head, to view me, then loped off on the path ahead. It hid its body behind a stately oak. With massive antlers scraping the lower branches of the tall tree, it held up its head to listen. I thought the deer would not become aware of my presence if I stayed quiet enough. It remained in place. I did too. Neat hoof prints on the ground. No sign of horse prints. Then again, you couldn't expect the Headless Horsemen to be prancing about the wood in broad daylight.

Wanting to get a picture, I approached the deer stealthily with my phone. I was no deerstalker. My first move sent the stately animal plunging down a slope of thick trees. Disappointed, I sat down on a rock. Long time since I had seen a deer. I tried not to take it personally. A cardinal swooped down from the upper branches above my head, streaking its flaming feathers across the path. It landed high up in the branches of a huge oak across the way. As he tweeted away, a tiny chipmunk, with a warm, reddish-brown body, scampered over my feet rushing for safety under a tree stump. Come nature; come fill up my head! I started to sing, "Come fill up my sensibilities . . ."   Take that, nature. There was no echo. I needed a cave.

Oh no. Don't tell me I am becoming the kind of guy who, at the sight of a deer, puts his hands over his heart, to sigh, "Ah! Bambi." What a lonely man I had become. All alone except for my woodland companions. A little stream gurgled and ran. Was it Gory Brooke? Had someone died here? Had someone shed blood here? It could have been me for all I knew. I felt entirely bloodless. I couldn't say that I felt dead, even back in the city, because I didn't feel my life at all. There must be one of those "carry on" aphorisms for this state of being, but all I could do was carry on. So down the road, I went.

How far would this path take me? Where would it take me? Maybe for once in my life, I shouldn't care. You work hard to manage, no, to micromanage life, and it all results in chaos anyway. Any sense of control that I thought I had over life was an illusion. It was just life's nasty little trick. Then, I realized that I wasn't so alone. A senior man and woman were walking on a parallel trail high up above me on a ridge. That must be the Croton Trail which runs from Yonkers, or maybe White Plains, up to Croton-on-Hudson. In the city, I walked between wall-to-wall people. Seeking fresh air in parks meant choking on the tobacco fumes from the nicotine addicts who pressed into outdoor areas, having been banned everywhere else. If it wasn't the nuisance of smokers, the panhandlers came up from under rocks and cracks in the asphalt to stick their hands in your face. They didn't ask for money; they demanded it. Any precious green space left should be as valued as an emerald, squared off, cut up and placed in the Museum of Natural History. Look at what was waiting for me at home? A dehumanized, and dehumanizing, city. A saner man would have thrown himself into the brook, and have done with it.

Down the sides of the path were picnic tables and a pagoda. A pagoda? How civilized. Looking up, I found the branches overhead curling into thick arches. The phrase "cathedral space" came to mind. Maybe it was "woodland cathedral." Simplify it to a sanctuary in the woods. Something from Thoreau or Emerson. Wordsworth? Something I had read back in college. Certainly, Brooke Deering would know. Dave would call her a "lit chick." "That's what you need, Richard, a lit chick." A man standing in cathedral space had to have a backstory. Oh no. That's a place I am not prepared to go.

Elements of a fairytale appeared. Every six yards or so, someone had strewn bread crumbs. They looked fresh. Perhaps that Hansel and Gretel house, the Victorian, Gingerbread, looming over the gates had been the real thing. Anything could happen here. Here was Richard, who hadn't checked his phone in twenty minutes, wandering down a path away from his destination, and, he doesn't even mind. Of course, he knew there wasn't any service available. People, though not too many people, will ask, whatever became of Richard Post? I tell you. He became a wanderer, a happy wanderer. He sang. He whistled. I should sing. I should whistle. There it was. The big chill. Things couldn't stay up. All fall down. I had to mock my happiness before someone else did.

A horse neighed. A horse neighed? Up above my path, there was a bridal path. That explains that. The end of the woods came into view. A mismatched second gate heralded the end of the line. Like the universe, there really could be no end. How would it end? With a wall? There would always be something behind the wall. This structure could be a gateway to something more. In reality, it was a dead end. A dead end, for what lie beyond the gate was Sleepy Hollow Cemetery. A broken hasp, a dangling padlock, a large, but redundant, hole in the chain link fence indicated that someone wanted in. Or out. No time to go around to the main gate. Take the back way in just like the devil. Maybe something wanted out. Cleary, the town planners, wanted a clear separation between woodland walkers and the dead, walking or not. Hopefully, it had been the living who took issue with that barrier. What was a gate to spirits who could waft across the evening dews and damps to fly as freely as the crow flies? Cue the crow. Oh, yes. One just flew overhead. Caw. Caw. Caw.

Yes, the living had broken through. So impatient were the bereaved o lay wreaths, place rocks, or pray for people who left them too soon, they found a second entrance. If I had my way, there would be a towering brick wall, well mortared, without a chink, to hold the dead in, and keep the living out. Out of sight, out of mind. That's how it should be. Take my wife. Take my fiancée. I mean it. Take her. Oh, that's right. You did. Oh, Richard, this is too much. You know her name. Diane. Just say it.

Long, skeletal fingers of death started grabbing at me, coming up out of the trees and up from the ground. Steady now. I quickened my pace. Like the deer, I was on the run. The ground was stable enough, but rocks and dirt scattered about as I flew. Abruptly I started to spin on my heel, then spun myself back. Suddenly superstitious, I turned around to touch the gate. I took myself completely by surprise. No need for a doppelganger to trail me. I could take care of that myself. I could scare myself out of my wits or back to sanity with no help from the spirits at all. I should go back to town, back to city sidewalks, to druggies and stoned vets to be the Richard I used to know, the one, who like hope, could almost float. Just go!

This movie was being played backward. Everything went into reverse. There was a brook, a gory brook, bread crumbs, a scurrying chipmunk, a swooping cardinal, and an immense deer walking toward me. Maybe he wanted to take my picture. On the trail, and out of the woods, back to Broadway, back to the fork in the road where I saw my mistake. Broadway was Route 9, but it branched out into old Broadway which led to private residences, and New Broadway which led to Douglas Park, the wooded area. Broadway itself was a broader road which pitched itself down to the river and Philipsburg Manor. An older and wiser man, I stood near the sign posts seeing how easy it was to follow the arrow to the Manor, the Old Dutch Burying Ground and the main entrance to the cemetery. Off to the manor, I went. It was all downhill.

Chapter Five

A Few Oohs and Ahs

Just as I was about to step into the street, a man came running by dripping blood from his right arm which was hanging limply at his side. One look at his bloodied clothes and wild eyes, and I wanted to flee back to the woods. "Look out behind you, man. A bear! A bear! Run for your life!" As I turned around to look, all I saw was a Mobile Station, trucks, cars, and a large, white, tour bus. "Bear!" he yelled as he loped across Route 9.

"In Westchester?" I shouted out. Lunatic. May the wind be at your back. A Smart Car practically ran up his back but screeched to a halt just in the nick of time. Cursing the driver, or the car for not having enough hood to pound or both, he headed south. Did I attract crazy people or were they just everywhere? How did he injure himself? Not much I could do about that. Now that I was back on track, I was able to follow the sign to Philipsburg which did look grand all spread out before the Hudson. Supposing it would prove worth all this trouble, I headed down the slope. To the right of the Visitor's Center, tourists were boarding a small, white bus marked, "Kykuit," the private Rockefeller Estate open now to the public. It was located somewhere up in the Pocantico Hills. I think I had read about a church up there with Marc Chagall windows. So much to see and do.

After purchasing my ticket for the manor, I inquired about Kykuit. All tours were sold out. It had to be booked in advance. I guess I will have to come back another day. If I was going to make a habit of this, I should consider buying a car. Where would I keep it? Entering Philipsburg meant leaving all the hassle of cars behind. Animals pulled carts, not caskets. The manor was inviting enough. Sheep were roaming freely. There were rather unusual breeds of hens with odd mottling. I recalled seeing birds like that in old master paintings. Later I learned they were rare breeds, the kind that was raised here when America was young. There was a barnyard cat.

"Watch out for Moses," warned an African American guide dressed in colonial garb. He introduced himself as Elijah. "Moses has long claws which he is not afraid to use on folks, especially if he doesn't know you. Let's go to the barn to milk the cow. A tour of the house will begin in fifteen minutes. Just assemble out front after we get this cow milked.

Don't forget, after that, to see the demonstration of the watermill down at the Millhouse." I fell in with the crowd.

We scrambled over to the barn where a sweet-looking cow with long, eyelashes waited in her stall. A thickset guide in a tricorn hat greeted us. The guide asked for a volunteer. A boy held up his younger brother's arm, then shoved him forward. The mom, who looked ready to scold, held herself back. I really should call my mother.

"Oh, well, OK. Meet Clover. She's a sweet-old girl. Sit down on this stool. Let's put the pail down right here. Now grab on and pull." The little fellow didn't seem too keen on reaching out under the udder. He screwed up his face. His brother laughed. The cow turned her big head around to check him out. With a now-or-never look, the boy grabbed the teat and, lo, the milk squirted out. The look of open delight on his face was priceless. The adults here wouldn't have been this amazed if they witnessed Moses part the Red Sea.

Now, this is the way it should be. Kids learning by having hands-on experiences. Adults beaming at them. That boy will never think that milk comes from the supermarket.

Was that Moses lurking about hoping for a mouthful? Time to move on. We left Clover and took off for the tour of the house. I started kicking the dirt about while waiting. People were content to stand quietly, keeping their thoughts to themselves. Of course, such calm can't last. A hearty, hale-fellow-well-met fellow started asking everyone what they did for a living and where they lived. His bold plaid pants muted mine. His red vest made him seem part of a show. Not this one, thank God. He narrowed his eyes a little when I responded, "New York City." He was good at slapping people on the back. Then we had to listen to his story.

"I'm from Pennsylvania. Not too far away. Came to catch a glimpse of the Horseman. Guess I'll have to sneak back in tonight. Anyone care to join me?" His saucy eyes scanned the group. A little girl backed up, grabbing at her mother's skirt. A few people laughed.

"I'll pass. The living dead is enough for me," I offered. As a guide opened the door to the manor to us, a group of people trickled down the stairs to exit out the back.

All the rooms were roped off. We started tramping our way through the house. The colonial exterior had a calming effect, so unlike our modern homes. This space was dark but snug. Without all the clutter, sounds gently echoed. My sojourn in the woods was still playing about my mind. I had trouble concentrating. Anyone could get lost, but had I dug up the ground? Something about Frederick Philipse taking the wrong side in the Revolutionary war, not losing his head, but being sent back to Britain. I think the guide said he went blind. What a shame. A green, quilt, a replica of the one the Philipse family had, covered the canopied bed. The guide said a college professor made it. The world sure was upside down when a Ph.D. does the work of a seamstress.

The smell of burning leaves wafted in through the open window. Do they burn leaves here? We had to save our dying air. I doubt they would make an exception here. Glancing out the window, I saw women in period dresses and bonnets cooking what look like grits on an open fire. Suddenly the cozy interior seemed suffocating. The rooms closed in. The great outdoors was calling. Green grass, sheep safely grazing and baaing, smoky air, the blue Hudson, the hazy, purple, distant mountain, drew me off. This beauty of nature, this feeling of being transported back in time, could only go so far. The call to stay in the here-and-now came from the guide who moved us down to the pantry and out the door. Like happy sheep, we all followed.

The good-looking millhouse guide looked quite at home in his colonial, broadcloth shirt, and knee breeches, wooly stockings, and handmade leather shoes. The shoe leather and belt bucket competed to outshine each other. Here was a man who loved his work. With that certain slant of his tricorn, casting could have used him in Poldark. His clothes could use a cleaning, but then again, you couldn't expect clothes to be whiter than white back then, so the stains added to the sense of authenticity. He began his presentation by holding up one of the products of the mill, a hardtack biscuit. He banged the biscuit against a wooden post, producing a satisfying thwack. This food, hard as nails, could last for years and keeps sailors alive as they crossed the oceans or feed armies as they marched off to war the guide explained.

"Would anyone like to try one? Step right up. Let me warn you hardtack biscuits are also know as 'molar breakers.'" People grimaced. There were no takers. I could just feel the crowns on my teeth shattering off their posts.

"Okay. Listen up. Who wants to help me grind some corn?" the guide asked with a friendly, down-home, grin. A girl and boy, about eleven and nine, perked up at that offer. The boy caught himself in the act of showing enthusiasm, then damped it down. That wouldn't do. The guide placed some corn under a small wheel and told them to start turning. Only the girl was willing to try. When she proved too weak to turn the wheel, the guide put his hand over hers to get it going. Deep grooves had been chiseled into the wheel. Soon some genuine, stone-ground, corn meal appeared. The boy remarked, "I don't believe that is corn. That is not corn." The guide gave a hearty laugh. "You're just used to popcorn, corn on the cob, and corn muffins. This corn is the real thing. Real ground corn brought to you by, er, what's your name? Ah, Megan."

"What do you do with it?" asked the boy with a skeptical look.

"You make cornbread, corn muffins or grit, of course." It's coarse. The mills of the gods grind more exceedingly fine than these. Hard work. Eh, kids? Not like buying a corn muffin at the bakery. Now, these smaller wheels do grind corn, but this might take all day. Let's get those big mill wheels working by opening up the gate to let the water in to do the job for us!" There was no resisting his enthusiasm. Up the wooden steps we went, while behind us, a new group entered the lower floor.

The guide stood before a small window. Then the guide unlatched the sluice gate. The soft, gurgling sound of the stream outside rose to a loud rushing roar as the gate went up, and the water started to move. Cogs and wheels meshed. Soon the force of the water had the huge stones going around and around. Corn started falling from the hopper to the wheels, then spilling out as flour into a large, wooden bucket.

"Wow!" cried the older boy. The little one laughed. Even the adults gave a few oohs and ahs. Though he must have given the same demonstration hundreds of times, the guide's eyes just sparkled. Pointing out that small sacks of dried corn were available for sale in case we wanted to make some bread at home, he bid us farewell. Time to move back down to allow the next group up.

It was getting late. Why didn't I get off to an earlier start? The shadows across the grass were growing longer. A man was trying to coax a sheep off a log so that he could sit down. Some kids ran passed. It went baaing away. A gentle calico cat with green eyes allowed people to pet her, while Moses swatted away at a fly. The sun was setting earlier these days. People started heading for the parking lot. A glowing light spread across the Manor. I felt drowsy and numb. The gift shop at the Visitor's Center looked inviting, but the crush of people was too much for me. They'd be enough crowds back in the city. Time to call it a day.

I was thinking of getting a train at the Phillipsburg Manor Station but, on second thoughts, I figured I had enough confusion for one day. I would stick to what I know. I headed back down Broadway to Tarrytown. Already I started to regret not having picked up a souvenir. I thought a bookstore or secondhand shop might have an old edition of Irving's works. Better than a trinket which would just clutter up a drawer. A book might prove satisfying. I might even get back into reading. I would prefer American history. You can keep the legends. I'll take just the facts. Still, it was Sleepy Hollow.

By the time I got to Main Street, the shops were closing. On the opposite side of the street, I could see the proprietor of The Villager shop tidying up. Maybe he would let me in. I would have to hurry. I crossed the street and headed to the door. The young shopkeeper saw me through the glass. He put down the box he was sorting to welcome me in.

"What can I do for you?" He ran his thin fingers through his curly, blond hair and fussed over the frilly front of his shirt. The ruffles wouldn't stay flat. He had a mop of blond hair to rival Harpo Marx's do. He must have painted on his black jeans.

"I'm not sure. I was thinking of getting a souvenir to remember my day here."

"Not sure if we have anything like that. You mean something that says 'Tarrytown,' or 'Sleepy Hollow' on it? We had a few pieces marked 'North Tarrytown,' which is what we called Sleepy Hollow up to 1996, but the locals bought them up. Some folks still call it North Tarrytown. They do not like change. The name Sleepy Hollow is for tourists and carpetbaggers."

"Those kinds of souvenirs just wind up in the drawer. I was thinking of something more useful. Perhaps a collection of Irving's works. An older edition would do nicely," I said. I glanced around the shop quickly. There were some impressive Toby jugs in assorted sizes and a large German stein on an upper shelf. Or, maybe it was Dutch. Nothing else caught my eye.

He pointed out some shelves near the door. There were books, mostly paperbacks, in between assorted tchotchkes. These included varied diet and cookbooks, some wellworn, hardback, Agatha Christie mysteries and Harlequin Romance novels. The thickest book of all was Lucky by Joan Collins. Nothing by Irving.

"The public library has some handsome, leather-bound sets. The delicate, yellowing pages will take you back in time. They're designated as reference books now though not too long ago, they circulated. Philipsburg Manor sells a variety of works including, The Legend, of course. Bracebridge Hall does well at Christmas time, and that perennial favorite, Rip Van Winkle is available with charming illustrations. They even have children's editions. I could have recommended Scribner's or Brentano's in New York if you're looking for fancy leather volumes with gilded edges, but those bookshops are long gone. They would have ordered them up for you if they weren't in stock. Here we just get what the locals discard. There is always the Internet."

"Before I get around to doing that, I will probably lose interest. Anyway, a book purchased online would hardly be the same as one chanced upon in town." I was holding him up.

"Hmmm. Something came in today that seemed interesting. Not the usual run of the mill. I haven't finished sorting things out. It's still in the carton." He started rummaging through a cardboard box under the counter. "It may not be Irving, but it's one of a kind. First edition. Out of print, I'm sure. He pulled out a clothbound, dark red volume with much wear and tear along the edges. "It came in with a complete set of the 1955 Encyclopedia Britannica from an estate up in Kingston. Someone snapped up the Britannica Set right away. Good thing too because what with all those hefty volumes, there was no room for anything else on the shelves."

I took the fragile book from his thin hands. The Book of Damen Willem. I flipped the pages. The copyright date was 1953. A note from the editor indicated that the journal had been penned in 1789 by a Tarrytown lad of Dutch heritage. No publisher. Selfpublished?

"Book Surge or Createspace?" I quipped. Though the shopkeeper offered a wry smile, he was too serious to laugh.

"I haven't priced it yet. 'Might be worth something, but I suppose I could let you have it for ten dollars." Then he added, "It was probably destined to find its way into your hands." I wished he hadn't said that. He tried hard not to look anxious to close down the shop. I decided to buy it. I was so used to using credit cards in the city; it felt odd to hand over the cash. There aren't too many shops left in the world which don't take plastic. It felt kind of quaint to exchange money for merchandise.

"Ten even?" I asked drawing a ten dollar bill from my wallet.

"Yes, even-Stevens. Not really, though. I think you are getting a real bargain. I am sure it is worth more." He wrapped it in a plain brown bag. His expression wasn't so simple as it looked. I was thinking of saying, you get what you pay for, but why bother?

There was a smarminess about him that turned me off. I was on the verge of telling him what he could do with his precious book, when he disarmingly added, "Come back and see us again, real soon. Trees are going to be in their glory soon. It will be fall soon. Most beautiful time of the year here."

Outside, the air felt crisp. It was growing dark. Was it that late? I heard the shop door slam behind me. I turned to see the young shopkeeper turn the open/close sign over, and gently snap the lock on the door. He looked apologetic. I appreciated the cooling down. It felt more like October than August. A mist was hovering over the river and creeping up the street. Streetlamps came on. Under one, I saw the slender blond boy, the one I had seen the day before on Beekman Avenue in Sleepy Hollow. Some very fresh graffiti on the base of the lamppost. The boy palmed a black marker. Hoping he wouldn't try tripping me up, I kept my eyes on his dirty, white converses. The Tappan Zee Bridge looked like a necklace spanning the waters. The new one looked too modern for the setting. It dwarfed the old one. What was on the other side? Nyack? Two historic towns joined by a contemporary structure.

The station was pretty empty. There was no one at all on the Poughkeepsie side. Do folks get mugged here? I made my way over the overpass to the New York side. There was a smattering of folks. Some young folk heading for the city, for a night out. A few people in Yankee gear were going to the stadium. Everyone was quiet. Soon the train came in. It was pretty empty too. I took a window seat on the side facing the river. A woman changed her seat complaining that she could not face backward. It made her dizzy she said.

I gave it all I had to look sympathetic. The towns became less green and more congested. It was too dark to see much out the windows. Gazing out on the rippling Hudson, the apparition of the dead marine's face floated on the water. I shook him off. Holding the book in my hands, I tried to relax, but I was too tense to read. Soon I dozed off, waking up at 125th Street where I saw a policeman walking up and down the street below.
Bright light flooded the street. Loud music surged up. Must be some street party going on. Last licks of summer fun.

Getting off at Grand Central, I found the wall of people overwhelming. I couldn't even think of taking the subway, so I walked home. Every block or so I found myself gazing over my shoulder. I thought someone was following me, but every time I turned to check, there was no one there. Just my imagination. No one is trailing me, I should say. There was always someone in front and behind you in the city.

As I entered my apartment, I flicked on the light and placed my new purchase on the card table. Chester immediately jumped up to sniff it. Then he tried to curl up on it, but it was not a good fit. "You're too wide, Chester." Jumping down to the floor, he led me to his dish. I petted him as I put out some fresh cat food. I refilled the water bowl and folded my clothes up on the chair. Getting into my pajamas, I flicked on the Yankee Game. The neighbors started arguing. I was going to make chicken soup but settled for dry toast. Chester went over to the window to look through the bars, down to the street. I drifted off on the daybed. When I awoke in the middle of the night, the game was still on. Did they go extra innings or something? Chester was snuggled up beside me. Carefully I reached over him to turn out the light. Something slowly rose up in the corner of the room. It couldn't be the cat. He was right beside me. Was it in the corner or the bathroom? I thought it was the small box of electric curlers on top of the medicine chest, the only trace of Dianne; I had left. There was a swirl of dust rising around it. Diane. I must have had you in mind when I got spooked in the woods. I forgot to remember you. Is that a deer I see? Or a small boy crouching? Two sparkling eyes, like jewels, stared back at me in the dark.

Chapter Six

These Streets

I fell back into the usual, deadening routine. You don't need a hot climate for decomposition to set in rapidly. The weeks passed by in monotony. A rainy Sunday found me trudging the wet pavement over greasy blobs of gum and spiritless people. There wasn't much to do but carry on regardless as they say. Pumpkins were appearing in florist shops, a blur of orange in a sea of gray. You disapprove of your life, but endure the lost weekends so you can make it to Monday with its dulling regimen. The last people on earth I wanted to speak to were the last people on earth who wanted to hear from me, the debtors. Would it help to reinstitute debtor's prisons? Get them all of the streets. To them, I was some demonic harasser of Seventh Avenue.

My partner, Dave Powers, good old Dave, took the subway from Queens to our office at 34 St and Seventh Avenue. He was in a good mood every day. Mondays didn't get to him. One day his sister stopped by to join him for lunch. It must have been her birthday or something. "Dave's in the wrong line of work. Don't you agree, Richard? He's just too kind. Right, Richard?" I held my words. You don't see him in action, I thought.

As usual, he had arrived before me though I live about tens blocks away. He sat before a pile of folders spread out like a fan across the top of his desk. "We're as welcome as death on a bright spring day, eh, Richard? We got law degrees to do this?" What was he, a mind reader? Then the invitations started. We should play golf next weekend, or take in a Yankee Game. Better yet, I should consider going out to Queens to see the Mets. He knew a good restaurant near the stadium. Do you want to see a real ball stadium? Only Citi Field will do. The new Yankee Stadium was a slab of cold, concrete. For every six or seven invitations, I might take him up on one. Once in a blue moon, irritation in the brain reminded me that I should invite Dave somewhere. I never did.

"Assuming we make it through the week, how about golf on Saturday, Richard? " He started singing song lyrics, something about wishing it was Sunday, not manic Monday. Something like that. He sang in tune too. "Too bad about Prince." That was his second reference to the grim reaper in two minutes. Suddenly, he seemed embarrassed. That was Dave. He even had a sensitive side though it didn't surface too often. He plopped back down wringing his hands in mock despair, then stabbed the folder on top with his thumb. I wanted to say I would play golf but held myself back. I would have asked him how the Giants were doing, but why prolong the conversation. I couldn't get worked up over sports. I only watched the Yanks out of habit.

My lack of enthusiasm created an awkward silence. All the monochrome days of my life spanned out endlessly before me, as I fixed my gaze on the rural New England scene on the wall calendar. There was a cabin in the woods behind a stone wall. The stones needed no mortar. A field of wildflowers filled the foreground. Over my shoulder, I called out, "OK.

Let's play some golf on Saturday, Dave. Weather permitting." I need an escape clause. "We should enjoy the good weather before the cold moves in." I was rewarded with one of Dave's lop-sided grins.

I might have to put this golf date off for a week or two so that I could spend a weekend with my brother Stan and his wife in Philadelphia. Was it six months ago they had adopted a Mexican boy? Though he was Mexican, they picked him up in Texas. Not sure how that deal went down. I had yet to see my new nephew. Fifteen years of happy marriage without kids. Stan was probably all right as things were. He never forgave dad for taking up with a young woman during a midlife crisis. Dad was down in West Palm Beach with his bimbo now, while mom was on her own in Orlando. Mom liked to say that Stan was a "meat and potatoes kind of guy." He took what he got. But his wife Edie wanted to be a mother. I suppose Mom wanted to be a grandmother. All Edie's failed pregnancies were heartbreaking. Stan called one night in tears, in tears mind you, because she had miscarried again. Since when did Stanley cry? It wasn't the failed pregnancy that was breaking Stan, but her shattered heart.

All these abortion mills. Women's rights led to big business. All these dead fetuses, with or without souls, thrown away over there, whereas over here, in a compact, starter home, were two kind people who wanted children. Was that too much to ask? Unwed mothers used to cast their babies away, but now they destroyed them. Still hoping to get pregnant, Stan and Edie registered with a noted adoption agency. Mom said that many women conceived after adopting. She wasn't sure why.

Soon there was talk of going to China, possibly South America. They considered Korea and Vietnam. Children were available in Ethiopia. I couldn't keep up with them. In the end, they only went to Texas. I must have revealed too much concern, because when the "child find" phase of their adventure led to a boy named Manuel, Edie told me over the phone, "Relax Richard. We're not going to such an exotic or forbidding place. We're only going to Texas to bring our child home." I wanted to say, "Tex-Mex kid," but I remembered Bush 41 getting into hot water by referring to his grandchildren as "little brown ones." Here he was a loving granddad who accepted kids who were a few shades darker than people with his New England roots had, and they got at him for being politically incorrect. At least, that's how people saw it. Who knows what is in a person's heart, I wondered. Does anyone still care?

As for Stan and Edie, they have that rare thing, stable marriage. They might have accepted that parenthood wasn't to be. Just get on with it. Many people choose not to have kids. But, here they were, pushing forty, and pushing the baby stroller. I started Googling toddler toys so that I could send a present. Toys that would arrive ahead of my visit to minimize the fuss. None of this Baby Einstein stuff. "Bath Fun Octopus" might do. Encourage him to be clean. Drop and Go Dump Truck. Now you're talking. Manuel could grow up to be an oceanographer or a trucker. Anything but a bill collector. I found their address on my phone and started typing it in.

The day dragged on. Debts and deadbeats were the names of the game. Sometimes I thought Dave was getting bored with this job. He went down our list of goodfor-nothings and tapped on a name with three check marks next to it. Three calls with no response. "Lawrence Hollander, today is not your day. Today's the day your fate catches up with you!" Dave declared with glee while speed dialing the phone. This time someone picked up.

"Must be our lucky day, Dave," I whispered.

"Lawrence Hollander?" David inquired with all the warmth of Macy's Santa asking some cherubic little boy what he wanted for Christmas. He had his man.

"This is New York calling." Dave started breathing heavily. He sounded like your toddler's worst nightmare.

"Why are you breathing like that?" he asked the defaulter. Obviously, the person on the other end wasn't coming around as readily Dave expected.

"Offer me something. Anything. It could be the widow's mite, all you have. It could be your wife." The other end of the line was quiet, but it hadn't gone dead.

"Guy probably looks like a deer in the headlights. Ask him if we can go to Facetime, Mr. Powers," I threw in.

"Yes, Mr. Post. Do you have Facetime, Hollander? You want to see who is on the other end? Stop breathing like that. Didn't you hear me?" Dave huffed and puffed, breathing through his mouth like a pervert on speed. "I am going to call the police if you keep mouth breathing like that. Do you know that you could be sued, you could be sued," Dave shouted at the end over and over. The trick was to get the person to go as far to the edge as you could without sending them over it. It was so easy for these lowlifes just to hang up. This time out it was Dave who slammed the phone down.

"We'll just have to drag this one to the bar." He smiled, as he threw on his jacket. "I'm going down to get some coffee. Can I bring you back something, Rich?" My back went up.

"'Richard,' please. Sorry, Dave. Must be a neurosis or something." I think my partner must have had a split personality. There was no accounting for that phone voice. It was something unnatural from the other side. How could it come out of a good guy like Dave? You could always count on him to return to the office in fifteen minutes like clockwork. No matter how many coffees and bagels he brought back for me, he always refused to accept payment.

I took a colder, more analytic approach to getting clients to ante up. I spilled out numbers. You owe blank. The interest rate per diem is blank. The attorney costs will run blank. The court costs, when we win, and we will win, will be blank. Whether they hung up on me or not, they would have some impressive numbers spinning around in their heads. Sometimes it worked. Sometimes it didn't.

The day dragged on. We called client after client, wrote up report after report. Around four, Dave went out again for some lattes. Nope, don't pay me. Get me next time. Told you. Dave's caffeine fix made him playful. He took the electronic BB8 robot down from the bookcase to let it circle the office. Beep, beep, beep, BB8 went as he bumped into the glass partition base. We were a republic of two with a secretary who often called in sick. Rita sat behind the glass, buying shoes from Zappos. I hoped they might prove more comfortable than the stilettos she had kicked off under the desk. As soon as our secretary started typing, no doubt, she would start typing our correspondence. Dave cautioned me not to take Rita for granted because she was studying to be a chiropractor. There was more to Rita than you see on the surface. Was he serious? I couldn't see that.

"At least, I paid for this little sucker," said Dave picking up BB8 in his arms to cuddle the little robot like a baby. This was all there was: Dave operating the robot with his iPhone, looking up the stocks with his IPad, checking up on me to see if I was too much alone, checking out Rita from time to time. Dave frowned when he saw that Apple stock was down.

"Apple's down again. What are they without Steve Jobs, Richard?"

"They are nothing without Jobs, Dave." Everyone knows that. That should have satisfied him.

"It was that watch. Thirteen points down because the watch was too expensive. Everything is tanking. They need to come up with something colossal. A homerun out of the park is what they need, but what that would be? You tell me." I had no answer.

"Lower the price of the watch," I hazarded.

"Who wants a cheap Apple product? That's an oxymoron." Dave shook his head, then grabbed his phone to spin BB8's head around. The little head started traveling all around the robot's round body. Then Dave turned back to the phones. When I could stand it no more, I stretched and walked over to the window. I saw people walking, but there was not a tree in sight. They were scurrying in and out of Macy's. From this vantage point, there would be no way to tell if the leaves were starting to reveal glimpses of red, orange, brown or gold. The only red I saw was the background for Macy's large white star logo. No orange, brown or gold. They'll be cranking up for Christmas soon. World famous balloon characters will fill the streets for the Thanksgiving Day parade. Chestnuts will be roasting on an open fire as vendors appear on street corners.

"We're lucky we have a window, Richard. We could be in cubicles facing blank walls. Eh?"

Either Dave read my mind again or felt my restlessness.

"That's true, Dave. Thanks for saying, 'Richard.' And, what a view. The World famous Macy's Herald Square, 'World's Largest Department Store,' as the sign says though someone should paint in, 'Not counting Shinsegae, Korea.' Look at the crowds. Before we know, Macy's will be all done up for Christmas. Just try walking down the street then. It's a wonder more people don't get mowed down by cabs and buses. Here comes one of those huge, doubledecker tourist buses right now." Dave joined me at the window. He heaved a sigh.

"It's bad enough now. Look at all those people. Macy's must be having one of those 'whale-of-a-sales.' The Macy family goes back to Moby Dick, or something like that."

"You mean they made their money in whale oil, right Dave?

I think so. Fancy starting out in Nantucket with a whaling ship, then owning the largest, or what used to be largest, a department store in the world."

"I could call you rich, then. Ha. Ha. Now you get filthy rich by dropping out of school and tinkering around in the garage to avoid to the tropical California sun. Or producing reality shows."

I guess I turned a little red myself. Looking back out the window, Macy's looked like a whale, no, a proud ship edging out from Herald's Square to cross the ocean. Or, should I say sea of people. All those shoppers embarking and disembarking. It did take up an entire city block. We would never make money like that or see our surnames up in lights or on shopping bags all across the country. I might be standing here in this spot, twenty years from now, or maybe, even forty. At least I wouldn't be watching the last leaf fall, signaling my demise. There still won't be any trees.

The day wound itself down. Dave seemed a little agitated as I started closing up shop. He looked like he wanted to say something. I kept shuffling papers around.

"Doing anything special tonight?" he asked. That was unusual.

"Nothing. Nothing much," I said, curious to see where this was going.

"Let's go over to Spillane's on Thirty-Third for a drink, huh Rich, Richard. Okay?"

"I don't know. I gave up drinking a few weeks back. I feel better without it," I responded.

"You got to be kidding. Come on. Have a drink with old Dave. Loosen up."

I didn't want to go, but I agreed anyway. Off we went to the Irish style pub over on Madison Avenue. A loud blast of music and glitzy young people sent me reeling back. Stunned, I wanting to revolve right back out the door. They were getting their groove on with thousands of dollars' worth of apparel on their backs and gadgets in their purses and pockets. There must be a big game on at Madison Square Garden. Lots of wood, surround TVs blasting sportscasts including postseason baseball, rugby from the UK, and, of course, football. Was it preseason football? I was looking track of things. Just get me out of here.

As we headed for the long, but narrow bar, a platinum blond started motioning for Dave to come over to her table. She had a friend with red hair, the same shade as Ronald McDonald. It was a setup. I looked at Dave who just had this stupid grin on his face. I couldn't walk away, but I couldn't take it either. After Dave had introduced the girls, Amber and Issy, we exchanged pleasantries. Like Rita, Dave's choice, Amber had flashy hair and a splashy top. Spillane's had the feeling of an Irish pub, so I ordered a Guinness. The girls wanted Martinis. I quipped, "When in Ireland . . . " Dave started to run his finger nervously along the dark, dusky brick wall. I began to trace a figure eight on the dark wood of the table. I brushed my hair back. My nose might be a little pointed, but my boyish, sandy hair is my best feature. The girls were laughing at something.

I excused myself to go to the men's room. I longed to go out of the window, straight into the street like an escapee. Or to just stay in the restroom forever like the guy who lived in the airport. If I stayed in too long, I would have to face wisecracks and smartass comments. No puns are intended, but no matter how I express this I keep falling into the crack. I had to steel myself to go back; I threw myself some moral imperatives. Have one drink, act like you're enjoying it, then get out. Go home and read a book. Make sure this never happens to you again.

When I finally returned from the restroom, Dave was alone at the bar. He was watching, or pretending to watch, the Mets on one of the ubiquitous giant TV screens.

"What happened? What happened to the girls? Where did they go? Off to take a powder?"

"No. Amber, you know, the one with the blond hair, got pissed at me. I guess I took the wrong tone with her. Her friend, Issy, left out of loyalty, I suppose. I'm sorry Richard. We could have had some fun tonight. I was just worried about . . ."

"Well, at least it's not me," I interjected, cutting Dave off.

"Of course it wasn't you. What, you think maybe the chicks left on account of you? No. It was something I said. Imagine her just walking out on me like that? Her friend too. What kind of act is that?"

"You don't look well, Dave. What's going on?" I asked with concern. He didn't look right.

"I don't know. I have these symptoms. Thought they would go away but that's not happening. Fever, fatigue, sore throat on and off. Symptoms get worse on the weekends. It's not too bad. I just keep pushing through it."

"You do look a little pale, Dave, especially for early fall. Your tan faded fast. I haven't noticed any changes in you, though. What do you think it is?" In the back of my mind, I was thinking of letting him know that I couldn't make it for golf on Saturday since I was going to Philly. I let it go.

"HIV? AIDS? The worst I'm sure. I should have stayed with Rita. I don't know why I pick up these women. I can't help myself. I want Amber, and I want to get rid of her. I

just thought we could have some fun tonight, but I've been so worried about myself, I just started spilling it out. In front of Issy too. I don't know what I was thinking."

The waiter brought over four drinks. He put the Guinness down for me, one Martini for Dave, and two for the girls. Dave told him we would order food later. As the waiter walked away, Dave spread out his arms to draw in all the drinks, including the ale, for himself. I was grateful that my cell phone rang though it was only the receptionist from the dentist office asking to change my appointment. It hurt to see Dave looked that foolish. It hurt. And that was before he started getting sloshed.

I took the Guinness, while Dave quickly downed the first Martini. I took a sip of my drink but didn't want it. The crowd was loosening up. A tipsy, old guy, floundering about, bumped my back. His son called him over to the table. His group sang Happy Birthday to him. At least they were having fun. After downing all three Martinis, Dave looked a little green. The people swirled around, the sports broadcasts and music got louder. My head ached.

"Dave, forget the girl. They're too young for us anyway. Nothing but trouble. Give Rita a call. See a doctor. Could be the flu. The more you worry, the sicker you will get. It's probably nothing. You can have the Guinness, too. I don't want it. I've got to do something. See you tomorrow." With that, I turned to leave.

"You've got something to do? You said you had nothing to do," Dave remarked grabbing at my arm.

"See a doctor Dave. It will be alright. I am not ready for this scene." I offered to pay for the drinks, but, of course, he shook me off.

I was never so happy to find the door.

Now I didn't feel like going home, but I went over to my apartment to put some fresh food and water down for Chester. It seemed everyone had seen the latest James Bond movie, *Spectre,* except me, so I went over to the quad theaters on Fourteenth Street to take it in. It wasn't playing in theaters anymore. Not sure why they had it. The movie would kill two hours, and get the girls out of my head.

Unlike the bar, the theater was empty. Dead silence. My footsteps crunched the stiff carpet. The soundtrack might be audible. If only it would stay like this. I bought a large soda and popcorn. That's a large popcorn? Oh, please. I checked the carpet to see if it was clean. It was just passable. I took a center seat in the middle of the theater. Mustn't eat all this popcorn up during the endless coming attractions. Pushing the seat back, I waited for the show to begin.

An elderly couple entered. The man was very shaky. He held onto his wife's arm as they made their way to my aisle to take the end seats. Then an unkempt, middle-aged guy, took a seat on the opposite end. We are the kind of misfits who missed the film's holiday opening. Virtually every seat in the theater was available, but here we were, four New Yorkers sitting like ducks all in a row. Not this duck. The walls were closing in. Of course, there were several seats between us, but I felt sandwiched in the middle by perfect strangers. I got up.
"Excuse me!" I said to the bum sitting at the end. He looked up at me with startled eyes. "Excuse me," I repeated. Turning his thick legs to the side, allowing me two inches of space to pass through, he looked like he was doing me a favor. My legs were in a vice. There go some ligaments. What did he want me to do? Make the old folks on the other end get up?

"What? You think they are going to cancel the show? Not enough people?" he asked.

"No, the show must go on." What was I supposed to say? Was any movie worth this aggravation? Daniel Craig is too old to play Bond. Britain is not a major player anymore. The hero is a WASP, the villain, is Germanic. He is either effeminate or a metrosexual. Not Bond of course. The bad guy. One day perhaps Bond will be too.
Christoph Walz is fit for a Tarantino flick, but here he is threatening to take the world away. Ernst Blofield. Blofield? No Pussy Galore? What's the point? Well, you can't kick the women in the G-string anymore. Still, I was hoping for a juicy Bond girl in this one. It didn't have a theme song to stay in your head. Ever since the last summer Olympics, it's been clear that Bond is protecting the Queen. Can we have Helen Mirren since they bumped off Judy Dench? The real enemies are ISIS and the banks, and we're watching this Cold War crap.

My next step proved to be a terrible mistake. As I exited the theater, I was surprised by how dark it was. The sun had set. A few slices of pizza will do for supper, I thought. I walked up to Twenty-Third Street for a few slices. Bad idea. Like the movie theater, the pizzeria was pretty much vacant. A girl was stumbling around at the back. Two men in suits were bullying her. She was experiencing a wardrobe malfunction. One breast was popping out of a bright orange tank top. Practically out on her feet, she steadied herself against a table. The two men exited with looks of disgust on their faces. Then I noticed a designer purse, lying on a table across the way. It was half open with a wad of cash just visible at the top. It had to belong to her. The woman slumped down into a chair. Her head fell on the table top. A man in carpenter jeans and construction boots ambled over to the table with the purse. Taking an inordinate amount of time to pick a beverage from the cooler, he kept his eye on the money.

Why did I choose this place? I was in the right place at the wrong time. If I wanted to see stupefied, young, stoned, numb, people who were knocked out and frozen in their footsteps, in other words, the walking dead, I could have gone a few blocks east to the

Veteran's Hospital. There you could take in a whole show of folks who would come to a complete stop in the middle of the sidewalk, eyes rolled back, knees bent just enough to lock them in place. They wobble but don't fall down just like those silly toys my mother sentimentally held on to, Weevils. They must think it is a judgment day when they come back to their senses. No matter. They just start moving forward again. There must be little angels holding them up, or more likely they are cruising on autopilot.

Of course, I couldn't just return the purse to her. She was completely out of it. Even touching it could bring on accusations of theft down on my head. So, with one eye on the purse, and the other on the suspicious man, I back myself up to the counter to tell the pizza man what was going on. He took me seriously. He strode over to take possession of it just as she slid so far down in the chair; it was a miracle she didn't hit the dirty floor. There must have been another one of those angels holding her up. Awkwardly he started pushing her breast back into her top. Realizing I was watching, he opted for pulling the material over her exposed tit. He didn't want anyone to accuse him of perversion, sexual harassment or rape. She would at least have her purse when she came around again. Or would she? Who could you trust? The pizza guy seemed OK enough. You never knew. He might return the wallet to her saying, "Here I kept this for you. There was no cash in it."

It was just terrible to lose control of yourself like that. Somedays I think half of Manhattan is out of control. I waited at the counter to place my order. The manager kept calling out, "Lady, lady, lady!" to no avail. Shaking his head, he returned to the front of the store. I had lost my appetite but ordered anyway. Placing two slices in the oven, and the purse under the counter, he rolled his eyes at me. As he took the slices back out, the woman began to moan. I took my pizza to a table as far away from her as possible. I watched as he started rummaging through the purse. He might find an emergency contact number. What would he do if he couldn't find one? Call 911?

I ate the first slice, but could only manage a bite or two of the second one. I took a few sips of Coke and headed back out to the streets. The evening had a kind of Sunday emptiness about it. There was another Starbuck's opening up where the Dunkin' Donuts used to be. Stores seem to morph in Starbucks overnight all over the city. They were like mushrooms after rain. Is that simile too clichéd? Vestiges of the city were disappearing every day. I bet you couldn't find one Chinese laundry left. Or a folk singer in Washington Square who had any talent. Here and there, you might stumble over an ancient cobblestone.

A young man blew smoke in my face as he asked for directions to The Bottom Line. A couple who looked and sounded like they were from the Midwest, was looking for an ice cream parlor. A boy of about sixteen was puking in the doorway of a derelict building that only last year had been a gay bar. Kind of early for that. Stink of a homeless man hit me as I crossed at the corner of Twenty-Third and Third Avenue. He stuck his hand out for some money. Whiff of stale whiskey. All these beggars. I couldn't support them all even if I wanted to so the maximum was two handouts per day. You had to be careful not to get flocked. They were like pigeons that way. You were just feeding their drink or drug habit anyway.

As if they weren't bad enough, the prostitutes, pimps, and drug dealers were coming out. Excuse me. Coming through. Make way for a reasonable person, please. No way.

Women, free from work, laughing in each other's faces, and blowing smoke in mine, crowded the sidewalk. They were office girls just biding their time, waiting to join their boyfriends for drinks. I mustn't forget to mention all those starry-eyed dreamers who were heading uptown to the Great White Way, where they hoped to see their names up in lights. Unknown young actors and actresses from backwater towns that weren't on the map. Dominicans and Puerto Ricans filling the streets up with Spanish. Why couldn't they move closer to each other when they wanted to speak instead of shouting out across streets? I know, it's a cultural thing. It's harder to move in the tropics.

There was yet another one of those walking dead, out cold on his feet, near my building. The way his body suddenly crumbled down, he looked more like he was going to plunge off Mount Everest, then stumble over a curb in front of the Flat Iron building. Weary and ready for sleep, I wondered if I was the only sane one left in the city. Yes, "there are other Annpurnas in men's lives," or something like that. These streets were made for beggars, buskers, druggies, and thieves. Young lovers, hustlers, and theatergoers can have them too. The homeless make themselves homes here in these streets. These streets were made for street merchants, street walkers, dealers, wannabe models, and Broadway dreamers. These streets were not made for me.

Chapter Seven

The Book of Damen Willem

I canceled the golf date with Dave. I never made it to Philadelphia. Since Dave tested negative for the common STDs, he went right back to being his usual self. We were obviously both relieved. He started dating Rita again. I don't know if he strayed. I wasn't going to ask. They were both so casual about everything. His unexplained fevers went away. He stopped badgering me to get out of the house. The weeks dragged on. The leaves started turning; the temperature fluctuated wildly. If I wore a jacket, the heat came back strong. If I didn't, the temperature dropped. I stopped going to the movies and stayed out of pizza places. I just wanted to be left alone. I don't know which was worse, the dull work days or the boring weekends. Bright sunny days with crisp air pushed my spirits up, but rain brought me straight down. I was a real barometer.

The second Sunday in October broke cold and gray. Chester looked like he had a headache. I rustled up his fur and stroked the thick stripes between his amber eyes. I fell into myself. In pajamas and slippers, I padded down to the lobby to pick up my copy of the New York Times. I had to grab it fast to prevent some other resident from swiping it. Through the lobby door, I peered through the foggy glass at a steady drizzle. The lobby was cold. What happened to the heat? As I walked back up the stairs, I heard those lousy neighbors on the second floor starting up again. She called him a bastard. He called her a whore. He whacked the wall; a chunk of plaster broke off. Over the years many pieces of plaster broke off. He called her a whore, and she called him a bastard so many times, you know it had to be true. Good day to stay in bed.

Splitting an English muffin, I put it in the toaster. Then I put the kettle on for instant coffee. Hope you won't mind having me around, Chester. Hot on the trail of the muffin, Chester's nostril's flared to take in the full aroma of hot butter. He jumped into bed with me. I pulled the blue, plaid blanket over me. As I placed the tray on the bedside table, the book I had purchased up in Tarrytown hit the floor. It had been hiding in plain sight. While I leaned out of bed to retrieve it, the cat made a mad dash for the English muffin. I let him lick a little butter, then pushed him off the bed. I started on the Times.

There was an article about hurricanes. They were still rebuilding New Orleans. The injustice and stupidity of it all. Can you imagine people rebuilding in a hurricane prone area where the land was below sea-level? Pitt/Jolie was on board to rebuild the Ninth Ward. That's an accident waiting to happen again and again. I flipped through the sections to find the crossword puzzle. Taking a pencil from the drawer, I finished off the muffin. Before beginning the challenge, I had to check the answer to thirteen across from last week's crossword. "Jobs for underwriter for short." Four letters. I couldn't get that one. "IPOS" "IPOS?" I was still stumped. Need to look that one up. Hurricanes stayed on my mind.

Katrina was not soon to be forgotten. The dead were buried; their suffering ceased. The failure of the levees blamed on the Army Corps of Engineers but no consequences to date.

I guess Katrina started a train of thought because the Irving story came to mind. I was thinking of reading *The Legend of Sleepy Hollow.* I'd have to remember to pick up a copy of the story. Curiosity about the book I bought in Tarrytown got to me. I reached down to the floor to retrieve it. Chester jumped up on the bed again. I patted his big head, then ruffled up his fur. He pawed the dark red book cover. The binding was cracked, but holding together. They made books stronger then. I hope we're in for a good read, Chet. It couldn't be a magical book because I didn't purchase it in a magic shop. What if I opened it to find fairy dust bursting out into my face, spiraling me back to the Sleepy Hollow region in the times of the Revolutionary War?

I ran off with my awakened imagination. In earnest, I would have to go back up to Tarrytown to find the shop. The proprietor would be an old, elvish man with wispy hair and beetling eyebrows. He might say, "You don't choose a book. The book chooses you." There could, or should, be a mascot, a cat or a raven, or a crow pretending to be a raven. Or a mynah bird up on a high perch, trained to cry out, "Nevermore." My return to the shop would bring complete bafflement. Instead of learning more about the book's provenance, I would stand in the street with my jaw dropped. The proprietor would have disappeared along with the shop. There would be a laundromat in its place. People would find me weird standing on Main Street stopped in my tracks. I would ask the locals what happened to the secondhand store. What secondhand store they would say? Chester's eyes met mine. If this cat could talk, I am sure he would say, "Get on with it." I cracked open the book and began to read.

Editor's Note

This book was given to me by my elderly, Dutch uncle who stubbornly refused to speak, read, or write English. It was penned, he said, by a young Dutchman who caught the anglophilia so badly he recorded even his most intimate and meaningful thoughts, in English. Dutch, or Netherlandic, was our language in the old world. There was no reason it would not do for the new one. According to Uncle Joop, people here, especially the upper classes, want the fashions of London. Long before they adopt them here, the good people of London have long abandoned them to move on to new styles and crazes. The book, therefore, being in English, was not worth the pain of perusal. It should, however, be preserved, my uncle maintained, because it did contain information regarding both postrevolutionary war and family history.

Taking my uncle at his word, I accepted the book. I did not intend to give it much thought. I casually flipped through the book, reading phrases here and there. The pages were brittle and yellow. The once black ink had faded to sepia. Our ancestor, Damen Willem, had apparently fallen in with some hooligans who had nothing better to do than to prove the old adages, an idle mind is the devil's workshop, and that, sparing the rod, spoils the child along with the land and the Republic. The young man did write in a neat hand. The hand that held that pen was skeletal now. According to Uncle, Damen Willem's remains rested in the Old Dutch Cemetery in Sleepy Hollow. I placed the manuscript on an upper shelf under the eaves of my cottage up in Hudson Highlands.

There it would have remained except for the fact that certain elements contained within, such as wandering spirits of Revolutionary days, odd usage of native vegetation, and the mysterious disappearance of a community member, remained in mind. Curiosity got the better of me. So, one day I took the old pages down from the shelf under the eaves, shook out the dust, and blew out the cobwebs. I read the manuscript with increasing interest. Growing fond of my distant relative, I decided to type it up with minimal editing, and then to publish a limited edition. Though I took the time to translate the Dutch words Damen retained, I did not entertain expectations of much readership. Preserving and presenting the journal was a labor of love and a demonstration of familial duty. I entitled it, *The Book of Damen Willem.*

Johannes Van Crickenbeck

Kinderhook, New York, 1923

November 1, 1789

Little Cuz came today. Mama was getting Enoch ready for church. Whenever Mama was in the room, Roos was demure in her petticoat. Carefully, Roos patted it down with care to signal that she was a good girl. The moment Mama left, she lifted her petticoat up to shake it in my face. Her eyes flew wildly about the room. The walls might have eyes and ears. Butter would not melt in her saucy, little mouth. This little minx is always hungry, ferreting out anything she can put in her maw. Scraps will do if there is nothing else to be found. She will slip out the door without telling anyone to go off and hide in the forest. She says she runs off because of all the chores Mama gives her. For me, this is unfortunate because I too long to steal away to the solitude of the woods. Roos dashed all my hopes of getting her to do my chores today. Little Cuz is too smart for us. I accept the necessity of chores, but I have much on my mind. I did not get to be alone until the sun had set.

In the evening, I went wandering about like a spook in the gloaming. When the light failed, I wound my way back to the church. Last night had been a wild one. The evil spirits had come out to have their run of the place before the saint's day commenced. All was quiet now. There were smashed pumpkins along the road.

November 2

In bringing back a stray cow, I passed the old, gnarled oak tree which faces away from the main road and toward the river. The golden leaves were browning and drying out on the ground covering up acorns which crunched beneath my feet. Twas not so long ago the schoolmaster sat under this tree with his long back against the trunk reading old leather volumes which he carried about in his worn satchel. He was often to be found there. The words on the page would bring a pleasant smile to his face as threw off all his worldly cares to sit in the timothy and clover. Sometimes the warm rays of the sun would bring him down into a deep sleep. The book would tumble out of his hands to splay out on the grass. Children would merrily dance around him, having their fun. He would sleep until the sunset.

It may be that some of the books in hand contained dark matter, for he would rise quickly, all affright, stashing the book quickly away in his pack so that he might make his way to safer ground posthaste.

I wished again today that I might have more time to be idle. Little Cuz does no chores. She rolls her eyes about and trolls her tongue. Behind our backs, she puts lampblack on her eyebrows and the red color from crushed cochineal beetles on her lips. She looks quite the whore. She rubs it off before Mama and Papa can see. Mama and Sister Margreet do all the women's chores. She has an innocence that I have sorely lost. I doubt it can ever be regained.

"We live out our time in darkness," I remarked today at breakfast.

"Damen, your head is soft, and your heart is flinty. The days are filled with light. Darkness comes at night," Father responded with a hard look on his face.

"Mahalalel, Damen is a good boy, an angel who fell out of heaven to abide with us here on earth," scolded Mama. She cannot see what is in my heart.

"

Pray, pardon me, wife. Every day Damen gets less done. He is not yet twenty and does less than Old Man Kroll. Who has time to worry about dark days? It is not the starry plow we wield."

"Good husband, I do not know what is wrong with him. Tomorrow he will work harder. A little angel has promised me this." Mama winked.

"Little Cuz thinks Damen is bewitched," Sister Margaret added.

Talk of bewitchery made my little brother Enoch laugh so loudly; he had to hide his face in his hands. Whether or not the devil has gotten inside of me, I cannot say. I only know that I am a man more fit for graveyards, who is obligated to work all day on the family farm from sunup to sundown. Dark, unholy thoughts lurk in my head and press down my brain. Relief comes in writing them down in secret. I draw strength in the belief that I will become the man who can see his way through to a new day.

Mama knows something is wrong. I make her sad. She says she is concerned that my betrothed, Josefien, is growing unhappy with me. Josefien is a thoughtful person who is too good for me. When she chews cloves to sweeten her breath, I tell her there is no need to add sweetness. She is a true woman, a quality person, who was not bred up just to dress and dance.

Father has demons of his own. I am not the only one lying awake in the house. He is digging his ragged little claws into his palms right now. In the morning there will be little spots of blood on them. A sharp crescent moon, tipped a bit, hovers in the sky in streaks of pale light. It is just visible at the top of the window. Father is swinging his only leg to form shadowy half-moons over his wooden one which lies beneath him on the floor. His peg leg bites into his stump. It is a daily torment not unlike my conscience, which eats at me all day, beds down with me each evening, and rises with me in the morn. Though he has Mama as his bedfellow, and I will soon have Josefien, I cannot abide the thought that I will have to share my darkness. Before the snow flies, we will be wed. The candle I have lit is bothering father. He is crying out for darkness. He sounds like a screech owl. Snuffing the candle out, I secret my papers in a wooden box under the bed. I am also keeping a book that the schoolmaster had lent me there as well.

November 3

After feeding the chickens, I came across Margreet and Little Cuz talking outside the barn. The sky was a dark shade of blue with wispy clouds billowing. The morning had been cold, but the afternoon warm. The leaves were falling, and the wind was still. The girls were in the middle of a buzzing conversation.

"I fear that something scared him not half to death, but all the way to the next world. Do you think so? There was more to Saturday night than we will ever know," said

"

Lil Cuz. She lowered her head but raised up her eyes to see if anyone might hear. No doubt she had been running about the woods last night.

You know something that we do not know, Little Cuz. You must not tell what you know. It may not even be true," said my sister.

I interjected, "Margreet is right. Do not tell tales out of school, Roos." Why I could not keep my mouth shut, I do not know. My heart was beating like a runaway horse.

"You know something too, Damen." Little Cuz flashed me a look of sudden revelation worthy of a prophet.

"I wish I knew nothing at all. How good it would be to be a child again, even a bad one who evades chores. I wish I had no learning, no lessons, and no more knowledge than little brother Enoch," I declared.

"There are things about you, Damen; I do not understand. Why is Abraham your friend? I would like to know. You say that you do not understand anything, but you know more than he. You are a better man, a smarter man who is above him and his ways. Mrs. Van Vleet days you have soft curls around your delicate ears. She thinks you look like a scholar. You walk like a man and do not strut like a peacock. Not like some people I know who put on airs. I know this," asserted Little Cuz sounding wiser than her twelve years.

"Cousin, you speak of things of that do not concern you. You are speaking for someone else. I would not be surprised if the things you say came from Josefien. Why do you bring Abraham to mind? What has he to do with anything?" Josefien looked away. I shook inside.

The uneven thumping sounds on the path warned us that Father was coming. Quickly we dispersed.

November 4

Father tells tales of the war. At evening, overwhelming memories of the Revolution carry him off to battle in his mind. The darkness comes on so early now. We sit at the kitchen table while the candle burns down. Our glowing eyes focus on Father's face. The mouser, Binx, purrs by the hearth where the embers glow. Why do these old folks keep looking back? When it comes to war, the young look back too. Nochi cannot get enough of these tales. Margreet and Mama do not care for them but listen with love and devotion.

"Right where we worship, and I beseech the good Lord to give us lasting peace, a cannon stood in the grass on the ridge above the church. Little boys were running helterskelter all over the grounds bringing water bottles, pounds of bread, powder and shot

"

to help the troops defeat the enemy. They were yelling 'the British are coming.' If you had been old enough, Damen, you might have joined the fight. Nochi, who might not have even been born yet, would have made a better soldier, than his older brother. The thing Damen is good at is sitting in the corner reading. Instead of pitching in to fight a war, he might be better off staying home to pitch the hay. Were you born then, Nochi? Do you remember the war?" Nochi shook his head.

The war could spook a man like a horse, or cat. Did you ever see Binx leap straight up into the air or huddle in the corner with his back arched? That is what battle can do to a man if his bravery falters. If you ever do go to war Damen, resist the temptation to run all the way home to bolt the door and hide under the bed alongside your books and papers. Stand son with brave men like me to drive the British away."

Nochi laughed so hard he had to double up.

"Bang, bang, bang! I would kill more Redcoats than you can count. The brook would run as red as the Red Sea," Nochi boasted as the candle burned out.

Mama lit a new candle for she knew this would prove to a long night.

"T'would be the judgment day when I would let Damen or Nochi run off to be soldiers," Mama admonished.

"All the houses were dark. We blew our candles out." Father ignored Mama to continue his story.

"Did you not want the British to know people were at home?" Nochi asked.

"Son, do you remember the war?" mother asked turning to me. "You were not troubled then. It was such a terrible time people did not have a chance to worry about anything else except staying alive. Do you remember?"

I went deep inside my thoughts. "I think I remember the cannon. There were men in red coats, and shiny, tall boots. I remember coming up to here to you, father." I said, drawing my hand across his waist. "You had two legs then, father. And, I was not afraid. "

"Yes. You knew that brave men and boys like Enoch if he had been alive then, that is, and I would save the farm. Now children, be careful not to laugh, even though it was a funny sight, but when the British came, all the farmers came out to fight with mops, broomsticks, shovels, hoes and pitchforks. We were even sharpening tree limbs to make earthworks. We were determined to hold the British back. Even Old Man Kroll, old as Methuselah as he is, came out all covered in hay holding up his pitchfork. He may have slept in the hay all night, or fallen in the grass in the fray, but all I know it that he was a veritable straw man. He has gone to meet his maker since."

"

Mama said we must go off to bed. Blowing the candle out, she took Father's hand to lead him off to their bed in the corner. Enoch and I went up to the loft. Nochi was mute. I think he was still thinking about the strawmen and battle. The sky was pitch black with a few streaks of red running across it. Father's disembodied voice called out in the dark: "Revolutionary days. You will not see such blackness at the break of day again. Black smoke and red fire blowing over the Tappan Zee. And, I do not mind telling you now, what I would not have said then, that I was very much afraid."

November 6

Father takes nothing by halves. He is either too serious or too foolish. This morning at breakfast, as Mama served pancakes and apple sauce, he plucked a sugar cone out of a dish and started sucking on it.

"This tastes so zestful and delightful now, though when first I tried it, it burned my tongue. I do not know which I would give up first: my wife, my pipe, or my sugar." Smiling at him, Mama put a thick slice on bacon on the corn bread for him. From sugar cone to the pipe, Father's mouth was always open. Licking the sugar off his fingers, he drew on his pipe and blew a smoke ring across the table.

"The Dutch should take over more islands in the Caribbean because the whole world will soon be devouring sugar," Father said.

"Waste not, want not. It is enough to put a little in your mouth while drinking tea, Mahalalel," Mama cautioned. He was having none of that.

"The doctor says it is good for the health. It has medicinal properties, Hennie."

"Husband, I think you have a sugar demon inside you. We knew how to make do with little during the revolution, but now everyone demands sugar, rum, white bread, and chocolate."

"Good wife, women want that and more such as mirrors, books, clocks, curtains on the window and pictures on the wall. We all want what we want. Sugar devil, indeed."

Sister Margreet covered her mouth to laugh, but little brother Enoch broke into gales of laughter. "Where is this little sugar Demon, Mama? Can I see him?" Nochi went down under the table to look for it.

Mama traced her finger around a knot in the pine table where the gray paint was wearing away. The inside of the cupboard was painted dark orange. Though pale in sunlight, tonight, in candlelight, the wood will glow out at me like hellfire. An image of a big devil with a pitchfork jumping out of it to get me flashed into my imagination. I was unnerved. Do they come even in daylight? I dropped a plate which almost broke in half.

"Damen has the whim-whams!" laughed Nochi.

A sound of shuffling outside the door made me jump. Nochi guffawed again. It was just some wilden (Indian) squaws selling baskets made of strips of reeds and sweet grass. Mama rushed over to the little spice box up on the shelf to retrieve a few coins to buy one. Opening the top of the door, she bought a new basket. After the squaws had left, she sat down at the table laughing at herself.

"I do not know what business I have to buy this basket. There are enough of baskets stored atop the cupboard. Do not tell Papa," she pleaded as she placed the new one behind the others. Then her laughter died. She looked sad. I knew what was coming. When she is sad, she thinks of Amsterdam, especially the leaving of it.

"Good family, does anyone remember all the ships in the harbor at the Port of

Amsterdam, and the smell of fish and spices that filled the air? There were ships from all over the world. People from all over the world. There were even Jews. So many languages. It was like the Tower of Babel. Teeming warehouses reaching to the sky. The city was all steeples and masts. And the windmills. Oh, the windmills."

Even Margreet, the eldest, said she did not remember Amsterdam. It was too far back. Nochi was born here. I did not remember, but I said I thought that I could recall the fishy smell. I wanted to add that I could remember well my good heart that was then free of evil deeds. That would only worry Mama. I resolved to keep my unease to myself.

"Papa and I were young then. We visited London because Papa thought he could claim property there. Someone had married into an English family, but no records could be found. We had to let that go sailing off to the New World. Perhaps our kinsfolk had gone there before us. The world was turning upside down," Mama concluded.

November 11

Laundry day. I hauled heavy tubs of water out to the yard so mother and Little Cuz could wash the clothes. The sun was bright. The air felt thick. As Mama prodded the clothes with her stick, Little Cuz, sat down on the grass to watch.

Mama handed her one of my shirts to place on the bush to dry, "Clean clothes and a clear conscience. Tis what we need."

For me, that was the last straw. As Mama carefully smooth out the wrinkles in my shirt, I threw myself down on the grass next to it. I held out my arms.

"Tis a white shirt now, Mama, one that is not fit for a black man like me. Some of my dusky color may come off on it, and it will have to be washed all over again.

"What are you saying Damen? You are not a black man. Clean clothes and a clear conscience," cried Mama.

"I am a man black at heart. There is no clear conscience to be found in me. I do not think it will fit either because I have become a smaller man than when I wore it last. I am no better than a Wilden, Mama."

I tore at my shirt and upended my hair. I made my mother cry. Father stomped out from the barn. He looked from her forlorn face to mine.

"Hendrika, Hendrika. Do not be sad. Damen, what are you doing to your mother?" Empty the buckets. Put them away. Do your work. Work! Work! Work! The clothes will not wash themselves. Now is not the time for talking." Turning my back upon him, I walked out of the yard, down the road. He may or may not have called out to me. All I heard was a drumming in my head. I went walking. Passing the empty school which looked so lonely at the foot of the wooded hill, I threw a rock at the oak tree where the schoolmaster used to sit, then scurried down to the river. I watched a big ship going down the river wishing I was on it. All the way to Amsterdam I would go if need be.

November 12

Today, at breakfast, I sulked and complained about the way of the world. It was musty, so Mama opened up the top of the door. A smell of apples and wet leaves wafted inside. "I do not think this life is worth living. All this eating, drinking and working to stay alive. What for?" I questioned.

"The drinking is alright. I will take the food too. The work is not a choice. Have you forgotten the scriptures, Damen? It is not a man's choice. A man will labor, and a woman will give birth in pain. This is the price for falling from grace," said Father.

Mama cried out, "Son, I do not like to take food when I see how unhappy you have become. You were my candle burning bright with a steady light, my Damen. Now you are flickering and fluttering all over the place. I fear you in danger of going out. Until you become your happy self again, I think I will not take food at all."

Hardening my heart, I got up from the table with a steely countenance. Striding to the door, I noticed that Mama's prettily arranged ringlets were graying. I wanted to kiss the top of her dear head, but just then, she pushed herself up to go to the window. She turned about again and went to sit at a small, pine table in the corner. Lowering her head upon her arms, she began weeping.

"Mahalalel, you must do something about this boy. You must do it now," Mama beseeched. Father looked as stricken as a dog that had his bone snatched away. Mama sobbed audibly and gave her little body a shake. He raised his arms above his head as if something was going to fall on it. I wanted to both comfort her and take comfort myself on her ample bosom. But, I knew that even if I could not yet become a man, I could not act the child. I stood stock still.

Mama sobbed a little louder. Father raised his hands straight up above his head as if to bring down the wrath of God on us all, then let them fall limply to his sides. Then he balled his hands up into fists.

Grabbing a study chair, he placed it before himself for ballast. Looking down at the stout chair legs that looked not unlike his wooden, peg leg, Father announced, "I am a fit man of not two, or four, but six legs, who can spare a leg to throw at your foolish, pumpkin head, Damen. Damn you." Father tried to remove his wooden leg while standing. He tried to steady himself against the chair, but lost his balance and fell back into it. Feverishly, Father pulled on his leg until it came off. Firmly grasping the back of the chair, he stood up again to hurl it across the room at my head.

I cannot say I did not deserve this, but to preserve my foolish, pumpkin head, I ducked. The leg struck the door with such force that the table rattled. One of the delicate, blue and white chocolate cups fell from the cupboard to the floor. It shattered to bits.

"Sit down Papa! You will fall over like a hacked tree!" cried Margreet whose hands flew up to her mouth. Her lips formed a perfect letter O. Papa fell back to his chair, then down to the floor on his rump. Margreet started to gather up the pieces of the broken cup. "Help your father, Enoch," pleaded Mama. "You too, Margreet." It took Mama, Margreet, and Enoch, to raise father back to the chair. He made mumblings of such senselessness that I thought he might be going crazier than his older son. He fell back to the floor.

Mama stood paralyzed. Margreet took charge.

"You must get Damen to the minister, Mama. I am afraid he has one of those little devils in him as the people of Salem, the ones the schoolmaster told us. There may be an amazing range of spirits here in town. Someone might even have made a poppet that looks like Damen, one with oak-colored hair and slate blue jacket. They might be using it to control his behavior." Margreet said.

"The minister might be able to get it back out again," cried Enoch excitedly. Even in a crisis, Margreet was ever the practical one. There was always something to do. There was always something that had to be done. The mention of the teacher froze up my blood.

November 14

Mother has not stopped eating. She has not stopped threatening to do so. Mama picked at her food at breakfast, taking larger bites, I suspect when no one is looking. As for the chocolate cup, she said that as sad as it was, she was reconciled to losing a member of a set.

"Soon we will all stop eating because President Washington has declared November 26th a day of fasting and thanksgiving to acknowledge the care God took over us as we strove to be a free and independent nation," Papa said. Making a grab for the butter and raspberries, he looked at his pancakes with regret at the coming fast. I struck my hand to my forehead, ground my teeth, and then pressed my fingers deep into the sockets of my eyes. Everyone ignored me.

"See Mama. We will all have to give up our dinner, but it will not have anything to do with this silly Damen and his sulks. But you are not fasting, are you Mama? Somebody eats the ginger cookies that are left over at the end of the day. That somebody is not me," snickered Nochi.

Father gave him a cautionary look. Nochi started to brush his thick wheat-colored hair off his forehead so he could more clearly discern Mama's expression, then snickered again. Margreet was silent. Would that she had kept quiet yesterday instead of telling Mama to get me to the church. It is clear that before the week is out, the dominie (minister) will be taking time out of his most precious schedule, to address my malady. The thought that the dominie could help me cheered Mama up but brought me down.

Chapter Eight

November 15

As I sat in the pew at church today, I felt that horrible shouts of derision were going to spill out of my mouth. I knew that when the sermon was over, Mama would not forget to ask the dominie take the time to talk to me. A desire to loudly curse the entire congregation rose up from deep inside me. I removed myself from my family. Up to the balcony where the slaves sit, I took myself. The desire to speak freely was so overwhelming that I soon withdrew from the sanctuary. Running to the rail, I glanced down at the congregation below. I wanted to cast myself down onto the pious people as they bowed their heads in prayer, so I ran down the stairs only to meet the devil at the door.

"Come back Damen. Come back to church right now, Damen," Papa shouted.

"Come back Damen, Come back," Mama echoed. Though my parents ordered me back to the church, I took off for the woods. Was that a devil I saw hiding behind the door? I could not tell my family that I had become a man unfit to take communion at the table before the altar. I should not have gone to church at all. The sun was warm for November. My head felt as if it was on fire. That was not the result of the sun. Not knowing where to go or who to turn to, I took off for the woods with my hot head.

"I am on fire," I shouted. I ran around the trees. Someone with a deep voice yelled, "Go down to Andre's brook." I walked to the site with my arms held out in front of me like a spook. All proper spirits wait for the sun to go down before they go wandering. No one paid much attention, not even the wilden.

At supper that night I told my family I was sorry. My little brother Enoch laughed at me. He said I was crazy as a loon.

"No," said Father. "He is more like a maize thief, taking his mother's heart away instead of corn." His leg was back on. He had calmed down. The blue and white pieces of the shattered cup were piled on a shelf near the window. I could not bear the sight of them.

"Some believe those starlings are members of the Lost Tribes of Israel. Be careful what you say," scolded Mama.

"Yes, and this fair land is the New Jerusalem. And it would be if New Amsterdam had not fallen to the English to become New York," Papa declared with disgust. Annoyed with Father for clinging to the old ways, I waited until he was filled up with his mug of beer to ask why we did not hold on to the new nation. Pushing his mug at me, Mahalalel, stood up, splaying out his good leg and wooden stump. "In the old world, we were very tolerant. We took in dissenters of all kinds. Baptists, Anabaptists, Palatines, anyone who was fleeing England was welcome to Amsterdam. For our gracious acceptance, we received no gratitude. When New Amsterdam fell to the British, they attempted to make us Anglicans. They went so far as to dictate who could minister to us in our churches. They had no tolerance at all. We Dutch were great administrators who did not know how to plant our feet. Trading we knew, but settling had no charm for us. Our feet were too far off the ground Damen. We were too much of a track and trade nation. They did us in. We will lose our heritage entirely with our President Washington. When they think of beavers, they will think of us Dutch." He spat.

Enoch got up now too to start laughing. "Papa, you only have one foot. And you speak of planting feet. The enemy will knock you down like a bowling pin. Ha. Ha. Ha." Father smiled. He always took tender care of Nochi.

"Yes. Men like me. And Peter Stuyvesant, before me, who wanted to stand up against the Duke of York, wooden leg and all. His leg even had a silver tip. We are the ones who were most able to see the sense of settling and securing the land. It was the men with two feet who would not stand with Governor Stuyvesant to urge on the fight. All they could say is we are gaping into an oven. In other words, there were too many British troops," said father.

"Let us be grateful for what we have. Let us eat this nourishing food," remarked Mama. Mother grew happy when I smiled. At least she was eating more. It was not over. It never is.

Later, at dinner, talk of the British came back. After swallowing a big bite of ground beef, and washing it down with his beer, Father to rant.

"We lost hard to the British, but soon they lost to us. We became Americans. That is if we concede that we are all Americans. I might not care which side won at all if they would just keep the taxes down." Mama gave him a hard look.

"Well, the British were a nasty people, riding out with those monstrous Hessians running at their side like a pack of banshees. Hessians eat children, Nochi. Do you know? Damen knows."

"I know nothing of the sort, Father. Those who have level heads do not think such things to be right." His mouth turned down into a frown. I smiled at Nochi, but he was having none of it. He believed father.

"Did you fight the Hessians, Papa? Did you send them back to hell?" asked Nochi who could barely contain his excitement. He started to climb up on the table. Mama told him to sit back down. "Eat your soup," she shouted.

Sister Margreet, like Mama, could sit like patience on a monument. It was as if they had engraved the words of our Lord on their hearts. "Blessed are the peacemakers . . ."

"Yes. I sent those Hessian hounds back to hell where they belong. I did. As General Washington liked to say, 'I am a warrior. Not a politician.' Mama looked low now. She knew what was coming. So did I. If he had lived a hundred years ago, he would have convinced people that he was Peter Stuyvesant, the governor of New York. He had played the hero so much time up in his head, he, no doubt, believed that the tallest Hessian, the one with a dark, smoldering face, had swooped down on him to slice at him with a sword.

"Children, I had never before encountered a uniform like that one. It was not Red. It was not blue. Half of it was black. And the other a burgundy as dark as blood . . ."

At that, I stood up and shoved the table at him.

"Yes, father. You won the entire war all by yourself. They asked you to advance to the highest honor of serving a free country, to become the president of the United States, but you were too busy telling your yarns."

By the time, Father got to his feet; I had stalked out the door. Peter Stuyvesant lost his leg leading an assault on a Spanish fort on the island of Saint Martin. Father lost his leg because he slipped and fell on the ice one night when he was crossing over from Nyack to Tarrytown on the frozen Hudson River. Father was not too far from the shore when the ice gave way. He must have been in a panic though Mother does not say so. His right leg snapped. A bone came through the shin. It is a wonder he did not fall through the ice. He said that a little devil tripped him up. Mama says a little angel held the ice together. It was fluttering there just above the surface, pulling the jagged edges together. She saw a large head with tiny wings.

That was the worst night of my life to that date. I did not think a worse one was yet to come. Father was in bed, howling like the wind outside. The snow was coming down again. Big snowflakes were blowing under the door. When the doctor came, he had a hard struggle to open, then close the door. He sat down by Papa's side and drew off the covers. He did not have good news.

"I do not know if I can save that leg, Mahalalel. The wound is festering. I will have to take it off below the knee. Be a brave soul for me now, man." Margreet wanted to help, but mama told her to go to bed. Nochi had not been born yet. Putting the covers over my head, I tried to smother the sound of sawing. The room smelled of blood and guts. Mama held his hand, and her nose as well. There was still blood on the bed and floor the next morning. He lay in bed for days after that. Clinging to my covers, I evoked the protection of the benevolent St. Nicholas to save us all.

November 16

Today mother was happy. A letter came from her great friend, Mrs. Byron, whom she met in London years ago. I wish a letter could have that effect upon me. Twill not be a letter from this world that could do that.

"Oh, children, listen to news from England. Mrs. Byron recalls how her husband Jack, "Foul Weather Jack," fought here. He would sing, 'America! My newfound land, my America, my America.' He told her he would bring his Catherine here. She says, 'Jack, you fought against America in your red coat.' Says he, 'I fought to keep it,' then crows like the scoundrel he is. Oh dear, she writes that the French have a new device to execute people by slicing off the head: 'It is called the Guillotine, after its inventor. Heads will roll. It may be that even heads of kings and queens will roll. It happened to Charles I. These are the unsafe times.'"

I turned my back on Mama. No matter what side of the Atlantic they may be on, the last thing on this sorry earth that I wanted to hear about was heads rolling. Mother remained wrapped up in her letter. I looked down to the floor.

"Listen to me son. It is not every day we receive a letter like this. If I could cry loud enough, she might hear me and come over. Years ago, she had come down to London, from Aberdeen. And, there, in the short time given to us, we became friends."

"Why did they call her husband 'Foul Weather Jack,' mother?" asked Enoch.

"Because every time he went to sea, storms loomed," said Margreet who must have heard stories of the Byrons before.

"He is a dark man, children. Dances on the Sabbath. When his first wife died, he said, 'Black becomes her.' Her baby is as beautiful as a cherub but has a club foot. It is as if an angel fell to earth, but a piece of hell came up to meet it in the shape of a cloven hoof. Mrs. Byron says they took Jack to the King's Bench Prison for his debt. His tailor bailed him out. Children, can you imagine that? He has run through her fortune now. As she says, he is 'a rattlin, roarin' man.' He reminds me of your friend Abraham, though in marrying a Dutch girl, he will have a Katrina instead of a Catherine. I promise you nothing will be lost. Imagine an upstart Yankee thinking he could wed the daughter of a wealthy, Dutch burger. The schoolmaster was not thinking. Catherine had more wealth than any of them including a castle in Scotland. And a title to boot, Laird, for her father was a laird who had no sons. There was a dark legend:

"When the heron leaves the tree, the Laird of Gight shall landless be.' Do you know the thing about legends, children, is that they are wont to come true? Jack made her so poor that my friend had to sell her castle to Lord Haddo.

"Poor Jack. Poor Catherine. Catherine has the northern way of talking, and the English do not think much of that. She is an aristocrat who looks more like a peasant." Nochi screwed up his face into a knot.

Paying him no mind, Mama continued.

"For Jack she sold her castle. There is yet another legend which foretold that the castle would slip from Lord Haddo's hand: 'At Gight three men a violent death shall dee. After that, the land shall lie in lea.' Now she lives in Nottingham."

"Did three men dee, I mean, die, Mama?" asked Nochi. Even Margaret revealed a sense of wonder at this pitiful prophecy.

"Oh Yes. Lord Haddo himself fell from his horse cracking his head. Two servants died soon after that." Nochi started to tremble.

"Oh no, Nochi. You need not show any fear. We put reason over revelation. No legends exist about us Willems, just a prophecy that we will live happily ever after in a fair place called Tarrytown." Nochi and Margreet smiled.

"Our blood is lower but purer, than that of the farmer King George. Now in Tarrytown, we do not put any stock in castles or titles, but Catherine Gordon can trace her lineal descent from the Lord of Huntley and King James the First of Scotland; they call her 'the Honorable Kitty,' and I warrant that she is a friend of mine."

"A fair place called Tarrytown? Mother? 'Tarwa Dorp.' Wheat town. We live in a little wheat town where we have tarried too long. Take my meaning as you will," I remarked. Mother was never as proud as when claiming she put no stock in titles. Sister Margreet looked hurt and surprised that I would speak to mother like that, especially after the letter from her Scottish friend had lifted her heart.

"Do legends come true, Mama?" asked Nochi. "Is there why The Honorable Kitty lost her castle? Oh what a shame to have a castle, then lose it!"

"It is not so much the legend that took her castle away as her husband. If she comes to America with her husband Jack, he will make nothing of himself and nothing out of what she may have left," Margreet, who is usually a sphinx, enlightened us. Then she drew me into the fire.

"Why did she marry a man who had nothing to give? Was it because he was handsome and charming? Could she not do better? What women want is beautiful clothing, so they will look so pleasing when they travel to faraway places. Cupboards filled with silver and gold, servants to do the housework and to strut about the town on the arm of a good looking man will do. Her Jack did not give but take away. Damen will not be able to give much to Josefien, either," said Margreet added bitingly.

I did not think that those were the things that Margreet wanted at all. Why was she so mean? I never thought about such things. I only knew that we had been tenant farmers until the revolution when father bought the land. Father worked very for many years to save the money to buy it. One day I suppose it would be mine. Like the sun going behind the clouds, my thoughts darkened. I did not even want the farm.

"Do not look at your brother Damen, when you speak like that, Margreet. Damen will make a good husband for Josefien. Since when has your mind been taken with the treasures that moth and rust corrupt?" asked Mama.

"I wish Josefien came with a castle. We could all live in it," said Nochi excitedly.

"You were not listening, Nochi. In America, you do not come with anything. You have to make it. You earn money by using your head. The Phillipse family made their money by selling wheat to the British army who required in more bushels that you can count." Mama shook her finger at us.

"But they lost their riches, Mama. Mr. Beekman has the upper mills, now."

"Yes, Nochi. He has the upper hand. Someone always has to come out on top. Twill always be."

"I reckon Papa is not going to buy Mama a castle. I will build you a castle, Mama. You can be queen."

"Oh, Nochi. Spoken like a real prince. Come over here and give your queen a little kiss." Nochi ran over to hug and kiss her.

It was a good thing that father was outside taking his anger out on the British by stomping around the field. America is not a land to keep castles or kings or queens. We are not like the British. Nor will we have a Guillotine like the French for we do not like to make such a show.

November 17

Oh, all the things I did. Here I stand with my conscience seared and burned like a pig on the hob. "No hope for them that laugh," said the preacher on Sunday. I reckon that, therefore, there is hope for me. It has been a long time since I laughed. What is all this nonsense about, my talk of being a black man who cannot wear a white shirt, walking about the woods like a spirit?

Was it only two weeks ago that I was proud to be a Sleepy Hollow Boy? Given a dare, we could do anything. There was Abraham, Hobnail, Caleb and me. We thought that since we will soon be putting away our childish things, we should whoop it up now. Until the night we went too far, it was silly prank after prank. We only stopped laughing when work needed to be done. We only wanted more fun. Only Abraham had more stake in it than a laugh, but we rode out down the post road to scare a man half to death. It was a bargain made with the devil, and we got more than I can bear. Wrangle it about in my mind as I may, relentlessly the thought comes back to me that in our harum-scarum ride, we killed Ichabod.

Chapter Nine

Most Haunted

"We killed Ichabod?" I shouted out. My glasses slid down to the end of my nose. It's an odd expression, but I think I experienced a frisson of horror. Chester flew up from under the covers rocking the cold cup of coffee which sat neglected on the table. Then he saw the half-eaten English muffin. As he made a swipe at it, I warned him off. "Chester!" He started licking the melted butter out of all those nooks and crannies. Of course, he did not take me seriously. What cat would? After I pulled the muffin out of his maw, Chester jumped down to the floor to daintily lick away at his paws.

What kind of manuscript was this? Had I purchased an eighteenth-century journal describing actual events, or a work of fiction? Was this meant to be read as a sequel?

Wouldn't it be something if it had historical or literary, even monetary value? I might have to invest in an appraisal. I could bring the book to the Antique Roadshow next time they came to town.

I might be laughed out of town. The journal could be a hoax like those early, black and white photos of the Loch Ness monster. Every so often some book came out purporting to be the diary of someone famous. There were the Hitler diary and even a Jack the Ripper journal. Those were the ones I could recall, but there were probably others. No one even cared if they were real or not. Books like that made news, flew off the shelves and then disappeared. I never bothered to read any of them. What did it mean, or what was it worth, if the author rode out as a wild Sleepy Hollow boy, and subsequently felt compelled to discern the true fate of Ichabod Crane to assuage his guilty conscience? They were fictional characters who managed to stay alive for centuries through books, paintings, cartoons, movies and now, even the medium of television. Or were they?

Whether the characters were real or fictitious, I was hooked on the story. The kid with his "seared" conscience, the old man, swinging his remaining leg over the wooden one in the dark pretending to be a war hero, and the funny, little brother, held my interest. That older son wouldn't feel such guilt if he lived nowadays. He might take drugs to control his posttraumatic stress disorder. Chester stretched his body out over the book, butted me with his big soft head, then gave a big yawn. The kid had no one to look up to, Chet. Today he might take his story all over the networks to tell his tale of woe and sell his book.

Then the phone rang. It was Stan calling from Philadelphia.

"Hey, Richard. Glad I caught you. How's it going?" You OK?" We hadn't spoken in a while. Even though it was my brother, I felt awkward. Speaking to someone who matters was a rare event in my life. Then again, there was all that baggage of childhood.

"I'm just plugging away. Not much is new. How about you?"

"You have a few minutes Richard?" Chester butted me again with his ever loving head.

"Yeah, sure Stan." Small talk wouldn't put Stanley off. I knew what was coming.

"Good. Are you getting out to enjoy yourself? I hope you're not just going from home to work, and back again in a daily grind, Richard."

"You didn't call me to nag, did you? Or, to give me a good, old pep talk?

"Nah. Sorry Richard, but I have my agenda. We would like you to come up and meet Manny. He's been with us a few months now. Edie could tell you to the hour and minute. We've spoken about this before, but I can never pin you down. Manny's getting bigger every day. By the way, thanks very much for his Bath Fun Octopus. He loves it. And the truck too. You know all about boys and trucks. But he needs to see you. You're his uncle."

"Sure, Stan. Sounds like a great idea. I'd love to visit. Just the other day, I was telling Dave at the office that I was going to Philadelphia. I said I couldn't wait to meet my nephew." Of course, I did not add that I said it just to get out of playing golf with Dave.

"We'd just love to see you, Richard. Can you set a date?" I told you Stan was not the man to be put off.

"Hold on, Stan. I'll check my calendar."

I fumbled in the card table drawer for my small, leather notebook. I already knew there wasn't much happening on any weekend, holiday, or any day after five for the rest of the year for that matter. Possibly for the rest of my life, for all I know. Flipping to October, I saw the Columbus Day weekend coming up. I figured that since there was no way to get out of this visit, I might as well face up to it now.

"Ok, Stan. I meant to ask how Edie's doing. Is she okay? I see Columbus Day is coming up. How does the weekend of October 8th look to you guys?"

"Fine Richard. Gorgeous time of year. Fall colors will be coming out well then. We're a bit of head of you being south. Come on down Richard. We can have fun. I can spook you out with our Mutter's Museum."

"OK, Stanley. I'll pencil you in." As soon as I said it, I regretted saying 'pencil.'"

"Ok. You made my day, brother. Now don't go bringing anything except yourself. I'm looking forward to seeing you. I can't wait to see the look on Manny's face when he meets his Uncle Richard. I have been missing you."

"Me too, Stan. Have you heard from mom?" It was true. I had been missing myself.

"I spoke to her last week. She doesn't want to push you. It would be nice if you gave her a call. She worries about you. Mostly she's still getting over Dad. I hope she's not hiding away too much. Like mother, like son. She promises to meet her grandson by Christmas. If she doesn't come to us, we will go to her. Florida is her cocoon."

"That's what people do. They withdraw. I'll be in touch, Stan."

We signed off. If I couldn't be the doting uncle, I would at least be the dutiful one. Couldn't just send a Hallmark card in this case. The kid probably didn't speak much English. I guess it's too soon for him to read anyway. I think he's three.

It was about seven. The evening stretched itself out before me. Carefully putting the manuscript away in the card table drawer, I started checking emails, messages, and voicemail. How easy it was to text. No emotion, only those infernal emojis. It was almost like Morse code compared to talking on the phone. Texting kept everyone and everything at arm's length. Thought of taking up the Times again, but opted for TV. Ninety-nine channels and there's nothing to watch. Or, like going 100 miles per hour down a dead end street? Dylan or Springsteen or both? They always get it right. I started channel surfing.

And there, as if in hot pursuit of me, the Headless Horseman filled up the screen. That dense, blond girl from the *Most Haunted* show, the one with the sloping, blobby eyes, was planted in front of a huge, dark orange statue of the Horseman up near Sleepy Hollow Cemetery. I missed that one. What kind of metal was that? It looked like fruit rind or pumpkin guts.

Now I was amazed. Here was the British up in the Hudson Valley, treading on enemy territory. Obviously, they were there to investigate a haunting. Maybe the patriots who gave their lives for the cause of American independence would rise from their graves to haunt these British nutcases back over the ocean. This situation was delicious. Worth a few laughs. Grab a beer and some chips, Chester. We're in for a hoot. I even felt a pang of momentary jealousness. If anyone was going to sniff out anything supernatural up there, I wanted it to be me. Ok, cat. I'm losing it. I had to laugh at myself for wanting to join in the chase.

The *Most Haunted* team was pitching tents to spend the night. They were close to the cemetery, but not actually in it. I figured they were bedding down in Douglas Park. Could you dig up the ground close to the gates? You might find something there. Again, I felt that jealous pang. If that dark cloth had any significance, I should get the credit. Ha.

Here came the pitch: According to recent reports, locals started hearing sounds of hoof beats in the vicinity of the Old Dutch after dark. Midnight, of course. Who could it be? From their vantage point in the woods, Sleepy Hollow appeared to be a wilderness. They couldn't fool me. I knew just how close to civilization they were. A BP station was just around the corner. I felt ill at ease watching the show. Chester had curled up next to me on the bed. His fur was soft and warm. A little chill went up my spine. I got up to close the window. It was October now. Chester shouldn't feel chilled.

They no sooner settled in when the ghostbusting team started jumping up and down as if to get out of their skins. Yips and screams were coming from the tent. The taller man took out a flashlight to examine the ground. Talk about your anti-climax. They were unnerved by the Daddy Long Legs which were scampering across their campground. Of course, the camera man's shot magnified the insect to heroic scale.

Ghostbusters who were afraid of bugs. Most ludicrous. I guffawed right out loud. Chester jumped up from his slumber vertically into the air, giving me quite a fright. Reaching down, I scooped him back up into the bed. Sorry, Chester, old boy, I said while giving him a hug. They have just got to be kidding. We bedded down.

So did the team. Then, one of the women stirred again. Telling everyone to be quiet, she listened for a sound in the woods. Hoofbeats. Shhhhhh! I hear hoof beats." It was certain now that the Headless Horseman was making a beeline straight for them. The one with the funny eyes sure looked scared. It struck me as ironic that intrepid ghost busters were scared of ghosts. They would have more to worry about if no spooks showed up. Ratings, ratings, ratings. Now they had me going. What is it about the ghosts that perplex the imagination and defies common sense? Spirits keep a hold on our interest, even when we know better?

The night was dark. A microphone was picking up sounds. Their ghost meter was vibrating up a storm. Something was up. Devices were beeping and lighting up. The viewer could hear something that might have hoofbeats, but the camera caught nothing. Sounds would have to do. We wouldn't want to focus the lenses on hoof prints now.

Small, triangular prints would indicate white tail deer, a creature prevalent in the area. Tarrytown had a deer crossing sign right off Main Street. As the show wound down, they brought out their expert, a Ph.D. in something. It was his job to decide whether this ghost hunt had produced any empirical evidence of things that go bump in the night or not. Did their findings have validity? I was on the edge of my seat. Nah. With eyes spread out even wider than the blond woman's, if that was possible, and gap-toothed mouth, the good doctor, gave the verdict. No, there was no evidence of supernatural activity that evening in Sleepy Hollow. What a relief for America. And, Britain as well. I hoped Brooke and her friend Bonnie were watching. Now they could go back to sleep resting assured, that legends withstanding, Sleepy Hollow was spirit free.

All good things must come to an end. There was the blond standing in front of that huge, rust-colored Horseman statue again to sign off. They had survived the night. Give them a hand. I don't know if they used any technology to enhance the color, but the valley was glowing with an almost supernatural lighting in the final shots. The grass was greener than green, the metal of the statue glinted in a bright copper gleam. Most alluring.

Nature was enough for me. The Hudson Valley would soon be at its most beautiful with fall colors to challenge those closing shots of the TV show. No pun intended, but the show put the bug back in me. Not sure if it was the Revolutionary War history, or the simple, natural beauty, that attracted me most. It was not the city or the country. It was the town. Long before the Most Haunted team had set foot up in the hollow, or even seen the light of day, young Damen Willem was busy up there haunting himself. I just might go back up again on Saturday if only to check out the Daddy Longlegs.

The still life painting on the wall started to bother me. What had it to do with me? I had to admit though that my life was at a standstill. A landscape of the Hudson Valley would be more pleasing. I took out the laptop and started looking on Ebay. There were hundreds available, but a reproduction of a painting by Frederic Edwin Church popped out.

Dramatic pinkish, gray clouds took up almost two-thirds of the picture. The valley below, the river which ran through it all, the puffy trees snug against the winding paths, might have been anywhere in the country. That was a good thing in case my interest in the region should fade. I would have to find a new place for the still life. After all, it was a gift from my mother. I couldn't just take it down again. Above, the kitchen table might work.

As I turned out the light, I heard Chester jump up to the foot of the bed. He circled a few times, then settled in. My huge shadow was hovering on the wall over us. It disturbed me. I tried lying down as flat as I could. The shadow almost disappeared. On the floor below, a baby cried. A cat mewed next door. That opera singer who was performing in a local production of *The Phantom of the Opera* was rehearsing up on the fourth floor. Have you to practice at this hour? Really? I would have banged the broom against the ceiling, but I didn't want to get out of bed. I went down to sleep reminding myself to continue reading the manuscript.

Chapter Ten

Sick in the Soul

We were just lads running wild in the hollow. Our pranks were innocent. We stopped up the chimney to smoke out the singing school, then returned in the night to turn the classroom topsy-turvy. We spilled out all the ink and overturned the desk and chairs. The next morning we snickered behind the trees as Ichabod announced, "There will be no school today, children." The youngsters laughed much to their delight. We did too. Thus, we earned the appellation, "The Sleepy Hollow Boys." There was no end to the mischief that Brom's head could conjure up. The next prank would take a little more time and planning.

"Let us go out into the night to lead all the horses out of the barns, and change them out. Twill be something when old Farmer Battus stumbles out in the morning to the barn. What would I give to see his countenance when, instead of Heriold, his mighty stallion, old Bat finds a changeling mare rolling in the hay? He will cry, 'Oh, where is my horse? Oh, where is my horse?' What have they done to Heriold the Mighty?" I laughed with restraint, but Caleb and Hob roared. It was to me he turned.

"Damen, horse trading. It is not an honorable profession?" Putting his thick arms around us, he continued, "Boys, tonight we become honorable men." The big man lifted Hob up into his brawny arms in a huge bear hug. Caleb slapped his knees and guffawed. Raising both hands up to push my hair back from my forehead, I looked at Brom. I was astonished. I shook my head, but I wanted to do this. There was all this harvesting to be done, and we playing at being fools. Many good folks may have judged us, but many envied us as well.

It was true that people sometimes accused Brom of things he did not do. He did not throw pots of paint at the blacksmith's door. "I might have been having a tumble in the hay, that night, boys. But that I can't say." Brom cared not. He laughed it all off. So, off we went into the dark when all good folks are in bed, to do a little horse trading. We rode some. We walked some. It was a little tiring, but we were still guffawing and slapping our knees, as we trudged back home along the Turnpike road. In the early morning light, I spied the little hollow down the steep hill, at the border of our farmland. A little house was soon to be built for me there. I would live there with my wife Josefien when the spring comes. And, here I was acting more like a wild thing than a man about to be married. It was still September. The evening air was warm, and winter seemed far away.

"We are not done yet, boys. Before the frost is on the pumpkin, we will get in our last lick. There is a certain schoolmaster who could do with a lesson of his own." And then he laid out his scheme. We would wait for Master Crane to leave the merry-making, then pursuit him down the Turnpike. Through the dark, we would move as quietly as the Wilden.

Not a branch would be broken. This prank would involve legends, costumes, and pumpkins. We listened with awe and excitement. Caleb predicted that the big man would outdo himself with this one.

"Was there ever a man like Brom Bones?" posed Caleb. We repeated this question to each other over and over. He was becoming the stuff of legend. We never stopped to think. We just followed anywhere that he would go. And, when we rode out under the harvest moon, to scare that scarecrow of a schoolmaster half out of his wits, it never occurred to us that he would not come back. It has been over two weeks now, and there is not a trace of him left, but his hat. Yes, Abraham topped it off. Now I am gripped with such fear that I cannot swallow. We enjoyed a bountiful harvest. Now I might be harvested myself. I was sure that by now the schoolmaster would have shown his face. Would to God out pranks had ended with summer!

November 19

Things have jagged edges. I am always snagged. When I walk into a room, people go quietly. When I step outside the door, tongues wag. I would give a good deal to know what they are saying. I caught a snatch today. Going inside the barn, I heard Margreet say, "Oh, he loved the ladies, but he loved to eat even more." I do believe she is referring to the schoolmaster.

"I hardly knew him . . . " I blurted out. Oh, no! I had spoken my thought again out loud.

"Cousin Damen, who is it you hardly know?" asked Little Cuz. She should have been gone with summer, but here she was still staying with us long after the frost was on the pumpkin. Her eyes were glowing like a cat's in the dark. She was trying hard not to smile, but her lips were curling up in spite of her effort. Mama entered with Josefien. This distraction might have saved me if little Cuz was only as curious as a cat. Unfortunately for me, she was as cross as a bear when thwarted. Little Cuz will have her way.

"Look who has come to visit us. Josefien, have you met Damen's little cousin, Roos?" After introducing them, Mama withdrew from the room. Little Cuz resumed the torment.

"Damen says he hardly knows someone. Who is it you hardly know? Josefien, he wants to keep secrets. Do tell us now."

"Damen will not keep secrets from me. We will soon share everything," said Josefien.

"The teacher!" I shouted before Roos could say anything naughty. I wanted to lie. But like an aching tooth, the truth will nag, then rage, to come out.

I did not think Roos' saucer eyes could get any rounder, but they did. With the solemnity of Solomon, raised up both hands to shape them into claws, to announced, "The schoolteacher? You should not trouble your head about him, Damen. He is not coming back to get on your wick. The Goblin Horseman took him to get a more learned head." Roos almost laughed her head off at her joke. I was not amused.

"Hush! Hush! Hush up your mouth!" scolded Margreet, compressing her lips tightly.

It was too late to be quiet. Father had heard us. "How can it be you have all this time to laze about while the chores are crying out to done?" he demanded shaking his fist.

"Oh, Uncle Mahalalel," said Cuz drawing out each syllable. "The chores do not talk, but if they did, they would tell you that Damen would prefer to talk about hoo doo rather than do his work today."

"Hoo doo?"

"Father, Little Cuz is familiar with local lore such as demons who ride out on horses to snatch up heads right off people's shoulders. I was about to tell her not to believe in such things," said Margreet. Josefien nodded.

The chores were going to have to scream out to get done because Father started in against the English.

"The English say that we Dutch take stock in old wives tales. We do not. They reckon we are backward Germans. They even think we speak German which shows just how ignorant they truly are. The only one without a head is that Hessian who got struck by a cannonball. They buried him in our cemetery. Foolish folk says he rides out with his troops out to battle after midnight when Godly folk is tucked up in bed," explained father. He sat himself down on a bale of hay to rub his leg above the stump. His talk of battle must have irritated his old wound.

"I think I saw him riding past the farm last night," said Roos. I could not determine if she was serious because her lips were, as always, curled into a smile.

"Well, it may be that he questions why he was fool enough to leave his homeland to cross oceans to fight a losing battle for the English. His mind is addled. I do not know if a person can have a mind without having a head but, Roos, I leave that to you to decide. It is the English, not the Dutch, who have permeated the air of the hollow with such legends. A man may not walk in the woods after dark without frightening himself with these tales. The Bible speaks of Celestial beings, but the English prefer demons," Father continued.

"Do the English believe in The Headless Horseman? What about the Woman in White?" Josefien asked.

Some of the English believe. Some do not. So enamored of spirits are they, that prayer at a loved one's grave does not suffice. They must tell their tales of the dead over and over. The Dutch just laugh. One day, one of them, probably one with Scottish blood, will write them all down in a book."

"Uncle," Little Cuz began, then dissolved into laughter. Checking herself, she continued, "People who scoff at such tales in the bright sunlight, are not so sure of themselves when the sun goes down." Placing her hands on her hips, she laughed and stuck out her tongue. Roos was proud to have the last word. The look of triumph on her face did not last. Her saucy expression fell off. She looked scared. It was growing dark outside. "I think I did see the Horseman flying past in the night."

I confronted her. "You are right to be scared. The Headless Horseman bore away our schoolmaster's head, leaving us no peace by day or by night. Most folks are too busy to ramble on about such matters in daylight for there is work to be done. Though exhausted by day labor, they toss and turn in their beds all night. But why? Are these true tales? No. These are things that people put in your head. Cotton Mather put the superstition of witches and warlocks in Ichabod's head. The schoolmaster put them in ours. Brom Bones added the legend," I added. My anger was boiling over.

"Cotton? What kind of name is Cotton?" asked Roos.

"I do not know. You should ask the Minister since we have no schoolmaster," I replied.

"Yes. Master Crane's head was so filled up with witches and apparitions, that, all the talk of the Horseman scared him off to the next town. He is probably taking the birch up against the naughty little urchins down the river in the next town right now," Margreet remarked.

"No, Margreet. You may be bigger than me, but you do not know everything," declared Little Cuz. She stood next to my sister to compare heights.

"Do you think they will fish him out of the Pocantico Creek, Roos? Twill not be his head that he starts blundering about to find, but his hat. He was always crying out about the poor wages. He will have to see Van Ripper about that. He is holding on to all his earthly goods," said father starting to yawn. Then he turned to me.

"Why is it that Van Brunt hides his face to snigger whenever the schoolmaster's, name comes up. Most folks do not even care, though some do. Brom knows something that he will not tell. You are his friend, Damen, though I do not know why. You might know this." I put my head down.

"I would like to know the answer to a better question, Uncle Mahalalel," Roos interjected. "Why are they, friends? Damen walks like a schoolteacher, with his head bent down in a book, though he is far too handsome to be mistaken for a runaway scarecrow who escaped from the cornfield. When you put on your spectacles, you even look smart," continued Roos turning to look at me.

"You sound as if you are half in love with your cousin. Damen, being a thoughtful man, is the better man. I would not give a button for Brom," said Josefien, giving me a sidelong, fond look.

I looked to father to see if he would agree, but he had curled up on the bale of hay to fall asleep in the noonday sun. Roos had stolen his fire. Shrugging, I sat down on a bale of straw. Everyone followed suit. Now, Little Cuz would have her way.

"Damen is the better man except in when it comes to riches. Katrina, with the beautiful hands and hair, will cook and cook for her father. When he is all fattened up like a bullfrog, he will blow up, leaving Brom in charge of the farm. Brom will work hard enough to buy up all the farms in the valley. Before the blink of an eye, he will have as many acres of land as Frederick Philipse. Then, instead of saying, Philipse-his-Castle, it will be Van Brunt-his-Castle. He will buy up your farm. Then one day, Damen, you will work for him," says Roos.

Suddenly Binx the mouser ran across the field in pursuit of a crow. Nochie, laughing hysterically, was trying to catch Binx. He ran so fast he took a fall. He began to cry. When I ran over to see if he was okay, a look of terror spread across his face. He started to cower, a thing he never did. Father kept a birch rod behind the door for thrashings but never used. Our usual punishment consisted of having to copy out Bible verses. Was there something in my eyes that frightened Nochie so? Suddenly remembering that he was supposed to be pitching the hay, he picked himself up and ran off. I rejoined the ladies.

"That day will never come. No one says Philipse-his-Castle, anymore. It would be Castle Philipse, except that it will soon be Castle Willem. Damen is a hard, working, conscientious farmer. He is just like Father who works so hard that he falls asleep in the afternoon. When Father grows too decrepit to work the fields, Damen will dig, and plow and seed so well that the next frolic will be held right here. Of course, twill be under the harvest moon. We will have such an abundance of crops that we will share our good fortune with the entire Hudson Valley," declared Josefien with glowing pride. I looked away to hide my blushing cheeks.

Margreet came over to push my hair off my forehead as tenderly as mother did when I was little. I felt like a lad again. Then she took my hand and sat down beside me. Straightening her shoulders back in her chair, she hinted that I should do likewise.

"Margreet, Josefien, I am not the good a man you make me out to be. Someday I might grow good again. Tomorrow, Mama has arranged for me to visit with Dominie Hunthum at the church. She, at least, believes there is hope for me." I slumped down and had to plant my feet firmly on the ground to avoid slipping off the bale of hay.

November 18

Mama made a fuss over my clothes, brushing off my coat, saying that it matched my slate blue eyes. Father walked me to the church where he left me on the bench outside. I should wait, he cautioned, until Dominie Hunthum came out. By no means should I bother the door. Yes. Yes. I sat on the cold bench clutching my stomach as I watched Father stump away. There was a chill in the air. The white washed stone was cold to the touch. A cardinal streaked by over my head.

Growing tired of waiting, I knocked on the door. No one answered, so I started wandering amongst the graves. The dead started talking to me. An epitaph for one Dirck Hoogland caught my attention:

Death is a debt
To all is due
Which I have paid and so
must you

If the dead talked to me, I would talk back to them. Twas, not death that bothers me, Dirck but the dying. Looking across the road to the slave burying place, I thought that only by dying could they be free. Then Dominie Hunthum appeared at the window, waving me inside.

"Come in Damen. How fares it with you" said the minister. Motioning to a table which was covered with books, paper, pen and ink, chunks of leftover bread, he said, "Sit yourself down. Your family has been worried about your welfare. Are you unwell?" His long dark hair, parted in the middle, came down over his shoulders. I watched his thick, pink lips which were easy to see despite his curly, mustache.

"I am well enough in body."

"I wish that I could say the same. My stomach is often unsettled, and my eyesight is growing dimmer." Withdrawing inside of himself, he fell silent. I would not give a penny to know what went inside his head. After an uncomfortable pause, he resumed.

"Well in body, Damen? Sick in the soul? What was it that the good Lord said, "The spirit is willing, but the body is weak?" He seemed befuddled. I quickly agreed.

"Is it a matter of the spirit or the heart?" Are you unhappy in the ways of your intended? Does Josefien Blomaert not please you? Does she have your heart? It will be enough if she has your thoughts."

"Dominie, I am happy with my Josefien. She has my heart and my head."

Despite my resolve to say nothing, I blurted out, "I have done something." My words hung in the air my head. Too late to draw the breath of words back. Would that he could have ignored them, but Hunthum continued to press.

"You come from a good, God-fearing, churchgoing family. You are still young and cared for, living under your father's roof. What have you done to unsettle your spirit and your family's peace, I wonder? You must have done something. You do not look like a proper villain. I will hazard that you broke a piece of crockery. Though to our good housewives, that might not prove to be such a trifling matter. It is not, however, the same as breaking a commandment," he teased.

"Yes, I did. How did you know this, Dominie? Did my mother come to tell you?" I seized upon the chocolate cup incident to unburden myself. When the preacher consulted his watch, I knew his patience had worn out.

"I roused my father's ire so much that he threw, eh, well, he threw something at me, and a cup was broken. There is nothing as heavy as the weight this has placed upon my soul, for the mother is so house proud, this loss has cut at her heart. Her kitchen is her special pride."

"Damen, I fear that it is more than that. Hendrika should not lay up her treasures here on earth, but you have broken the fifth commandment. You did not honor your father. You aroused his anger and brought down his wrath." As he moved forward to the edge of his seat, his fat belly relieved its weight by sinking in a space between his plump thighs.

I frowned. I said nothing. There was nothing I could say.

"Your mother has a sweetness about her. Mahalalel, despite his bluster, is a kind man at heart." He must have been running down the list of commandments in his head.

"There is more. Did you take something, Damen? Because if you did, I would call the thief catcher right now."

I shook my head. Surely I will find no mercy here. If I had anything on my side, it was time. I would waste his time. Knowing how much he wanted to be away, I placed my forehead flat to the table's surface.

"Look up, at me Damen. Do not avert your gaze. Whatever you have done will be revealed."

I looked up. Sitting ramrod straight, I placed both hands flat upon my knees, turning myself into the statue.

"I have not the time to run through the Ten Commandments or all the laws of Leviticus. Just tell me, Damen, what it is that you have done," the dominie demanded.

I sat stock still.

"You may be as silent as the tomb, but I will draw it out. I may not bring it forth out of you today for I have much to do that does not concern you. A sermon to prepare, sick people to give succor to . . . " His stomach gave a rumbling sound. Wanting to add, dinners to eat, tasty pies to swallow, I mastered my mouth.

"It is not easy Damen. Our Dutch is going. English was our work week language. Now we use it on Sunday too. We labor under the rule of the Anglicans and mother church in Holland. We cannot even hire a minister without sending him back to the Netherlands to be ordained. Not easy to raise money for the voyage. Salary? They might as well pay us in salt. The only good thing about the Revolution is that we got the old world classis, off our backs. But, we cannot convert the blacks. We cannot save the wilden.

"Then there is the matter of the schoolmaster. We cannot even keep a schoolmaster. All that trouble to hire that Pumpkinhead of a Connecticut Yankee, Ichabod, and, now he is gone. I have to conjure up another. Twill not be a Yankee. I tell you that. He was a Yankee, was he not? Schoolmasters arrange for the burial of folks. If he should turn up dead, who will bury him?"

Down went my heart. My chest shuddered and sank.

"I should have appointed a Dutchman. Did Ichabod teach you anything besides the supernatural, the legends and lore of Madame Hulda or the legend of your Headless Hessian? "

"Master Crane spoke of many things and for many hours. He read books with titles in Latin containing spectral evidence of possession. They were written by scholars, men of the cloth, with odd names, like Cotton and Increase Mather. Up in the North Country, there were Incubi and succubi. Young girls from God-fearing families were shaking, shuddering with fits because the community had not been vigilant enough. The devil had sidled up beside them. There was a red, translucent cat. Killer cats too. All they had to do to kill you was to look at you." The dominie's mouth formed a big O.

"In Boston? There were witches in Boston?" A little bit of spittle flew from his mouth. I found myself wiping my own with the back of my hand.

"They were in a place to the north of Boston. Salem, Dominie. Salem."

"Did you accept these nefarious tales as truth, gospel truth?"

"I am a God fearing man. I was one before I met Ichabod and a more God fearing one after listening to him. Have you read these books, dominie?"

"I have not. Tell me more."

"Well, there were brooms and black goblins up in trees that could send huge planks of wood up into the air. There was a woman in a red coat who made a pact with the devil."

"No! They sound worse than Baptists, Quakers, and Catholics. Oh, my good lord. Shelter me. That must have had a bad end."

"It did Dominie. With the jails stacked to the rafters with witches and warlocks, they brought the possessed ones up before a hanging judge, Judge Hathorne. He condemned them. So they took all these witches up on a high ridge, with the town all below it, and set up a gallows, and hung them high."

Suddenly the dominie's interest in my stories fell off.

"Cotton Mather? Succubi and Incubi? Mather was English, not at all sensible like the Dutch. His name refers to a cottage. We do not have names like that. We do not burn witches. We may have caught one in New Netherland, but there was not enough evidence to prosecute her. You are speaking of scholars whose heads were overweighted to the point of toppling over with ghosts, hobgoblins, folklore, and witchcraft."

They were ministers, lawyers, Harvard Men for Jesus's sake. Dominie, why was he named Cotton?" I tried to distract him.

"So that is how the schoolmaster's head got filled up with nonsense. Many a hot day, as I was trudging to do my duty, with the sweat beading up on my brow, I would see him lounging under the tree lazily reading. He lived not so much in a schoolhouse as in a Castle of Indolence. No good will ever come out of that. I would not be so surprised if some dark spirits did carry him off."

"It is not for us to judge. I trust in God," I cried.

"Do you have to bring God into our talk? What will you trust to God? How will you trust in God?" he shouted. I looked down to see a vision next to my foot. A camera obscura must have projected it. The fiend rising the fiery pumpkin up high in the air, aiming at the harried schoolmaster. I shook my head and rubbed my eyes.

Beads of sweat started appearing the dominie's reddening brow. He drew himself up out of the chair with no small effort. His waistcoat rose up to his chest. He pulled it back down, placed both fists on the table, and gave me his hardest look.

"I do not know what is wrong with this generation. You have no discipline. You are so stubborn, stiff-necked, unfaithful to God, disobedient to parents, that you are virtually sermon-proof. You, who live in times of peace, should not go to war with yourself. Did your precious schoolmaster teach you the story of our country? Not so long ago, down the Hudson in New York Harbor, the British had the waters red with blood. Redcoats and red blood were all you would see from sea to sky. Someone said all that red made it look like London.

"I have never been to London, but your mother has. It is a wonder that Hendrika does not put on airs. You must read your Bible to find such sights. Waste howling wilderness. Seas red with blood. It was like London floating over the Atlantic to our shores. And we were losing. General Washington on the run. Up to White Plains, he went. And there he lost again, boy. We were doomed. It was a judgment day what with the Continental Army prisoners starving and covered in lice in the prison ships down in the port of Manhattan at Fort Washington. 'These were the times that try man's soul,' said Thomas Paine. You are wasting away in a time of prosperity."

Finally, his little sermon came to an end. "Damen we will meet again. Until we do, you must give your mother no further cause for worry. But if you want me to heal you, you must put your troubles into words. Now thank me for what I have tried to do for you. Think over your deeds until we meet again. Whatever you have done must be dealt with in this world if you do not want to deal with it in the next. You will not have me there with you there to help see it through."

I stepped outside the church, carefully closing the door behind me. It had grown warmer outside. A light wind was stirring up the fallen leaves. My ears were ringing. Stunned, I sat down on a cartwheel across the road where the dark folks lay in their humble graves. I felt as if I had been cracked open like the fallen chestnuts that lay on the ground along with the brown leaves.

Chapter Eleven

Brimstone, Mama, Brimstone

November 19

My family was at peace. Mama made pancakes while Margreet scoured the table. Nochi played with Binx. Mama complained about the smoke from Father's pipe, so he took it outside. It was making her cough. That was that. Sitting in the corner and looking out the window, I watched dark clouds move over the river. Father's smoke curled up before my face. The future stretched out before me as an endlessly, unyielding and infertile as the field in winter.

Mama came over to put her hand on my shoulder. "Did Dominie Hunthum pacify your soul? I was so hoping he might be able to lift your spirit." No one, no matter how hard anyone tried, could succeed one whit in understanding or to alleviate the trouble in my mind. Not the dominie. Not Mama. "Trebly damned am I to hell, according to the dominie. I was not able to find much solace in that." Mother's hand flew up to her mouth. Like a bunny, Enoch vigorously sniffed the air.

"Enoch, why are you sniffing the air? Papa took his disagreeable pipe outside. You look like a little animal. Are you too losing your mind?" Mama pleaded with her voice breaking.

"Brimstone, Mama. Brimstone." Mama turned her back on me. Nochi wanted to laugh but restrained himself. I thought I should take a lesson from him. He had a way of either going completely quiet or of maddeningly repeating people's words. When he had a mind to, he could keep folks at bay. Feeling that I had not a friend in this word, I thought of our Lord upon his cross. He was a friend to all who suffer. He had suffered so much for the likes of folks like me who had gone so far astray others thought they could never return. Even a murderer would not be unwelcome at his table. I could throw myself upon his mercy and ask for forgiveness. How could I ask to be forgiven when I did not know what I had done?

I decided to confront the Sleepy Hollow boys one by one, including our leader, to find out what they knew. If Master Crane was lying in the grave somewhere, he deserved to be dug up and given a proper burial. We had haunted him by conjuring up those local ghouls and ended up being haunted ourselves. Well, I had. The other lads took scarce a care about the whereabouts or fate of Ichabod. He might arise from the dead to drag us down to our own. My jaw tensed up. Suppositions and superstitions could be damped down. Reason trumps fear. Not so my insatiate conscience. Dominie Hunthum was right about one thing, the need to avoid retribution in the next world. As for this world, the long arm of justice might reach out to drag us down if a body should be discovered.

Now there was no one to talk to about spirits. Who but Ichabod would concern himself with such visitations in this dull, farming community? We were tenant farmers who bought the farm which then saddled itself upon our backs. I suppose the farmers believed that doing good work day after day assured a good afterlife. Some Sabbath ranting served to keep them in place in case they grew unmindful. The world was alright with them. This world was not made for me.

What I would not give to see you, Ichabod, coming over the cornfield with your clothes fluttering about in the wind to take your place under the tree. Come back to draw out from those volumes all the secret and dark doings of evil spirits taking up residence in our world, and tell me about them until the sun goes down. Inform my soul of dark beings, grievous molestations, and other curiosities. Of witches and warlocks and creatures that stalked our beds to suck on us in the night, I could never get enough. What would Abraham be thinking today? Of marrying up to gain the plumpest, most succulent fruits and abundant fields, I reckon. All of your earnest seekings made you a singular being, Ichabod. You cannot be denied all those cupboard comforts. Will you not come back again?

November 22

Would Father never stop thinking of war? Approaching the church today for Sunday service, his proud heart again swelled up with memories. Stomping up ahead of us, he planted himself on a spot of grass. An afterimage of cannons and generals hovered and wavered over certain spots. He could not cross certain places without being carried away to earlier days. The times now were too workaday. I suppose Father's memories would hang on to him as relentlessly as my conscience, gnawing away like a worm in the wood.

"Do you remember, Hennie, when our President Washington stood here with his staff? The British were leaving New York, and Washington was our great hero. To think that once they referred to him as that leader of the rebel mob. Here, right here, Washington stood with Governor Clinton and Lieutenant Governor Van Cortlandt. He stood with his staff, I say." Father stomped his peg leg to mark the ground.

"Husband, I remember. Those blue and buff uniforms, with not a Red Coat in sight, were a comfort to the heart. Mahalalel, do you remember the changes that came after the revolution, here at the church? The bells rang out again, and when we entered the sanctuary, we saw, to our surprise, that the lord and lady's thrones had been removed. Straight-backed, pine pews had replaced our hard, oak benches. I said that Damen and Enoch, and even Mahalalel, will sit up properly now with hearts and minds as straight as their backs. Margaret already knew how to sit properly. Today, Nochi, you will sit up properly to listen to the holy word. I cannot say that I would like to see a king or queen here, but I do admit to missing those lovely thrones."

"Mama, we may not need a king or queen, but why not thrones and castles? I would still like to have a castle," Nochi piped up.

"A rich man could build a castle, Nochi if he has money enough. That castle would not make him a king. Did we choose, mind you, I say choose, to call our leader, 'your

Excellency,' 'the exalted one,' or 'your highness?' No. For no mortal man will have dominion over our souls or flesh. What did we call him Nochi?" asked Mama.

"Mr. President. Master Crane said that when the British sent him a letter marked, 'Mr. Washington' he sent it back. It was Mr. President." Nochi drew himself up to his full height to sneer down his nose at their ignorance.

"And, when he became president officially he wore a brown, homespun suit, and that no crown was placed upon his head," Nochi added looking disappointed at the thought.

"Mama is right. You cannot even begin to comprehend the changes. The upper mills over there were wrested away from the Phillipse family to be sold at auction to Mr. Beekman. Philips had originally purchased it from the Wilden for twenty-thousand wampum," Father remarked.

"Twenty-thousand wampum? I cannot even imagine that many beads, Papa," cried Nochi.

Father spread his arms out. "Look at these little graves. These new legislators wanted to take our very dead from us. Everything was up for sale. If we had allowed it, they would have auctioned off the burying ground, but in the end, it was deeded to the deacons and elders, and held in trust for us, for us, the congregation," Father continued.

"Is that when you bought our farm, Papa?" asked Nochi.

"Yes, Enoch. Mr. Philpse was rich, but in his mind, he was not rich enough. He was in cahoots with the Royal custom inspectors, smugglers, pirates, Willian Kidd, himself. It was all laundered money and captured goods. Honest families work the land."

Now we would exchange our history lessons for gossip. Mrs. Van Vleet came down the road to greet us.

"Good morrow, Willem family. How now," she gushed. After congratulating Nochi on his recent growth, and asking Margreet if she had found a beau, she butted into my business.

"I do not see you hanging around with the Sleepy Hollow Boys these days. You were always a little too intelligent for that bunch. You look more like a scholar than a farmer. Just look how your hair curls around your delicate ears. Though, if it is your lot, to run your family farm one day, I dare say you will make it grow. Hendrika, there is much promise in Damen. The Sleepy Hollow boys are so . . ." I supposed she wanted a word to describe them that would not imply something lacking in me.

"Robust. Abraham is such a helter-skelter person. There is not a thought in his head. Of course, marriage might calm himself down a little. He will never have your refined manners, Damen. There will never be much thought in his head. He is too high-spirited to run a farm. The Good Lord forbid that Mynheer Van Tassel should leave this world too soon," she concluded.

"Managing the farm will damp him down," Mama said with a smile.

"That brawny lad is a sign of the future. Only the devil himself will damp him down. The old Dutch families will not be around to pass their properties into proper hands. Marrying up and above his station! His kind will rule the world if we do not keep a watch out," Father admonished. He then pointed out the sad little graves with their winged, angel heads.

"In the future, the whole burying ground will be filled with people like him. They will want great monuments, as big as their puffy heads, to remind us who they were in this life when they have moved on to the next."

"Van Tassel is a self-made man, Mahalalel. He will pass on the fruits of his labor to his family. Here and now, we are what we make ourselves to be. We must be sure to make ourselves the people the Good Lord wants us to be. Stay in the here-and-now, husband," Mama reminded.

The church bells started clanging. I put my hands to my ears. As we entered the church, I saw that the marriage bans for Abraham and Katrina had been posted on the door. Speaking of, or reading of, the devil conjured him up. There was Brom, all spat and polished up, striding past us to be the first to enter the church. As he faced the altar, he wiped the grin off his face. The choir began to sweetly sing the last dulcet tones we would hear that morning.

Dominie Hunthum gave a howling sermon. Mounting the curved, oak steps to take his place in the pulpit, he glanced up at the hexagonal sounding board above his head. His voice was so loud and determined that he would not need it. It was cold inside. Mama passed Margreet a little box of hot coals to warm herself. They might not be needed either. The dominie practically belched forth flames. As the Ten Commandments were read out, I tried to count how many I had broken. The farmers, in their linsey-wooly jackets, all bent their heads. The sermon began.

"Time is winging away. To bring this wayward congregation back to the fold, I will have to baptize them all over again. That is how far they have gone astray." The words volleyed like cannon balls over my head with such force I had to duck down in my pew.

"Deceiving spirits call out to you. You listen. Hear the words from 1Timothy 4:2: 'Such teachings come from hypocritical liars whose consciences have been seared as with a hot iron.' They forge chains to bind your soul, and you submit. I have given you ample time, but still, you tarry in the haunts of sinful men. You think that you are not seen. Oh, hear the words of Isaiah who knew the sins of men like the back of his hand: 'I am the one who blots out your transgression for my sake, and I will not remember your sins.' He will blot out your sins, he says, and yet you refuse to come to him." As the dominie scoured the faces of the congregation, his gaze fell on me. Something distracted him. Raising up his grubby hand, he began slicing the air. "The air is so thick with devils, demons, and imps, that I can feel them. There is an amazing range of evil spirits in the sanctuary," he said.

"God will ferret you out. You know how the terrier dog ferrets out the rat hiding behind the barrel of beer on the immaculate kitchen floor? So out of place is the vermin on the waxed wood which the housewife so carefully tends, the little dog wants it out. He takes it and shakes it by the throat.

"God will ferret you out. The farmer carefully grows and harvests the apple, but the worm eats up the plump heart of it. The wife will core out the worm with a skewer, and make a delicious sauce." He licked his thick lips with his pink tongue. I lowered my head to look down at my feet.

"God will ferret you out. The wife cares for the flowers no less than her bonny children. The bad seed grows into a weed, then roots itself amongst them. You, farmer, yes, you. I am speaking to you. Do you not pluck it out by the roots?" A man in the first row readily nodded his head.

"Can an evil man find refuge? I ask. Ferreted out, skewered out, weeded out, where will he go? God will scoot his soul across the floor like the housewife who swatted away with her broom the rat the terrier found behind the barrel. He will skewer him out of his sin like a cored apple. He will pluck him out by the roots like a weed pulled from the garden. Chased to the edge of town and beyond, the sinful man will find no refuge but in Him. Come to Him now!"

Silence filled the room. Looking up, I saw a sea of lowered heads. Finally, I raised up my head for the sake of curiosity, if not my aching neck. I saw a sea of bowed heads. Brom was covering his mouth, trying to stifle a yawn. Perhaps he thought that joining the Van Tassel clan would get him off the hook. Dominie Hunthum glared out with an evil eye but overlooked him. If he did not hold his gaze on me, it was for my mother's sake. His plump fists went up above his hot red face which did brightly shine.

"To break that commitment is to separate from Him like Adam and Eve and the fallen sons of light. Do you think that God will fail to retaliate? Glory be to our union with the Father in heaven. If you want God's peace to enter your heart, then let him lodge in your bosom. He will lodge with you and leave you forever changed." The dominie lowered his head.

Prayers for those suffering from various physical afflictions were passed on a cane to the minister. The little cloth bags filled up with coins. Though the cloth muffled the sounds, the jingle of dirtied silver troubled me. Such coins were of no use to that blasphemer, Judas. The only solace he could find was in the taking of his life. No amount of riches in this world could buy me a clean conscience. The walls of the church were moving in on me like a vice. The sermon next week would be salvation. I doubted it would be of any use to me. I might not even be there at all. How do I take refuge in the Lord? What do I do? I rushed through the sanctuary seeking air. Behind me, Mother mouthed these words, "

       For as the rain and snow come down from heaven,
and do not return there but water the earth,   making
it bring forth and sprout   giving seed to the

sower and bread to the eater,   so shall my word be that
goes out from my mouth;
                    it shall not return to me empty,
but it shall accomplish that which I purpose,   and
shall succeed in the thing for which I sent it.

I would trust to the Providence which had always failed me before.

Chapter Twelve

The Heart of the Matter

November 22 (continued)

We spilled out of the church into the light of day. Caleb playfully jostled Hobnail as he ran down the path. Brom mounted his horse. With his muscular thighs pulsing against its flank, he turned the horse's head to the Turnpike Road. When the Van Tassels arrived home, he would be waiting at the door. Oh, the strut and swell of him. The sun was shining so brightly. I went to church feeling like a man facing execution. I came out as one of the damned. I wanted to take off to the woods to be alone with my thoughts. I muttered something about hell. Father went back to war. This time I had had enough. I planted my own feet on this good earth to challenge his lies.

"Hell? There was a time when Tarrytown was in hell. You, Damen, now live in the Ilium the Dutch hoped to find here. You were just a boy when Royalist Governor Tryon sent his wolf pack of Hessians to burn the town everywhere. Desolation warfare. Scorch the earth. Do you remember the cannon up on the ridge? The night was cold, but the barns burned with fire. They looted our homes and farms. The farmers ran into their barns to grab pitchforks, hoes, and shovels to stand against not only the Red Coats but the cowboys and skinners who were taking advantage of war conditions to steal our livestock.

"Their Dutch was up. Imagine the British screaming at us, "Dutch devils!" Our cry was, "Slay the English dogs.' They even plundered furniture. The snow lay deep and even. All inside was broken or looted even the furniture. This bleeding country. Cattle were left to decay. In the morning the   No Englishman will ever sit at this table. I wish with all my heart that we had a Dutch president, but I do not know what we would have done without General Washington. I still see him leading the Patriots up the Albany Post Road. Children, Washington slept here at David's Homestead. I fought for that man, eh, I would fight for that man again," declared Father.

The family remained silent. This time in telling the tale Father did not seem to mind that Washington was not Dutch. I could stomach no more of Father's tall tales. "Father, you have never fought at all. You do not know what it is like to kill a man. You fell through the ice and broke your leg which became so infected the doctor had to saw it off."

"Damen, do not speak to your father like that. You have ice in your heart," cried Mama as I stalked away to trudge home ahead of them. I wanted to say that if he did not know what it was like to kill a man, I did. What, I pray you, would be the use of that? There is no use of anything.

No hope for that laugh. There was no hope for me. Father could not help me. What was truth to him? He was happy to tell his tales his way, twice, thrice, for as long as anyone would care to listen, or even if they did not care to hear. The preacher could not help me.

God might give me a hand, but before I could go to God, I would have to find out the truth. Resolution set in. I would confront the Sleepy Hollow Boys. If I could ascertain that we had killed Ichabod, I would turn myself into the law. If Ichabod were alive, I would find him. If an evil spirit had taken him, it was beyond my ken.

November 23

The air was bitingly cold this morning. Two or three inches of snow lay upon the ground. Mama let us into the house early. Chores could wait. She lit the fire, then started to prepare dumplings. Nochi went out to play in the snow but soon ran back inside wearing a fox skin hat.

"Who am I?" he asked. He shook the tail. My thoughts darkened.

"Someone who knows better than to wear a hat inside the house?" I questioned. Little brother crinkled his nose at me. He looked to Margreet.

"The riddle is too easy. Brom Bones of course. Who else goes about in a fox skin hat, flashing the tail?" declared Margreet. Gales of laughter came out of both of them. I could not bear it being one who knew that he could never laugh again.

"Take it off, Enoch," I demanded. My sister interrupted by asking, "Who am I?" Dramatically, she spread her arms down on the table, then lay her head in them, making herself a picture of despair.

Sounding off like a redheaded woodpecker piercing the wood bark for worms, Enoch laughed, "Ha ha ha ha ha ha ha! You are Damen."

"Take that stupid hat off, Nochi," I demanded. He ran across the room. I flew at him. Pointing his fingers into his cheeks, he sassed me. "Is Damen in love? Is Damen out of love with his sweetheart?" He voice sounded like the screech of an owl.

"Does his sweetheart love another?" teased Margreet. Now my sister, who was always so good, was turning against me. My siblings set me to a rolling boil. They were not done yet

"If his sweetheart departs, she will not find another like him," said Nochi batting his long eyelashes. What did Mrs. Van Vleet say? Neat ears and with swirls of hair curling about them?" I swatted Roos for tugging on my hair too hard.

"Yes, and then there are his Mary-Queen-of-Scots eyes. That is what Mama says. Are they blue or are they gray?" Margreet added. I placed my hands over my ears. Nochi came over and pulled my hands away.

"Better go to your love now brother before it is too late. Brom Bones may not be satisfied with just one wife," added Nochi. This joke set the little fool off with another rhyme which had naught to do with anything: "Too late the maiden cried, who departed a maiden no more." Again I put my hands over my ears. He continued laughing.

"Enough Nochi. You do not even understand the words that are coming out of your mouth. What do you know about love? Take off that stupid, bestial hat.. Where did you get it? You look hideous. Tell me where you got it. I will have your head for a doorstop." I could stand no more. I flew at him to pull the fox skin hat off his head. He ran across the room, and out the door. I slid across the snow chasing him down. Cornering him between the shed and fence, I got his head under my arm. The hat fell off. Before he could retrieve it, I grabbed it and threw it into the well. Nochi ran to the well, jumped up on the ledge, and almost fell into the frigid water. I pulled him back by the seat of his pants. A tear started to form in the corner of his eye.

"It is just a stupid hat, Nochi."

"Damen, it was my hat." In tears, he ran back into the house. I was growing into such a mad, bad person, that the wonder was that I did not throw Nochi into the well. Or myself for that matter. I bent over the well to see the fluffy, red fur darkening and flattening itself, as it sunk into the dark, cold water.

When I tried to get back into the house, Nochi pressed his little body against the door to prevent my entry. I started clawing the door. I had hurt him. He was only a child. It may be time for me to put away childish things and become a man.

November 24

I walked up to Sleepy Hollow to the upper mills where I met Hobnail standing by the stream. Giving out a little whoop at the sight of me, he waved his arms up in the air. "What cheer, Damen? When my face looks as sad as yours does, my father cautions that my pack is too heavy. You are carrying a heavy load." He slapped my back.

"Yes. My heart lies heavy." Hobnail was not the brightest orb in the sky. Taking a direct approach, I began with, "I am worried about something."

"I am worried that you are worried about something." "What is it?" said Hobby shuffling his feet in the dirty snow.

"I cannot say. It is something. I am worried about something," I said. We were not making much headway.

"You are going to be married soon. You probably cannot wait for your wedding night." Like a true country bumpkin, he rolled his eyes, and in smacking his lips, almost bit his tongue.

"I feel unfit to wed. My intended should have a better man than me. Will you stay a single man, Hobby? That may be the way for me too."

"That is not the way our Abraham feels. Why Brom is practically crowing like a rooster, all ready to rule the roost, and eat up all the victuals, the Van Tassel kitchen can offer." He ran his tongue over his lips.

"It is Abraham who troubles my mind. Remember the night of the Van Tassel merrymaking when we . . . "

Hobbie's mouth, which had been curling into smiles, now went down into a frown.

"I recall tapping my feet to the fiddling, dancing, jigging about the floor, and drinking up the punch. The punch was sparkling red. The country reel was too fast, and the room was swaying. I may have even fallen when I swung Matilda Kiliaen around. Her lacy skirt did swirl around almost up to her breasts." His ruddy face took on a deeper, redder glow.

"Matilda may not be pleased with me. I remember that our friend Brom stayed behind to woo Katrina. By morning, we heard he had it all hollow, woman, livestock and household furniture." The corners of his mouth flew up to form the horns of the moon.

"Yes, there was tapping, fiddling, jigging and punch drinking, but Hob, do you not remember what happened after the tapping, fiddling, jigging and the punch drinking? After Brom left Katrina, do you recall us all riding out to scare the schoolteacher off? Hob, I think we may have gone too far. Ichabod never returned."

Hobnail furrowed up his brow and frowned again. I do believe he tried to remember. "We may have done something terrible for all. . ." I urged. Suddenly, Hobnail was reminded that he was a hard-working man who had to get to work at the mill. Bending down to poke his finger in a hole in his stocking, he avoided my gaze. He pulled at the uneven fringe of hair on his forehead. He was not taking me seriously. He buttoned up his jacket as if the temperature had dropped.

"All that I remember of that night I have told you, Damen. As for Ichabod, I think that when he lost all hope of love, his thoughts turned to food. All he wanted to do was fill himself up with food, food, food. You know how much he loved to eat. People say he went down to the harbor of New York City where food comes in from all over the world. There was a promise of more food than his eye can see or stomach hold. Though he was a skinny man when we knew him, he might be plump as Katrina now for all we know. Then again, he was a clumsy man riding an old plow horse that night. He may have been thrown and drowned in the creek. Hans Van Ripper may know something. You are a cloudy man now. I bid you good day now for I have work to do. I am sure you do too." He turned his back on me.

And so, I went off to see the man about a horse. I could not tell if Hobnail recalled anything at all. It was hard to determine what that man thought or if he thought at all. The thought of Ichabod eating all the good foods of the world down the river was pleasing. It might have just been Hobby's fantasy to go down to New York and stuff his maw. Now I was like a weathercock turning back upon the steps I had already made in the melting snow. As I was coming up the road, I saw Hans Van Ripper leading the oxen back to the barn. The big beasts were not paying him much mind and his temper was up. He took up his switch to strike the one on the right.

"Dumb beasts. What are you about, Damen? You look a rayless man. You put the sun, moon, and stars out about you," he said. Was there a cloud of darkness hanging over my head? I put my concerns before him.

"No, Damen, I do not know what happened to the missing the teacher, Master Crane. All I do know is that he never came back to apologize for not properly returning the horse and saddle I lent him. It is a Sunday saddle. I was very fortunate to get them back again. Old Gunpowder is as big a fool as these dumb oxen here. He did not have the sense to run off. I do think the schoolmaster rode him a bit too hard. I hope he was not the victim of the highway for he had his full salary on his person that fatal night." Van Ripper gave the oxen his evil eye just in case they wanted to do a runner.

"Fatal night?" I gulped.

"Tis an expression, lad. An expression. I have trouble enough keeping the farm together. I can hardly keep my wits about me. Should I worry about that arsy varsy school teacher? Tis a hard life boy. In this life, you make the best of a bad bargain, lad. I mind my purse and read the good book. I have Gunpowder and his saddle back. I keep watch over my soul. That is enough for me. I will say one thing in the schoolmaster's favor. Like the willow, he could bend, practically bend down to the ground, and still snap back. Now let me get the halter off this ox." He had no more to say. I felt dismissed.

I walked to town to the tallow shop where Caleb worked with his family. Caleb's mother did not seem very pleased to see me calling. She did allow her son to step outside the door to chat with me. "Do not keep him long from us, Damen," she said playfully slapping the back of his head as he joined me outside.

This time I would go straight to the heart of the matter. It was not that cold outside now. The snow was forming large puddles beneath our feet, but Caleb pulled his jacket tight across his chest as if he, like Hob, wanted to keep something out.

"I am sorry to have taken you from your work. There is something that keeps pressing in my mind that will not stop." Caleb did not seem to care very much about the pressure in my head. He started picking some wax off his nails. There being no way back, I rushed ahead.

"Do you think a man could fear his rival in love so much that he would take his life, Caleb? I mean, take his opponent's life, not his own. Would desire for a woman, a woman of property, be the motive for murder?" Worry rippled across Caleb's darkening face.

"Damen, what kind of question is this? What would I know about killing for love? What would I even know about love? Or killing? I am just a candle maker who tends his own business."

"But what if we were involved in that business?" I was driven to say.

"Whatever do you mean, Damen? To be involved in murder is to put the soul at stake. We could never again sit down at the communion table or show our faces at the church door. We were just there two days ago. We were fine. We were in church, Damen. We were, and are, fine. Everyone was at church except for Piet Godjin, who having been kicked in the chest by a mule, stayed in bed. The world was right. Is there a murderer in Tarrytown? I would not know such a man like that even if I could. Do you know a man like that?"

"I think that we both know such a man. I suspect we helped Abraham Van Brunt kill Ichabod." The color faded from his cheeks. His right hand clutched his jacket even tighter. "I think that Ichabod lost his love that night, but not his life. As a learned man who lost his love, he longed to be a smarter. He probably went down to New York City to enroll in Columbia, which not long ago was the King's charter school. Now we are free men who do not listen to a king, but our consciences." Caleb was building a story based on logic and reasoning. I started to speak when a surge of anger colored his face red. He cut me off.

"If you think Van Brunt capable of plotting murder, do you not think he would be capable of killing you for your big mouth? Do you not know that if you press on a man like that too much, he will press you down to hell?" No longer clutching his jacket, Caleb folded his arms across his chest and planted his feet firmly on the ground. His rocklike expression, his rigid body, the icy stare in his eyes brought murder to mind. He stomped in the wet snow spraying mud on my boots.

"He might press me down to hell for all I care, Caleb. He cannot, I say, he cannot annihilate me as much as my conscience." With a look of amazement, Caleb took himself back inside the shop. He was having none of me. I headed for town. There was one more fish to fry.

I saw Brom's bobbing head and broad shoulders as he strode along the brick wall on Broadway. Like King Saul, he walked head and shoulders above us all. I followed him. He must have felt me at his back for he abruptly turned to look behind him. I slithered behind a tree. Courage began to fail. He was not an easy man to approach about an evil deed. He kept on going and did not stop until he got to the Red Ale Tavern.

He sat down at the table near the window to order some beer. I summoned my courage. Sliding across the bench to confront him face-to-face, I looked him in the eye. Any surprise he felt to see my face before his, did not show.

"What is in the wind with you? In truth, you look a worried man." He flashed his healthy teeth at me.

"I am in search of a rare commodity, true colors, true colors that come out in daylight after the ball is over."

"Do you mean colors such as true blue, the color of your jacket? It looks faded to gray in the light of day, Damen."

"Never mind my jacket. Did you pay attention at church, Brom? Did you hear that God will ferret out all sin?" I blurted out. The suddenness of my inquiry baffled him. Brushing back his thick dark curls, he looked me up and down.

"What are you? Are you a walking conscience?" Brom asked looking more annoyed than troubled.

"I am a man who needs to know."

"What do you need to know? Which way the does wind blow? Step outside and look to the weathervane."

"I am thinking of our schoolmaster who has not been seen of late. Do you surmise he lives down by the river now, Brom, or do you suspect that he is in the river? I believe that if he is in the river, he will rise. Tell me true."

"Well, I think that if he is in the river, he will rise no more. Dead men tell no tales." He pushed the bench back to stand up. He towered above me. I stood up too. The proprietor brought a glass of ale. Brom sat down to drink.

"What do you mean he will rise no more?" I steadied myself against the table.

"I think the devil took him. May he take you too Damen along with your eternal questions."

"The devil may take me whenever he wishes. Right now will do. I am more afraid of God than the devil. What did you do at the edge of the woods that night when you asked me to wait nearby? It was too dark to see, but I heard you digging up the ground at the clearing near Gory Creek. What went down into the ground, Brom?" I shook in spite of myself.

"What should I say? Your precious schoolmaster? Oh, you are smart. You have always been smarter than others. You think us fools who sat a-dreaming, while you looked at Crane, listening in earnest to his stories. Did you scribble notes? Teachers make farm boys feel stupid. That is why they swat at flies and stare out the window when they prattle on. Did Ichabod laugh at the flat faces behind the big boys' full backs, saying he could better train up a horse than the likes of them? Well, it may be that one of them, or more, outsmarted him."

"Ichabod did not have a mean bone in his body. You thought he would win the lady's heart, along with the farm. Come, Brom. The hour is late. You had a motive for murder. I know there was a harrowing chase involving a mighty black steed, a plodding plow horse which did not stand a chance, and a flaming pumpkin hurled through the air. All these facts I know, but I do not know enough. Tell me more." I was completely carried away.

"Tell me something, little Damen. Stand up on tippy toes to stand with me, breast to breast and face to face, to tell me what you saw that night.

"I will not stand on tippy toes Brom for even then I cannot rise to your great height. You were just a giant boy, and we boys with little brains to follow you. I think you are but a giant boy now. There was a long, dark cape with a cowl and a high collar, and Caleb following up on foot with a shovel. There was bright moon behind the trees that night, and a spooked teacher singing hymns through the trees to comfort himself. There may have been a six-foot hole dug into the ground. I would not know for I was too busy keeping my eye out down the Albany Post Road as you instructed." I was stringing so many words together that I was getting out of breath.

Brom was flabbergasted and gobsmacked. He rubbed his chiseled chin with his large hand in consternation. The big man turned his wide back on me. He could not face the truth. I could not twist and turn like a weathervane but must ferret out the truth. I had to make the next move. I did not have to look at his back of his big, curly head for long. He spun to face me, slapping both hands to his knees to let out a thunderous guffaw which might have been heard around the whole world. Several times he started to speak only to find his words dissolved by gales of his laughter. He finished the ale in one long gulp. The only way he could steady his shaking, rollicking body was to clamp his hands upon my shoulders and press me down so hard I thought I would go between the gaps in the wide plank floor. He lifted me up, then set me down again. It took a few minutes for him to compose himself, but when he did, he returned, eyes wide open, hands splayed out in full story telling mode. I felt unmanly and small.

"Let me tell you what I saw that night. Master Crane was riding through the green wood like a knight upon a noble steed at a strong pace. We could barely keep up with him on our worn out farm horses. Suddenly, a huge Werebear jumped down on him from Major Andre's great tulip tree and tore out his throat. You, Caleb and Hobnail jumped from your horses to hide trembling in the bushes while I tried to get to him. I was not quick enough. The Werebear ate him whole disparaging only his hat. That it then loped off all bloodied to the creek to clean and preen itself like Grimalkin, the house cat.

I looked stricken. For the sake of our lost schoolmaster, I managed to keep a straight face. Was it not the time to stand like a man? Brom covered up his reddened, animated face and full cracking mouth with both hands. He then manipulated his features into a baffled look.

"I beg your pardon, Master Willem. I misspoke. It was not a shaggy Werebear at all. It was a great, slimy green sea monster that swam up the lordly Hudson from the great Atlantic to sneak into the creek." His hands started undulating like a sneaky serpent across breaking waves. I could stand no more. Did I not have any pride? Men in the tavern were turning to look at us. I wanted to disappear.

"Give regards to the Van Tassels for me, Brom."

"I will give them to the devil first sir."

I moved to the door. Brom headed back to the table to order another ale. I turned to see him dangle his muscular arm over the side of the chair. His arm was so long that his fingers trailed the floor. Was this the hand that threw the missile I wondered? The last thing I heard was a fist hit the wall and another gale of laughter as I stepped into the darkness of night.

I wandered over to the clearing near the Gory Brook and started digging with my hands. There was a stone wall with broken bottles in a row to keep people off. I looked to see if there was a shovel there. If we did take your life, Ichabod Crane, you should have a proper grave. I will dig you up and bury you in the church yard next to Higginbothen or some other dead soul. The moon was waxing full again. I did not make so much as a dent in the ground. The wind grew fierce as I wandered home. As I came through the door, Mother lit a candle to see who was coming in so late. I cannot say she was happy to see me, but she blew the candle out with a sense of relief.

Chapter Thirteen

Trapped

So this Damen character had quite a story to tell even if much of it was in his head. My growing interest in the manuscript and the hijinks of the *Most Haunted* team, inspired me to head back up to Sleepy Hollow on that Saturday. The weather was holding. Soon Halloween celebrations would be in full force, and the fall color would be peaking. So through the SOS, the vomit, broken glass and drugged out people, I made my way once again to Grand Central. Did I omit corrupt politicians? Wasn't that my crook of a congressman coming out of Starbuck's?

The subway was subdued; that in itself was chilling. Expect the unexpected. Maybe people decided to stay home on the weekends due to everlasting trackwork. Even Grand Central was hollowed out. That kind of calm in NYC could only spell trouble. The Papyrus Store with its beautifully embellished gift wrap was enchanting. I lingered window shopping enthralled by the wrapping paper I wouldn't be able to use. Any presents I sent for the holidays would be strictly through the internet. At least no one was riding up my back.

It seems I couldn't step inside the station without having flashbacks of 9/11. My partner Dave was here on that gorgeous September morning, a day as beautiful as today. Even after the first plane had struck, it was business as usual in midtown. I was heading up to Washington Heights for a closing when things started shutting down. News about the WTC was starting to spread across my subway car. The second plane hit the south tower at 9:03. About that time, I got on an uptown train, then experienced second thoughts. Getting off the train at Forty-Seventh Street, I walked back home. "Man, this whole town is going to blow up in smoke," shouted a man standing on the corner. How naïve I was to think that a small plane might have hit the first tower accidentally. "Terrorism, man. It's terrorism!" he cried out.

The city went into lockdown. Cell phones failed. The subway, Path trains, Long Island Railroad and Metro-North, shut down. Bridges and tunnels closed. Wherever televised coverage was available, people gathered around to hear the latest grim news. New Yorkers gathered around? Yes, live news coverage of this unspeakable attack drew people together like the colonial hearth, or television in its early days. There wasn't much talk, though. An eerie silence prevailed.

On Thirty-Fourth Street and Fifth Avenue, a group of people all covered in white dust trudged uptown. These men and women in business suits looked like sculptures by George Segal. Even their briefcases were covered in dust. I didn't know what to make of them. I kept going the other way. Only a mile and a half from the site of terror, I was in a safe zone. No one knew that at the time, though. Word of the Pentagon attack was spreading through the streets. People were reeling. The next strike could come anywhere at any time. I was so glad to see my block. I went upstairs, closed the apartment door, and sat down on the daybed to breathe out a big gasp of air.   After putting the kettle on, I tried to joke around with Chester. "I guess you're surprised to see me back so soon. Thought you were going to have the house all to yourself, eh? I hope your girlfriend is not on the way." My voice just rang hollow.

Then the landline rang. It was Dave. Of course, he was worried about me. People all over the city were worried about each other. Looking out the window, I could see the drug addicts leaning on a dirty, white van. For once, they were standing still. They weren't even fussing with each other. They had made a temporary peace. Maybe it wasn't even them. The phone connection was good. Dave spoke slowly and clearly. He was struggling not to let emotion creep inside of him.

"Richard, you're home?"

"Yes, Dave. Where are you? Home?"

No, Richard. I was determined to get to Dobb's Ferry. Business is a business. I arrived at Grand Central to find it closed. Word was spreading that it was going to reopen soon. I figured, no excuses, just carry on. I joined the crowd outside the Lexington Avenue entrance. Someone said there was a bomb scare. Another said the Park Avenue entrance was going to open first. Not sure why, but I believed him. So, I went around the other side. It's not very rational, but I thought that if I could just get to Dobb's Ferry, everything would go back to normal."

"Dave, at this point, it feels that nothing will ever go back in place again. Where are you now?"

"Rita's apartment on West 72nd Street. Waiting for the other shoe to drop."

"What happened at the station?" Chester was rubbing my leg. I was rumpling up his fur in an agitated way. I had to tell my brain to calm my hand down.

"I went around the corner to the Park Avenue entrance. The door opened like magic. I was the first one inside. The station was virtually empty. Can you imagine Grand Central without a soul inside? The emptiness was eerie. My footsteps echoed around the cavernous space. There was a Hudson Line train about to depart, so I got on it. It wasn't very full. A large, sweaty man started to panic. Grabbing at his necktie, he began shouting incoherently. He kept pulling at his tie as if some invisible force was strangling him. 'Get off the train,' someone shouted at him. When the doors momentarily opened, he exited. I did too."

"Is the subway running now? Are you going to try to make it to Queens?"

"Yes, Richard. I think so. Not sure."

Nothing else fell from the sky. Dave stayed with Rita that night to comfort her. At least that's what he told me a day or so later. Most likely, it was the other way around. We took two days off, then reopened our office. Normality crept back into our daily lives. The stock market bounced around, then stabilized. The flags rose up. Posters started appearing. The victims may have died quickly, but the signs stayed up for a long time. The September and October rains made the colors run. What was left frosted over in November and December; by New Year's Day, the paper froze as ice particles formed at the centers and corners. Under little chunks of ice, faded blues, purples and green could be seen. No mattered how decrepit the posters became there was no one willing to remove them. They were holy relics for this skeptical age. What business do we have in seeking out horror in mysterious places when the real thing finds us, slays us, at the heart of the city? You would think reality to be enough.

I sat on the train wondering what it was like in Tarrytown that day. I watched Riverdale go past. Some wag said it was safe up in the Bronx on 9/11 because there was nothing valuable enough to destroy. No impact. No one would even care or notice. The rest of the country may have felt that way about Manhattan. Did New York care what the rest of the country thought? Of course not. I tried to ignore the reflection of my face in the dirty train window. That was not the face I wanted to see. The Columbus Day weekend had come and gone. I never made it to Philadelphia to visit with my brother, his wife, and their newly adopted son. I never played golf with Dave. I would like to say that I called my brother to make my excuses, but I just let it slide.

The announcements of stations were like a litany to me now. I practically had them memorized. Since Washington Irving's home, Sunnyside was closer to Irvington; I got off there. I scurried down to the river bank on the road covered with a carpet of leaves, as cars and tour buses sped past. I was the only one on foot. A cornucopia of architectural elements from 'crow-stepped gables to a Spanish monastic tower, gables, turrets, and cupolas, and wisteria vines made the home every bit as wild and fantastical as the Internet promised. There was a grand view of the widest span of the Hudson where the new bridge was under construction next to the old Tappan Zee. From this vantage point, Irving would have had a grand view of the river. Glancing at the souvenir shop, I purchased my ticket and entered the grounds.

An affable senior dressed as Washington Irving strode across the grass in high boots to greet us. Removing his straw hat with a flourish, he took us into the foyer of Sunnyside which had floor tile imported from Europe. No matter how many feet had trod the impressive tile, there were very few cracks. Facts ran by me. I grabbed quite a few. If I heard right, the guide said that the region fed Irving's imagination which produced the book which sold so well it financed the house. It was always a work in progress. The house that is. *The Legend of Sleepy* Hollow was written in London. Nieces and nephews lived here with the lifelong bachelor, filling up the whimsical house with love and laughter, watching over it while the author spent long months in Europe. His last official position was ambassador to Spain. Irving, himself, has planted the wisteria, which virtually covered the house. The woodland setting was designed to look natural.

It seemed a perfect life. Then the sour note sounded. Of course, it did. Irving's fiancée, Matilda Hoffman, passed away at seventeen of consumption. Her family had a summer home in Ravenswood, Astoria; her father kept a boat near Hell Gate. This celestial being died drop by drop. Irving was, so grief is stricken, he couldn't even speak of her. Though he said he could write volumes about this loss, he never did. Irving engaged in lifelong mourning, Victorian style. The guide, shaking his head, informed us that Irving never married but, lived out the last twenty-four years of his life at Sunnyside with assorted family. Our "Washington Irving" strutted about in his nineteenth-century tan suit, hat in hand as if he truly was the lord of the manor. Here was a man who loved his job.

After admonishing a young man for leaning too heavily on the railing that roped off the parlor, the guide gave us an opportunity to pose questions. The delinquent who almost took the barrier down had a friend who asked if Irving was gay. "Let us go outside where I will be happy to answer your question and any others. It is such a lovely day." Was the question so delicate, the house couldn't hear it? It seemed that if this house could talk, it would not have much to say.

Coming out of the quaint, but dimly lit dwelling, the splendor of fall struck with full force. The glistening river, the carpet of red, brown, gold and green leaves and grass, the trees with gold leaves to spare, was overwhelming. We gathered around the guide who put his booted foot up on a bench to lean on his knee.

"There is no evidence that Irving was gay. He had close friendships with men, but there is nothing unusual about that. Of course, back then, people were discrete about such things. The fact that the author put his love life away after Matilda died has led many to believe he did not need women. He did court the widowed Mary Shelley, authoress of Frankenstein, later in life. Some speculated they would wed. That was not meant to be."

Good thing I did not take Dave up on his many invitations to ball games and movies. People would say we're in love. Not sure if anyone would care. Rita, I guess.

"What a union that would make. The father of the Headless Horseman and the mother of Frankenstein. Imagine what they would produce," a tall Japanese man offered. We all laughed along with the guide. A Metro-North train roared by.

"What about the railroad? It runs right by his house. Was it running when Irving lived here?" asked a middle-aged man who had some tic.

"Good question. It was not here when Irving started building the house. He did use whatever weight he had as a successful man of letters to prevent the railroad from putting down the tracks. When the railroad won, Irving reconciled himself to it. He often took the train down to the city. All he had to do was flag it down. It would stop right here, just for him." I followed the guide's pointed finger down to the river's edge where the tracks ran parallel to the Hudson. How wonderful I thought that here along the river bank, Irving could just flag the next train down, here along the river bank where the leaves were still falling. But it wasn't time to jump on the train. There was much to see.

Our guide left us to ramble about the grounds so that he could greet the new group waiting outside the house for him. It was still warm though the temperature was supposed to take a sharp drop that night. I sat down in a small, Gothic chair to watch the river flow. I pushed myself back up after a minute or two for I wanted to take in the Old Dutch Church and Burying Ground up in Sleepy Hollow. I didn't want the time to slip away again. I had gotten off to a later start than planned.

I hiked it up the winding, steep, path back to Broadway. As I walked along, I saw Christ Episcopalian Church where according to the sign, Irving attended service. They had a rainbow banner on the old iron fence, and bilingual services at San Marco, which I suppose was a church within the church. Interesting how the Old Dutch Church went from services in Dutch to English. Maybe Damen Willem walked here. What was it he called the Native Americans, wild things, Wildens? Crossing Main Street and Broadway, I was almost run over by a red Toyota. I swear that was the condominium seller, Joe Noggins, at the wheel. I shook my fist at him.

The Headless Horseman swiped his sword at me as I entered the local bakery for a latte. Well, a hokey life-size statue of him did. Local folks, mostly seniors, were yakking it up. I took my drink to a table outside to savor the fresh air. Good coffee. Golden leaves from an oak overhead started to fall. One leaf fell into my coffee, another on my shoulder. If I sit long enough, the leaves will cover me. Whatever happened to Richard Post? He went up to an enchanted region, was overtaken by falling oak leaves, and turned into a green man. Then I saw a familiar face.

A few yards away Brooke Deering was having coffee and pastry with a friend at a table outside the Golden Harvester deli. Brooke stood up to beckon me over. Grabbing my latte, I went over. Some teenager was staring at his reflection in the shiny deli window to primp his hair. Was that man walking like a panther reflected in the glass, me? Nah.

"Hello. Richard, isn't it?" said Brooke.

"Brooke Deering. I remember."

"Yes, and this is my neighbor Bonnie Drummond. Bonnie, meet Richard who helped me buy my condo. He had to straighten out some debts, long story." Bonnie said hello with a thick Scottish accent. This kind of accent, like the bagpipes, had the power to stir up strong emotions when it didn't grate on the nerves. My antennas went up.

"Come sit down," said Bonnie grabbing my hand. This thin woman with puffy, bright ginger hair certainly meant business. Checking my shirt for crumbs, and pinching the pleat of my khakis, I pulled up a chair.

"How's life in the hollow, Brooke? Any ghost sightings at The Milepost? You look like a townie already." I seemed to fall into an easy camaraderie with Brooke though I hardly knew her. Not sure why. It usually took much longer for me to feel comfortable with people.

"Ha, ha. Not yet. Sometimes local kids set to howling outside the window on the Croton Trail, though. Well, I am indeed settling in. I can thank Bonnie here who's been

living at The Milepost for about seven years. She's the real Tarrytowner and a big help."
"Well, with my accent, no one will ever take me for a local. I just open my mouth, and people ask, 'Where you from?' To the real townies, we two are just carpetbaggers," said Bonnie patting the Princess Diana hairdo which framed her babyish, though middleaged, face.

"Where are you from?" I asked.

"Crossmyloof, a town outside Glasgow."

"Bonnie runs a knitting shop up in Putnam County. She has woven herself into the fabric of this village, and that one, no pun intended. What brings you up here on a Saturday, Richard? You're not collecting bills on the weekend, are you?" asked Brooke with her eyes dancing. Studying Bonnie's attractive, but slightly lumpy Fair Isle sweater, I gathered it was handmade.

"No, nothing like that. I came back to take in the historic sites. I just visited Sunnyside. I am heading up to the cemetery and the Old Dutch Church next. I returned the Saturday after your closing. But I took a wrong turn and wound up in a wooded area. Spooky, or maybe just silly." Why did I have to add that?

"You felt you had been there before," Bonnie remarked. Her blond eyebrows went up.

"Not exactly. In a way. Maybe. It's a long story, but on that Saturday, I picked up an interesting journal in an antique shop which may or may not be the real thing. The young man who wrote it seems to have been one of the original Sleepy Hollow Boys. He even claims to have been present the night that Ichabod Crane disappeared. He's a sorry soul. The journal is dated 1789, the year George Washington became president. An uncle, a Dutch uncle, preserved it. His nephew edited, and published it back in 1923."

"How interesting. I guess you find the Hudson Valley a nice change of pace from life in the big city. A cop who has lived here all his life said something worth remembering. I shouldn't gush, and yes, the big chill won't be far behind, but he said, 'Sometimes it is so beautiful here I have to duck as an angel floats by.' A cop said this. So hard to keep a straight face," said Bonnie.

"You know Irving is buried here. The cemetery is about a mile up the road. There he rests or unrests. The Headless Horseman Bridge will lead you to it. You should see some smashed pumpkins up there this time of year. Some people say Irving invented the pumpkin," offered Brooke.

"What do you mean Irving invented the pumpkin, Brooke? No, it was the Indians. Well, they grew it and knew what to do with it. You know what I mean. It's your Thanksgiving. Dry it over the fire or in the sun, put it in bread, soup, pudding, and pies, and it will keep you alive all winter," protested Bonnie.

"I meant Irving made it famous. Started the association between jack-o-lanterns and harvest balls, or Halloween, causing people to fall under its spell. Ever since Starbuck's put pumpkin spice in the coffee, it's in everything." Brooke explained. She brushed a crumb off her pumpkin orange sweater.

"Oh no. You haven't fallen under a spell, have you, Richard? Are you going to buy a punkin' to bring back to the city? I think it was the Scotch who invented the jack-olantern, except we used neeps, not pumpkins. Do you believe in the Headless One?" asked Bonnie with her eyes widening. The smattering of freckles across her face spread out when she smiled.

"What? Believe in being chased by a Headless Horseman who wants to smash my head in with a fiery pumpkin if I don't make it over the Tappan Zee? Or is he supposed to chase me up and down the Palisades before plunging me to my death in the icy waters below? Is that how Ichabod Crane died?" Does anyone know?" I asked.

"Died? Died, Richard? Ichabod never dies. Every night he rides out to be chased all over again. We hear hoofs outside our windows around midnight on the Croton Trail, don't we Brook? He's alive," teased Bonnie.

"Hush! Hush! Everybody. If you listen carefully enough, you will hear Ichabod's nasal singing of the Psalmody being carried down the centuries on the wind. Pay attention," Brooke implored.

Sitting back to enjoy her coffee, and the expression on my face as well, Brooke smiled like a Cheshire cat.

"I'm sure you're right . . . " Brooke was about to defend Bonnie, but I put my hand up to stop her.

"I have seen a dark figure in a black cape chase a terrified, skinny schoolteacher from farm to the bridge in broad daylight," I declared. Brooke shot me an incredulous look.

"In fact, not just from farm to the bridge, but all over this town and the next. I have seen them on street signs, T-shirts, on firetrucks, police cars, ambulances and municipal buildings. He does not chase me." They cracked up. At least I had the ladies laughing.

"With a fox, in a box, whatever. This calls for another round of coffees and treats," said Brooke. She went inside The Golden Harvester. There wasn't a chance of declining.

"Well, it is a lovely legend. We have one in Scotland too, Tam O'Shanter, written up in a poem by our Robbie, or Rabbie Burns. Our story came first. Tam rides like the wind to save himself from witches, warlocks, the very devil himself, by reaching Kirk Calloway.

The Burns story even has a moral: stay away from John Barleycorn if you want your horse to keep his tail."

Brooke came out with a carton full of coffees, and assorted pastries. She set it down on the table, then started spreading out little cups of half-and-half, milk, and sugar packets on the round, white plastic table. At the center, she placed two pumpkin spice cups of halfandhalf. I wondered if they charged extra for that flavor.

"I was just telling Richard about Tam O' Shanter. You know that poem, don't you Brookie? She's read everything. She's a walking book. Poetry in motion. Yes, and I say it is a good thing we are just drinking coffee. In my edition of Scottish poetry, there are photographs of the ruins of the old Kirk, sinking into the ground. The tourists flock. Robert Burns and his father lie in the burial ground there. There's more. There are comical sculptures of the main characters like Souter Johnnie and Tam himself. It's a kind of theme park with the Brig 'O Doon in the background. In the dark, it does look haunted. I don't understand poetry much, but Burns is a kind of people's poet, *A Man's a Man for All That, Auld Lang Syne* on the New Year."

"Yes Lord Byron, half a Scot himself, said Burns was 'half deity, half dirt. But I don't think Richard is too much interested in legend. I imagine he prefers history," Brooke surmised.

I nodded. Taking out my wallet, I pressed Brooke to take a twenty for the treat. When she refused, I threw it down at the table's center.

"There is a monument to the local militiamen who captured the British spy, Major Andre. He was in cahoots with Benedict Arnold to turn over West Point to the British. It's only about a block away at Patriot's Park. You will pass it on your way up to the Old Dutch Burying Ground. Have a look," Brooke suggested.

"And don't forget the headless Hessian who rests, or unrests, there. That is if some ghoul hasn't dug him up," she added.

"Ok. I am interested in both fact and fiction. I am kind of on the trail of Irving as well as his creations."

"Look at that skinny man crossing Broadway with his clothes flying about him. That's Ichabod late for the ball. Or what about that burly fireman who lives on the second floor, Bonnie? Brom Bones to a T. The one with the six-pack. And that pink-cheeked man with the paunch down to his knees might be Van Tassel. Look at the beautiful, young blond over there. She probably goes to EF, the international school, near the lake. She's the reincarnation of Katrina." Brooke was getting carried away.

"You're going off the deep end, girl. Well, maybe it's not too farfetched. Fact is stranger than fiction. Some thought that Britain's poet laureate, Ted Hughes, was the Yorkshire Ripper. He was a kind of Heathcliff. They even put him in a lineup. You know, Sylvia Plath, your American poet? He was her husband," added Bonnie. I wasn't sure how we got from Irving to Burns to Plath.

I went somewhere in my head. Her husband. I would have been her husband if we had made it to the altar. Brooke started spouting Plath's poetry. "There's no stopping it." "The blood jet is poetry." Then, "Daddy you bastard I'm through." I seemed to be seeing them through cobwebs, though the sun was still shining brightly. There must have been something in the coffee, more than pumpkin spice cream and sugar. I blurted out something about almost being her husband, but somehow no one heard me.

"Brooke, we should put all this literary knowledge to use. Tell Richard how

Ichabod's flight started at our house. We could give walking tours like that bloke in Edinburgh, Robin, who does the ghost walks. We could guide people down the authentic route. Do you know there are condos down by the river called, Ichabod's Landing? They start at a cool million. The Legend is the town's selling point. Can you imagine that? Aye, we should definitely cash in." said Bonnie.

I came back to myself. "What did you say? You know Ichabod's route?" I rubbed my eyes. The ladies looked kind of blurry. Brooke took a deep breath.

"Ichabod started at our condo on Broadway or the Albany Post Road, where the Mott House stood. Mott House was the model for Van Tassel farm. Some maintain it was Cortland Manor. Of course, everything gets disputed. He paused at Major Andre's great tulip tree which stood a block north from here, where the Warner Library, that neo-classical building, now stands. He headed north to Sleepy Hollow though back in those days the main road went to the east of Broadway. He rode uphill at Bedford, or maybe Pine Street, then downhill to the old Dutch church, to Gory Brook Road, where goblin raised up his arms to fire off the flaming pumpkin as Ichabod thundered over the bridge." Brooke recited this all without a pause.

"Whoosh. Amazing. That is the route I took last week." I cut myself off, not wanting to reveal how muddled my walk became. Like Ichabod, I had veered east.

"Too bad we couldn't take the tourists to the schoolhouse. For that, you have to go all the way to Kinderhook, which means 'children's corner.' That would be quite a detour." Brooke continued.

"What are they trying to do up there? Steal our tourist trade? We don't have an old schoolhouse? Certainly, we could rig something up. What about that little red house building across from the high school?" Bonnie said sounding exasperated. Were they serious about going into business?

Brooke went on. "I think that little red house is the elementary school library. My head is filled with facts. There was a man buried in Staten Island named Ichabod Crane, but he wasn't the model for Crane. That was one Jesse Merwyn, a schoolteacher friend of Irving's who lived in Kinderhook. Or so they say. I don't know. Some say, Kingston. The Hessian lost his head in the Battle of White Plains. Cannonball took it off. Irving made it quaint, but the real horror is not on the bridge but the decapitation. Irving didn't include much of that. He was not a man of war. The severed head was on the horse's saddle, though, like it or not. The Disney version omitted that detail. He pulled out all the stops. I could get the tourists' heads to spin."

"Not scarier than your New York subway, eh Richard? Now that would give me the willies." teased Bonnie.

"And all this happened up above the river 'in the bosom of one of those spacious coves which indent the eastern shore of the Hudson.' Now that opening of the story makes a striking contrast to horror, doesn't it?" mused Brooke. If I had sat here long enough, I might hear the whole tale. I made a move forward.

"Before you go, step over there to see a grand view of the Hudson. A beautiful sunset is just around the corner. Just don't go looking for a pot of gold," suggested Bonnie.

Maybe it was the Scottish accent or the childlike enthusiasm, but I rose right up out of my chair to follow Bonnie's pointed finger to the corner of Broadway and Wildey Street.

Chapter Fourteen

Under the Spell

While Brooke looked on approvingly, I dutifully followed Bonnie's finger. Taking a seat on the rough-hewn bench, set at the corner, I looked to the West. It was too early for sunset, but the sky over the river was electric blue with some streaks of glowing, metallic orange. I should say pumpkin orange. A few streaks of purple underlined the clouds. I chilled out. Tangerine skies. Could you have a tangerine sky? Mellow yellow. I was in a Peter Max painting. Then I woke up. This time of year was beguiling but tricky. Colors would disappear. Darkness would come quickly. Better be moving on to the next site. Didn't want to mellow out to mush.

"What a pleasant view. All those colors before sunset. Something's going on here. Are you finished with this?" I asked as I started to gather up the coffee cups and sweetener, and pastry wrappers.

"Don't fuss over it. We'll get Richard to go under the spell yet. Richard, you will buy a condo or a romantic cottage at the river bank. You won't catch too many sunsets, though. You will return each evening in darkness, to trudge, briefcase in hand, up the steep hill from the station. You won't be able to see the hand in front of you. Right now you are sitting on an uncomfortable edge, just shy of a making a move. You will soon be edging toward Riverdale with a view of becoming a suburbanite," Bonnie prophesized.

"Watch yourself now, Richard. Bonnie has the highlander's gift of second sight. Even the rational Dr. Johnston had some respect for that. The real horror will be the encroaching wildlife. A bobcat was seen in Irvington running along the railroad tracks. Someone saw a bear in Ossining. The only remaining ghosts will be the ones already here. People don't stay long enough for spirits to roost. Recently, a neighbor complained that it is getting too hard to keep ghosts what with all these carpetbaggers," Brooke contributed.

She cautioned her friend. "Bonnie, you're going to drive him straight out of the hollow. But Richard, we do have a few extra tickets for the hayride for next weekend. Please come up and join us next Saturday night. The good weather is supposed to hold. Last licks of summer, Indian summer, with a nice creepy, chill in the evening. Take out your phone. I'll give you my number," said Brooke.

We exchanged numbers. I gave Brook a business card. Not sure why. A heavyset, dark-haired girl went walking by with her face buried in a large poster of all the main tourist sites. Simple illustrations of Sunnyside, the Old Dutch Church, the Croton Trail and Lyndhurst Castle, were so big I could see them from my chair. She bumped into a tree sending her companion into gales of hysterical laughter. A rather odd, spacey young man approached our table. Dressed all in black, he wore an earring and a nose ring. Just as I started making my goodbyes, Bonnie introduced her son Alastair. His stringy, dark hair was too dark for his pale skin. Must have dyed it. In that get-up, he could have been part of the hayride.

I started to say goodbye. Bonnie was going on about her son believed in the lost continent of Atlanta, so he was an Atlantean or something like that. The lost continent? Children. Brooke sensed my discomfort. Though she kept her gentle smile, she did not look too happy herself. Come up next Saturday. You know my address? Ring the bell to 4B around 4:00.

I guess that exchange of phone numbers bonded us. I would be coming up yet again. As I stood up, Alastair slid into my seat. Bonnie looked a little agitated. Picking up my unease, she flashed me a look.

"Run, Richard! Get to the cemetery. Run! Closing time!" said Bonnie. What she meant was, run from the horror that was her son. I was more than ready. Taking my now familiar route, I headed up Broadway. Figuring that I didn't want much for dinner, I stopped at the Galloping Hessian to grab a sandwich for later. A tourist came in asking for directions to the Old Dutch Church. A surly busboy bumped a tray into my back. The waitress was friendly. I heard the manager tell the tourist, "What's his name is buried in the churchyard." A local school was named after Irving. The next town was Irvington, yet here he was "what's his name." Maybe he was referring to the headless one who didn't even have a name. I paid for my roast beef sandwich and moved on.

Around the corner from a Mobile Station, I found the statue of the Horseman that had been featured on *Most Haunted.* It looked like a huge tree. The sculptor was probably thinking of Major Andre's tulip tree which Brooke said had been destroyed by lightning. I snapped a picture. Taking out the rumpled, green and white schedule from my pocket, I checked the train times. As I walked over the Headless Horseman's bridge, which wasn't much of a bridge at all, I took in the Old Dutch Church which sat on a grassy knoll. Now that made for a picturesque sight. According to the literature, it was three hundred and thirtytwo years old making it the oldest church in Westchester having continuous services. It was magical. It would make a great movie set, but I don't think most Sleepy Hollow movies used it. They were having an outdoor church festival. Some boys in red and white aprons were barbecuing hamburgers and serving up cider with the minister was hovering behind them. Delicious smells filled the air. Then I heard hoof beats. A real Headless Horseman, or a person dressed as him, came down the road up on a large horse. Or, should I say steed.

That blond kid was here too. The Horseman pointed to his head, then waved his hand, and shook his shoulders. Upon consideration, the boy's head was too empty. It wouldn't do. The minister took the opportunity to preach. Taking the boy's chin in his hand, he said, "I told you to get a better head on your shoulders. Even the Headless Horseman does not want your head."

"He's just horsing around, Reverend Bob."

Good comeback kid. The Horseman dismounted and sat on a large rock. I moved over to the sanctuary to get a better look at the whitewashed stone, and the fetching bell tower with the old looking weather vane. According to the cemetery map, Andrew Carnegie and the Helmsleys, Leona, and Harry were buried here. Near the church, there were a few stone effigies with big heads with colonial wigs and sprouting angel wings. They looked like old souls in fight winging their way to heaven. The pamphlet stated that the dead were laid out here east to west so that upon awakening their souls would face God. Some of the embossments on the tombs were still decipherable. I bent down to read Ann Couenhovens epitaph dated 1797.

My cares are past
My bones at rest
God took my life
When he thought best

I slipped in time. Young Damen Willem is sitting on the bench waiting for the minister, then impatiently walking about the graves. There wasn't any bench there now. Damen found no rest for the weary there. Services were only held here now in summer. The minister's office would be at the larger church next to *The Milepost*. It was something to look down at the soil and think Damen, Mahalalel, and their compatriots walked here over two hundred years ago. They had to be real to do that. That is, they had to be real to walk the ground anywhere else. Not sure if those rules held here. The whole region had a case of the vapors. If I looked hard enough and long enough, could I find Damen's grave? I bent down to touch the soil. I just might blink and see Brom Bones jumping the gate.

"Are you really from here? Is this a real place?" I heard a tourist ask. I looked up to see a boy wearing a Sleepy Hollow High School hoodie. No, I felt like saying. Sleepy Hollow is only a set for a Johnny Depp movie or a Tom Mison TV show or the inspiration for a Disney cartoon. Can't you hear Bing Crosbie singing? Of course, it wasn't for me to say. The boy and his father laughed. People were just flocking in. It looks like a gathering of the clans. A small sign indicated Irving's grave, so I started walking up the hill to view it. I was looking down at some smashed pumpkins when a heavy drowsiness overtook me. Sluggishly I moved deeper and deeper into the burial ground.

Like Ichabod of old, I sat down under a tree to lean my back against the bark. The sunlight was so concentrated that I felt I had fallen into a suntrap. All I remember is taking a deep breath. When I woke up, it was dark. I fumbled with my sleeve to look at my watch. To my horror, it was almost seven. The gates closed at four-thirty. These things only happen to me. The gates to the right looked mighty high. Quiet, unassuming, wanting to pass with stealth through life, here I was stuck in a cemetery in Westchester. It was embarrassing. No, it was unnerving. It was dark. The sky, inky black with just a few thin streaks of red and gold. It felt like midnight.

Screeches, screams, blood curling howling sounds pierced the air coming up from the hollow below. Something unspeakable was loping about the dark. Such horrors couldn't be. Had I lost my mind? Then the path lit up. A flatbed truck wound its way around the road. The back was filled with people sitting on bales of hay. It was the haunted hayride! Not wanting anyone to see me, I hid behind a tree. I expected lightning to strike me momentarily. As I scrunched my body down, my knees brushed a tombstone.

I didn't try to read the inscription. It was probably marked, "Richard Post." The truck was moving away from the main gate. I headed towards the entrance.

Of course, it was locked. On my left, there was a spiky gate. On the right, steep slopes led down to possibly a ravine, too steep for me, though I did see a lower, flatter fence near the church. But, this was the oldest church in Westchester with continuing service. There might be alarms and security cameras. That's all I needed. I decided to go the other way. I had to find my way to that broken gate that led out to Douglas Park. Historic Westchester, or not, I was losing my nerve. I increased my pace. I would have sung psalms like Ichabod if I knew any. My heart started beating fast. Now the temperature was dropping fast. The wind was whipping up the trees. Talk about your frisson of horror. If a dark figure on a black steed, wrapped in a black cape, with a high white collar, missing a head, should appear under a willow tree, I would tell myself: it's only a hayride. Only a hayride.

I moved through the graves. I started to run. I hadn't survived all those years in New York City to be done in by my fears in Westchester. Westchester is supposed to be a haven, a place where city dwellers go to escape the horror downtown. Where was that path to the open gate? Moving forward too quickly, I tripped over a little grave. Hoping it wasn't one of those preRevolutionary graves, worn to small, faceted edges like a rough diamond, I stood up to brush myself off. The little grave marker looked ancient; it must be priceless. I gently patted its head.

Then I heard another scream, diabolical laughter. The hayride was nowhere in sight. Hiding behind a large oak, I craned my neck to see who was there. Dried leaves and acorns crunched beneath my feet. The sound echoed throughout the woods. I could make out a large shape behind a tree across the path. There was movement in the bushes there. Someone, or something, craned its neck to take a look at me. Just before it moved back, I got a glimpse of an overweight, kid about twelve or thirteen years old. There was a shuffling behind me. More kids. Did these little punks pass for the Sleepy Hollow boys these days? I was much taller than them. But there was four or possibly five or them, a real wolf pack.

A small one with curly hair started pulling at my coat. Another began to pinch my hand. A third one started tickling my neck with what looked like a piece of straw though he had to stand on tiptoes to reach. Just then I saw the slender blond boy leaning against a tree. Appealing to their better natures, I started to ask, with my voice breaking in spite of myself, if anyone knew how to get out of here. With the moonlight bouncing off his light hair, he chopped his hand through the air. I got it. He was saying. First, you go this way, than that. Thank you, son. Oh my God, thank you. If I get out of this damned cemetery, I will become a religious man. No, better yet, I'll put the kid through college. Nah.

The biggest kid, possibly the lumpy Spanish boy I had seen on Broadway the date of my first visit, took his backpack off. He looked awfully familiar. Setting it on the ground, he pulled a plump, plastic pumpkin from the pack. A crude, the jack-o-lantern face had been sketched on it with a marker. Taking out a lighter from his jacket, the kid attempted to set in on fire. It didn't exactly flame on. It did give off a horrid smell. I broke into a run.

Something smacked into a tree. Crashing through trees, I stopped at a large rock. I was out of breath. What if that blond kid gave be the wrong direction? It was Halloween time. His motions could just be part of another Sleepy Hollow Boys' prank.

When I regained my breath, I started walking again. All I had to rely on was some crude hand gestures. I kept my gaze to the ground to avoid falling again. A large mausoleum loomed to the left. I hoped it wasn't the Helmsley Memorial. That Queen of Mean was scary enough in the daylight. There was a plateau with steps going down. I should evoke protection of St. Nicholas. What was it Damen said? Yes, that was it. Rushing down the steps, I turned to the right. There was water rushing below, a bridge, and the path to the woods. If only I could make it across the bridge without being seen, I could get out with something of pride and dignity left. The path was very different now from the quiet, nature walk I discovered two weeks earlier. Tableaus filled ax murderers, bloody victims, skeletons, ghouls and even a zombie family looking quite at home in their moldering living room, were stationed on both sides. The final tableau was a gallows with a limp body hanging from a tree, right above my head. At least the floodlights here gave me a safe path.

Behind my back, I heard a large crack. It sounded like a rifle shot ricocheting through the woods. It was the hayride truck crossing the wooden bridge spanning the creek as it made another round. Again, I tried to hide behind a tree. It was useless. Kids dressed as skeletons, werewolves, vampires and ghosts poured out near the exit. I started running. People might take me for part of the show. Someone yelled something. I put my hands over my ears and ran on. There may have been a lot of hooting, but that broken gate was open wide. I jumped to the side to let the truck pass. Some kids in black with skeleton costumes came out from the bush to chase the screaming riders down New Broadway. This parting scare evoked shrieks of laughter. I came face to face with one of them as he flipped off his skull mask. I shrugged. He did too. Long skeletal fingers of death reached out to hold me. If it wasn't death, it was a high school boy. I can't tell you which one is worse. All I wanted was a good night's sleep safe in bed.

Chapter Fifteen

Midnight Visitor

I didn't get one. Things went from bad to worse. I headed back home, with, no pun intended, a hollowed-out feeling. Passing Patriot's Park, I saw some crows lighting on the scarecrows the town's children had made in a sponsored event. Those crows had no fear. I hope they didn't see my tail between my legs. That ubiquitous blond boy was collecting water bottles from his friends to flood the sidewalk. Then he took his house keys out of his pocket and placed the tip of a key on the bolt at the base of a street lamp. Then he grabbed a tall boy's hand. That youth grabbed that boy's hand and so on until there was a chain of boys. What was up?

"Ready now? Prepare for a shock. And, I do mean, shock," said the blond boy. Oh no. It looked like he had figured out a way to get electrical shocks off the street light which could be passed from kid to kid. Maybe he wanted to electrocute them. I went up to pull him away.

"How did you get out of the cemetery so fast? What do you think you are doing? You must have flown like a crow," I yelled. He blasted off on me like a small bomb.

"Get the hell off me, pervert. Go back to the cemetery, dig a grave for yourself and die. Did I save you in the woods so you could harass me here in town? Did you follow me here?" he shouted. He pulled away from me, spreading out his feet and pumping his fists. His fat friend howled.

"You could get severely burned. You're messing with electricity," I admonished. The boy laughed off my concerns.

"When's the last time you got a shock? Just what were you doing in the cemetery all by yourself? Looking for cheap thrills? You're just another deadhead, old man," the kid sneered. His friends started to form a circle him. He shook his hair at me. So this pretty boy who always seems to be in the thick of things turns out to be not good at heart, but a mean SOB. Tarrytown should pass an ordinance to confine the hooligans to Sleepy Hollow. They have a tradition to uphold. Kids! I'm glad I don't have children.

There was a line of people standing in decorative corn stalks waiting to get into the Greek Restaurant on the corner of Main Street and Broadway. Concert goers were coming out of the Victorian Music Hall in droves. Drivers were circling the block looking for parking places. Good luck with that. The temperature was dropping fast. I scrambled down the hill to the Metro North Station. I couldn't get home fast enough. The train's windows were dirty, but it was too dark to see anything anyway. Darkness was okay with me. The plunge into the dark tunnel at Ninety-Six Street brought me great relief. I had had enough of the Hudson Valley.

Keeping my head down on the subway, I made it to Twenty-Third Street. I kept my head down all the way home because I didn't want to talk to anyone. Going up the stairs, I brushed shoulders with some big bear of a man in a woman's wig.

He looked worse than the hetero on the second floor who bullied his wife. I unlocked the door and sat down on the bed. I didn't feel like brushing my teeth or hanging up my clothes. I just wanted to go down into a deep sleep. If I fell asleep for twenty years, it would be all right with me. As long as I wasn't under a tree in Tarrytown or Sleepy Hollow, I'd be content to sit out the next two decades. Could I be so bold as to break my pattern? Would I regret not using proper hygiene or neglecting my clothing? Chester did not even come out to greet me. Cats!

Then there came a knock on the door. It was after midnight. Peering through the peephole, I saw my neighbor from the fourth floor, David Poole, a real queen who was known to bring home assorted mugs from Alphabet City. How many times had I witnessed him sweeping open his door in the early morning evening gowns and mascara, and letting the riffraff out who had spent the night? I was heading for work, but they were heading for the streets. When shouts, screams, and violent arguments weren't breaking out in his place, David Poole was the quietest of men. Not all his lovers were willing to flee like vampires with the morning light. He would scream at the top of his lungs beseeching them to get out. Some of them told him to do likewise though the apartment was his. The building must have rules against such people. I really should move uptown.

Now here he was at my door. Don't these people have a sense of gaydar or something like that? He must know I am not interested in him. I opened the door.

"Are you going to ask to borrow a cup of sugar?" I asked. When he looked wounded, I added, "I'm only kidding." He held up a delicate hand to brush it off.

"Am I making too much noise?" What was wrong with me? That made no sense because I wasn't doing anything but sitting on the daybed, head in hands, ruing the events of the day.

"No, no, no. Of course, not." He bit his lip. Against my better judgment, I let him in. Sweeping his bathrobe across his chest, he sat down on the daybed and stared at the painting of the Hudson Valley. I hope it brought redemption for the blandness of all the rest of my décor.

"I have seen you, Richard," the drag queen dramatically announced. What was he implying? He made it sound as if I had done something grand or subversive. I looked perplexed.

"I have seen you, Richard. I have seen you about the building, taking out the trash and picking up the mail."

I stood before him in baffled wonder. He moved to the table and sat down smoothing out his robe the way women tuck in their skirts. "Play mother, please," said David pointing to the teapot on the stove. OK. I decided to play along. So, I put the kettle on to make tea. I reached out to shake hands. He lightly brushed my fingers.

"Who was that burly guy going down the stairs? Was he visiting you? Does he live here? He almost knocked me off the landing," I said. Something outside in the hall distracted David's attention. Cupping his hand behind his ear, he leaned not toward the apartment door, but the closet, to listen. When he was satisfied that there was no one outside, he gave himself a shake.

David resumed our conversation. "Much of the time, I do not know who he is. I certainly never informed where he is or what he is doing. He might be out there doing anything with anyone. I do know his name. His name is Donald. Tonight he was here and not here." As I started to speak, he abruptly rose from the table. He turned his back on me to study the landscape. I got up to straighten it.

"Love should make us happy, make us feel fully alive with a certain *Je ne sais quois*. A palpable *joy de vivre*, I suppose. Sirens started up outside as if to underscore his outburst. But then again there were always sirens outside. He perked up his ears as if he had never heard a siren before. Feigning great shock, he jumped when the tea kettle began to whistle.

"They are coming for me. I am miserable from having few things to like and many things to make me afraid. Francis Bacon said that. Or something like that. I should be more original. Bacon certainly was. I am so sorry about that. I keep myself alone when he present. I mean, I keep myself low when he is present. I refer to Paul Bart, the thug you saw stumbling down the stairs. Not Francis Bacon. I lied when I told you his name was Donald." David rambled on.

"What do you do?" I wasn't sure if I meant for a living or with men. Oh, my God. What was I thinking? As I picked up the kettle, I thought there was blood on my hands. I recalled David helping one of those druggies who had a nosebleed. He held the handkerchief to his nose regardless of what diseases that blood may have contained.

"If I told you, you would not sleep at night. Oh! I am very sorry. You meant for a living, didn't you? I am such a silly Pooh Bear," he said looking stricken. Ignoring my question, he looked up at the still life.

"I like your painting Richard. The blue vase is very soothing. Possibly it matches my eyes. In any case, it adds a woman's touch to the flat." Wishing David would comment on the Hudson Valley landscape; I saw Chester peeling out at me from under the daybed.

"Yes, my mother bought it." As I scrummaged through the cupboards for teabags and crackers, Chester came out to jump up to the countertop next to the sink. He sat watching me with more caution than curiosity. Coffee won't do for tea and sympathy, I whispered. I set two cups down on the card table and poured the water in carefully. Chester watched as I placed a few Lorna Doone cookies on the saucers the way my mother did. David would have to go. That was the second time I thought of mother in as many minutes He had fallen into a funk.

"Are you okay David?" Startled, he looked up and blinked a few times as if he had been in complete darkness when the lights suddenly came on.

"I am afraid Richard. Lonely and afraid."

"Drink some tea. Have a cookie," I entreated.

The buzzer rang. It was a pizza guy. No, I told him I didn't order a pizza. I don't know who did.

"David Poole, did you order a pizza?" David swore it was not him. I didn't feel comfortable calling him David. Mr. Poole was too formal. So I addressed him Quaker style.

"No, I did not order a pizza."

"Try the thug on the second floor, 2A," I said to the pizza man who ran down the stairs.

"I was living inside a Hieronymus Bosch painting when you found the grace to bring me out to the golden valley. It might have been a Francis Bacon landscape but what does it matter now? I would be anyone but me. I take myself wherever I go." He spun himself around on his monogrammed slipper, to study the landscape on the wall above the table. It occurred to me that I had the pictures in the wrong positions. The Frederic Edwin Church should hang over the daybed, the still-life over the table. David's mood suddenly changed. "I shouldn't have come here. I have disturbed your quiet evening," David apologized. Chester snuck a Lorna Doon from my saucer. My quest pursed his lips together into a petulant sneer. I thought he was going to unleash a vicious stream of bitching vitriol on me in my home. Chester jumped to the table and butted his head into David's chest.

"May I, Richard," David asked holding out a cookie to Chester.

"OK with me." Chester took the cookie in his mouth, then jumped down to the floor to eat it. David placed the second cookie on my saucer. He took his cup and saucer to the sink. I told him just to dump them in, but David meticulously washed them. He simply said thank you with touching grace. He left. Those two words were the most sincere words I had heard in a long time.

The phone rang. It was Stan.

"Richard. I know it's late, but I've been calling on and off all day. Don't you check your phone? Or are you that busy on the weekend?"

"It's a long story, Stan. Let's let it go. How are you?"

"Angry at you. You were supposed to come down to stay with us. Remember? I can do without your visit now. I didn't mean that. The toys were great. Edie and Manny love them, but this is about family, not gifts. I can't even bring up Edie and tell you how she feels."

"I'm sorry Stan." He ranted on.

"And what about Manny's feelings? Huh? Dad doesn't care. He has his young girlfriend. She's all he needs. Our parents make me feel like an orphan. I don't want to be too hard on Mom. I can play it by ear with her."

"How is Mom? Have you spoken to her lately?" My eyes, straying about the room looking for a place to focus, gazed upon *The Journal of Damen Willem,* which was resting on top of a copy of Irving's *Sketchbook* which I had picked up at Barnes and Noble. I certainly wasn't going to have the liberty to throw myself into bed unwashed tonight. These unexpected visitors and phone calls bring on a severe case of insomnia. I would have to read myself to sleep as soon as I could get off the phone.

"She's still getting over Dad and adjusting to life in Florida. To her family means being grandma and grandad as a couple. She would rather be alone then be part of any family now that their marriage is over. And that includes mine."

"Wow, Stan. I haven't thought of Mom as a grandmother."

"As if you think at all." It hurt. It hurt. I had hurt Stan and his family. I held my phone away from my ear trying to find words to say.

Stan softened. "Mom will come around. She will be a good grandma. I can't say she didn't have her suspicions about Dad and his extracurricular activities, but she never dreamed he would make a fast exit. I have to give her time. Mom will come here, or we will go to her when Christmas comes. If Mom doesn't feel up to traveling, like Mohammad, I will go to the mountain, er, Orlando, with Edie and Manny. We are a unit. We stand together. Dad too, not the floozy. I can't be sure of the location, but when I know, I will let you know. I hope wherever it is you will be there. If it is not too much to ask."

"It is not too much to ask. I will be there." I would have said anything to end the conversation so that I could get into bed with my book.

Chapter Sixteen

God's Many Mansions

November 25

The boys did not give up much information. One notion they all shared was that Ichabod Crane had gone down the river to New York City. I would do the same. Placing my papers, including a treatise regarding my personal salvation which I had written out in the night, some stale bread, and a couple of apples, and one cruller in my pack, I prepared to foot it to Manhattan by following the river. It might be easier just to jump into the water. That cruller did make me feel not a little guilty. I couldn't tell if God would forgive me, but I was sure Mama would.

I threw in *Memorable Providences,* a book Ichabod had lent me about the witches in Salem. What pleasure it would bring if I could put it back in his hands. The hot guilt burning up my chest was bound to cause a spontaneous combustion if I did not act fast enough. Mama had some money hidden in a locked spice box on the top shelf in the kitchen. I was tempted to steal it during the night but did not. I could sense it over my head as I sat down to eat. We had an unusually quiet meal.

As my family began to tidy up after supper, I decided to take my leave. Tripping over Nochi's wooden toy horse, I steadied myself against the door. I would have to store up the warmth of this hearth and the smell of Mama's dumplings in my head. I could not know how long it would be until I saw my home again.

I crossed over to the shed to get a hammer and nail. Placing them in my pack, I took a last look through the window to witness what I was leaving behind. It was cold and dark outside and inside my heart. Mama swung open the top of the door to sell some lemon bread and gingerbread to hungry folks. Sometimes she would just give her food away. As I stepped into the outhouse, oyster shells and bones crunched under my feet. I stood still hoping Mama would not hear me. My resolve momentarily shook. How can I leave with the smell of apples and burning leaves filling the air, and with the little starshaped flowers blooming? It would be more comfortable to venture forth in the spring. My heart swelled with infinite longing, yet, I could not turn back. The resolve to I come back for my dark wedding coat to wed Josefien in the new year gave me heart. Not until Mama went inside, did I move forward.

I headed north to the church to nail my protest to the church door like Martin Luther of old. Some people say he did not nail his treatise to the door, that that was only a legend. But, Ichabod swore that he had, and that was good enough for me. When the schoolmaster told stories of history, you believed that he had been there as an eyewitness, though, when it came to Luther's defiant act, it could not be.

My protest stated:

No man of the cloth nor church as a body can save my immortal soul.

As I am the man who lost my immortal soul, I must call upon our Lord Jesus Christ to help me regain it.

No amount of money can buy my soul out of purgatory.

I will not return to my home until I had made recompense for the wrong doings that burden my soul.

Of course, it was childish. Everyone would think me mad. I knew I shouldn't do it, but I nailed it anyway. I could imagine the dominie saying I missed the date of Luther's protest, October 31st by about a month, and 272 years.

Preposterous, he will shout. What has that fool boy to protest? I felt some presence fluttering over my head. A bat was flying about the rooster atop the weather vane. It was too dark to see, but I know what it said. There was an F for Felipe, along with an inscription: If God is for us, who can be against us. I felt like Peter betraying my family by flying away in the night. The shadowy gargoyles above my head were mocking me, but a steady look at the image of an angel on a tomb steadied my resolve. That big head, cumbersome as it may be, was winging its way to heaven.

Sharp pine needles scratched at my ankles, as I began the trek that would take me over hills, down through hollows, across Wilden footpaths and grazing lands, and through many villages snuggled all along the river, the only guide I would have. I had not walked too far when I was startled by a dark form silhouetted against the horizon. A large man was coming out of the clearing wielding a big club. I could hear strange squeaking noises. He saw me before I could run. With wild eyes, he lifted up his arms in consternation to shout, "I am losing the light, boy. I am losing the pigs."

"Whatever do you mean, sir?"

"Look around you boy. Do you not hear the squealing creatures running amuck through the bushes? They have abandoned the poor pig farmer. I mean myself. Look! There they go running over your feet." I looked down to see a pig running as fast as its short little legs could manage down the slope. A larger one ran after it. I took off after them as if they were the disappeared schoolmaster or my lost soul. With some satisfaction, I can say I caught one which I passed to the farmer who ran off to put it in some distant pen. By the time he came back, I had captured another which he, all huffing and puffing, did take from me. He ran off to the pen with it tucked under his arm. When he returned yet again, I had another squealing one in my arms. I kept chasing the animals down until the farmer declared that all the porkers were safe. He gave me a dollar for my help. Would that God would find me like a runaway pig, and safely bring me to the end of my road and back again. He waved as I walked away.

As I walked past the schoolhouse, I noticed an eerie ghostly green color rising from the ground. I shuddered to think it might be evidence of Ichabod's ghost hovering about seeking redress. How did I go from our bubbling laughter at this scarecrow who walked the fields and wielded the rod, to fear and consternation in this lamented, godforsaken, space? Oh, that God would make such a creature as Ichabod, we mocked. A fox was walking along the side of the road with his head low. Suddenly, he lifted up his head to sniff the air with his long, sharp nose. I hoped he did not smell me. He reminded me of Ichabod savoring the sweet pies he was about to devour. The wind was singing hymns like the schoolmaster trying to calm himself in the dark. Run, Damen run, I told myself. Bodies putrifying in the earth give up green gas like that. Maybe it was a ghoul or the spirit spiraling out. I did want to know if the schoolmaster was dead but I was not yet ready to find out that very moment.

I ran down the road but stumbled, and fell down a ha-ha wall. Picking myself up, I turned to look behind me expecting to see a spirit hovering in the air near the schoolhouse back down the road. Resolving to steady myself, I forced myself to look forward. Loud, blood-curdling screams stopped me in my tracks. Smoke was rising from a hollow. My blood ran cold. Behind a copse of trees, the wilden were screaming to keep the devil away. They were whooping and jabbering when one of them saw me. He motioned for me to come over. Hoping they were not making war whoops, I went over to their campfire where they were roasting a bass. The wilden wore a worried look.

"I put this fish in the fire for the devil. 'Come, devil,' I say. 'Eat this.' I will get the devil to eat this fish, so he will not want to eat our children. His belly will be full of fish. Do not eat this fish, man," he said. The flames were dancing in his dark eyes. His flesh was glistening.

"God will keep the devil from us, my good sir," I declared. My voice sounded confident, but I was not feeling that way inside. The Wilden shook the feathers in his headdress at me.

"God is too busy chasing his woman up in the sky to worry about us. Do you have something to give the devil so he may eat?" I told him I had some apples in my pack, but he said the devil did not fancy fruit.

A group of braves came walking out of a copse of trees to join him. Walking with great dignity, they had no trouble at all seeing in the dark. The little bead shells on their moccasins glinted in the firelight as they joined the shaman. There were boy archers with bows and quivers on their backs. The fire suddenly began to spit and sizzle.

"Oh, the devil be very happy now." I smiled at him wishing I knew such a simple way to keep the evil of life at bay. He motioned for me to go. The wilden do not look for answers in a book or on weathervanes or tombstones. I suppose all the answers they were seeking could be found in nature.

I continued walking along the bank. The setting sun was flooding the valley with a golden light which, all too quickly, was fading. A silver afterglow remained at the horizon. In the blink of an eye, it turned indigo. Going down on my haunches before the river, I felt a chill coming up from the soil. It went up from my feet to the top of my head, spreading all throughout my bones. I left home as a boy becoming a man, but now I was shrinking down to be a boy again. Someone should stand on this spot to paint the valley in the changing light. Many painters, a whole school of painters, should set up their easels here to capture this beauty with their skillful brushstrokes.

Soft and holy is this place. God, who created all of nature, got here to paint it first. Suddenly, the whole valley seemed to shift though I reckon it was only the shifting light of the moon. Smokey, silvery shadows rippled across the water. The bulrushes rubbed up against each other, knocking on my heart. Canada geese were on the wing. A dead, red-tipt cedar bird lay at my feet. The hand of God was in it all. I went to my knees. "Oh! Who can stand when he appears?" the Bible asks. I know it will not be me.

I walked along the bend in the river. A dwelling that was little better than a beaver dam stood on the bank. I thought I might bed down there for the evening, but, as I peered inside through an opening in the twigs, a tall, gaunt man abruptly pulled the rickety door back. I looked in. The man swiped a Bible off a tree stump, which served as a table, situated in the middle of the hut. The stump was off kilter, so it reminded me of Father. There was hardly room enough for two inside. Waving the Bible over his head as if he was flagging down a coach or a rider in haste, he came out to talk to me. He wore a gray shirt that was once white with threadbare cuffs and a greasy, black coat. He said he was just about to cook some beans. I could share them if I so desired. The hut was so bare that I could not imagine he had much to eat, so I refused. A fox stopped to stare at us.

"You are all alone on an open road with a starry sky gleaming over your head and a fox watching in the clearing." He liked his saying so much he repeated it adding an admonition. "You are all alone on an open road with a starry sky gleaming over your head and a fox watching in the clearing, but if you move, there will still be a starry sky gleaming over your head, but there will not be a fox watching in the clearing." He lit a fire on the ground. Since I had no time for nonsense, I plunged into my mission.

"Sir, if I might, I am on the road looking for Ichabod Crane, the schoolmaster."

"Ichabod Crane. There is no Ichabod Crane or Ichabod whatsoever, here. Are you Ichabod sir?"

"No, I am not. If I were, I would hardly be out on the road looking for myself." I was growing peeved. My words delighted him.

"Imagine being all alone on the open road with a starry sky gleaming over your head and a . . ." Since he was at a loss for words, I prompted him adding, "Fox watching . . ."

'Yes, with a fox watching from the clearing while you look for God. Looking for God is an awesome thing. You are not looking for yourself or some schoolmaster. I am Gerard on my way to becoming a Jerimiah. I understand the hearts and souls of men. Come, give me your good hand," he said reaching out his. He gave me a sweet smile. Since my hand might be the hand of a murderer, I hesitated to take his, but reckoning that he was not a prophet, only a man on his way to becoming a prophet, I shook his hand. He could not know who I was or what I had done if he wasn't yet a prophet. I told him my name.

"Gerard, are you a man of God?"

"I am, sir, but church, I have none. I only have this sacred space. I would be John the Baptist, except that I disallow baptism. I do not worry who is fit to take communion. Communion I have none. Anybody can sit at my table. See this apple here? I made this ruddy fruit. This egg I could scramble, then make whole again." If there was an apple or an egg on the ground, I did not see them. Apparently, this man has lost his reason. I might have found more sense in a beaver dam.

"I wish you well, Gerard." I did nothing to encourage him.

The moon went behind the clouds. I was eager to move on. The fox, who seemed to be laboring under a spell which suddenly broke, ran off. Gerard stamped the fire out. It was so dark I could not see my hand in front of me. There was no road, no preacher, and no fox. The man of God was as fallen as any man. I started to pull away from him, but he grabbed onto my hand to pull me back.

"Come nearer, Damen. Do not turn your back on God no matter how uneven your road may prove. When the Wilden are troubled, they build a fire to smoke out the dark one. They send all the small, woodland creatures scurrying as they walk to and fro digging up herbs and plants for they know the healing properties of each and every leaf. Sometimes, they just wander out to the woods to die." He paused to look down at his feet.

"Do you think there is no healing plant for you, or that there is no balm in Gilead?" he asked raising his voice. Just when he seemed most filled with hope, his spirit plunged like the darkness.

"I am in a wilderness, a waste howling wilderness as scripture says. My God is an awesome God. The trouble is he is a jealous God as well. He is even jealous of all the gods and people we invite to sit down at our table to drink our tea, or beer, or of late, coffee. So many people are drinking coffee nowadays," he declared, pointing at the flat top of a large, oak tree stump. Pulling at the loose threads of his jacket sleeve, he bellowed, "I am unraveling." He bent down to rub twigs to start up the fire again. As it glowed back to life, he took my hand to lead me down to the river bank where he forced me to sit on the ground. A beaver was swimming toward the shore radiating little ripples out across the water, in the moonlight. Face to face; we looked at each other. I could see the whites at the tops of his eyes expanding. He stood up stroking his long, white beard. I rose to meet his glance.

"Your God is a jealous God too. He wants you, Damen, for himself. You are out on the open road while he is out looking for you. He will be more jealous if he finds you are looking for yourself or a schoolmaster. You are looking for God, are you not?" I must not have looked too sure.

"I am looking for the schoolmaster, Ichabod Crane, who disappeared up north in Sleepy Hollow on the night of October 31st. Some say the Headless Horseman spirited him away. Some say he must be in New York City. I live under a dark star, in need of a bright one to lead me to him so that I might once again be one of these people who rise in the morning to labor all day, only to go to sleep at peace at night to get up and do it all over again." My eyes fell upon a burnt out house in the distance made visible by an odd slant of moonlight. When Gerard asked if Ichabod led the choir, I thought for a moment that he knew something.

"He did." Gerard did not stay with this thought. He went off into his strange thoughts.

"You could just stay here in the woods gathering acorns like squirrels. You could live off acorns if you had a mind to do so. I will tell you your fate. You will grow so tired you will lay down your head on a rock. The stars in the sky will act as candles when you look through the colorful leaves which will sparkle like stain glass. You will look up to see your Ichabod leading heavenly choirs in sweet songs. You will be happy then." He then walked me back to the road where he pointed out some small, Indian graves.

"The wilden listen to the wind. A voice will come to carry you away if you stand here too long. A ghoul haunts here. He is naked with long hair caked with mounds of dirt and clawed fingernails black from digging himself out of the ground. The nails are so long they stick into his palms. His skin is black too from the ashes of the dead. His eyes like slits will remind you of a cat, and his shadow is so long you cannot run out from under it. In your mind's eye, you can see him."

The thought of the long body made me think of Ichabod.

"In my mind's eye, I can see Ichabod, the schoolmaster," I boldly declared.

"Do you see him on the road or in the bush cowering from the one without a head?"

"Of course I do not see him. If I could see him, I would not be looking for him. I turned my gaze to the distant landscape."

Up the valley, over the mountains, something was moving the clouds and the mist down the river to the city where I must go over byways and highways, over stiles and through gates. The wind blew the leaves off the ground exposing dried, useless patches of dirt. Gerard moved away from me walking to the edge of the wood with his hands behind his back. He wrung out his hands and raised them up to his waist. Gerard started swaying, dancing to some rhythms in his head. As he turned his head a little, I saw his cheekbones rise right up. When he turned to me, the wrinkles etched deeply n his skin, made deeper by his life outdoors, radiated out with pure joy. He broke into such a deep laugh, his belly shook.

"What is so funny, Sir?" He picked up a branch to draw a line between us in the dirt.

"The universe over there where you are huddling and hunkering down is a small, dark place. Over here, on my side of the line, it is bursting with newness and light. I make all things new. Come step into the light with me." His eyes were ablaze with such flame I thought he would consume everything in sight, including me.

"I would rather not. Everything is not new. Look around you, Gerard. The world is falling off. It is dying. It is past twilight. The fire does give us a small half-light at best," I said in a weak voice.

"Half a light is better than none at all," said Gerard.

"Back in the hollow, I saw the wilden light a fire to cook the devil a fish. You are standing in the light of God, they are keeping the devil out by cooking his supper, but I am in the dark with only the clothes on my back and some apples in a pack."

"If at the end of time, or the end of the road, you get your soul back, you will not care how much stuff you had on your back or in your pack. Take those spectacles out of your breast pocket to look around you boy so you can see."

Though he reached out his hand to pull me over the line in the dark to him, there was only one thing I wanted and that he could not give to me. Putting my head down, I stalked away. I ran through the trees, and did not look back though I heard Gerard calling out, "Damen, will you take tea?"

In the darkness, my foot stepped into the water. As I moved, my right foot made a squishing sound. Up ahead I saw a great blaze. Either the wilden were making one of their explosions to clear the forest, or a barn was on fire. Did I hear them crying or was it only the shouts of drunken boys? Every object stood out in the firelight with preternatural brightness. Whatever it was I was growing too tired to care. I threw myself down beneath a tall oak. My wet foot ached with cold. There were golden leaves all around me, on the ground and up above my head. I was glad to see many leaves not yet unmoored. Then, in one fell swoop, they all came down on me. I curled up under the leaves to sleep. My eyes started to close. I saw Hendrik Hudson's Half-Moon plowing down the river. Troops of Hessian soldiers came marching along the bank.

He came for me in my dreams. A skeleton appeared. He was tall enough to reach the sky. Tatters of his clothes were flying about as he came to me with great, awkward strides. He had his hands stretched out before him, and every joint was clicking. He was coming for me, so I said I am not me. I am not Damen. I knew it was Ichabod. If it be possible to die of fright, I would never have seen the morning light. The skeleton's knees

114

buckled, so he stumbled into a grave. He did not like that, so he got up and dusted off his dirty bones. Somewhere there was a fantastical house with statues of bears climbing trees serving as columns. At each base, there was a large, baronial shield. I thought it must be one of God's many mansions.

I woke up to find that a bright, crackling, hoarfrost had given everything white edges which could cut like a knife. The sky, bright blue and pink, appeared like a kaleidoscope through the oak tree branches. My limbs were frozen stiff, but I pushed myself up to shake off all the leaves that had covered me that night. I ate two apples, and a crust of bread then relieved myself against a tree and headed down the road to New York City. A flock of turkeys waddled down a side path. I soon arrived in Yonkers where the Palisades glistened over the water just as it did upriver. An impressive,

"What are you looking at, boy? Your eyes are about to pop right out of your head, said a man who came up behind me with a wry smile on his face. His cheeks were ruddy; his body was thick, his checked trousers loud. Like a tree, he rooted himself into the soil. He thought me a marvel. He must have taken me for a country bumpkin because he tried to frighten me by identifying the mansion as the Philipse Manor Hall, adding that Mr. Philipse would not like me trespassing on his estate. I could not find my voice. He gestured to shew me away. Then, I stood up to him.

"There will be no Mr. Philipse here, Sir. My name is Damen Willem, and I come from Tarrytown. I know a thing or two about the Philipse family. They have gone back to England with their tails between their legs," I stammered out. If I did not at least attempt a firm stance here in Yonkers, what would the people of New York make out of me?

"Well, yes. So, you are Dutch. It was a rise and fall story. The first Frederick was a self-made man who fled from persecution in Holland to America where he rose to be lord of the manor. The family did come to endure the vicissitudes of life. That is a big word. Do you know the meaning of this word?" I assured him that I did.

"Your hands look a little rough to hold the scholar's pen. There is a light in your eyes. It may be that you are sometimes a student, Lord of your learning with no land besides.

"A manor house, upper and lower mills, here and to the north, the Philipse family had it all. He built your church. Do you know how the family fell from grace?" Before I could answer, he jumped back into his oration.

"The great-grandson took the wrong side in the Revolution. Loyalty to the king brought all their glory to an end when we won the war. Do you know that George Washington wanted to arrest him, but that sly old fox managed to get away? He shipped himself back to his mad king and country. He slipped through the cracks, and his properties slipped through his hands. That property is American property now. The American government seized the farms, mansions, and mills. Property that belonged to one was sold off to the many. E Pluribus Unum." He ended with a flourish of his hand. I supposed he expected an ovation. I did not bother to tell him that my father had bought some of that land.

"I suppose you would like to make your way in the world too. You are a long way from home. Depending on your destination, you are either near or far. Where are you heading, young Sir?" When I told him, his face took on a look of consternation. His mention of how far from home I was, brought Mama to mind. I could see her standing at the open door giving me a look of infinite longing which still could not bring me home.

'You do know that Manhattan is an island, do you not?"

"I know that Manhattan is an island, but I am not sure how to cross the waters from the Bronx where I am now heading."

"Oh, there is a ferry and a bridge. An old black man named Diamond will row you across. His skin is dark, but his eyes do sparkle. The boat will cost you, boy. Frederick Philipse constructed the King's Bridge over the Spuyten Duyvil Creek, but the farmers did not want to pay the toll. Sometimes they waded over. You could do that, but your trousers would get all wet. You might take the Free Bridge built by Mr. Dyckman as a kind of circumvention to benefit the farmers. Go down the river. You will find a tavern near it. Do you have money, boy?" I hesitated to tell him about the dollar.

"Spuyten Duyvil did you say?" I asked in earnest.

"There is a spouting devil there, a tidal unrest, not as bad as Hell's Gate, but enough to take a boat down. When the British attacked the Dutch, a trumpeter swore he would get to the other side in spite of the devil. It is not the River Styx. I am not sure why he wanted to get to the other side. Things do look better on the other side. It probably had something to do with the war, strategic positions and all. I trust he knew why. Why do you want to get to the other side?" I was growing in confidence. I had made it to Yonkers, more than a third of the way.

"I am looking for Ichabod Crane, the schoolmaster of Sleepy Hollow, who might have made his way to Manhattan. He is a long, thin man with a sharp nose who walks about with clothes that cannot seem to rest on his body. Some say he is like a scarecrow.
Whether he be sunk beneath the waters of the Pocantico Creek or alive and well in New York City, I do not know, but mean to find out."

"Come, I will walk with you down the river a little way. I have not seen such a man but if he did not die up north, the devil here, or some mortal man, may have gotten him. Funny how folks try to pull others down into their predicaments. As for going down in the creek, I can only say that is a sorry state. Be a long time dead, boy. No need to hurry."

"I am leaning that way. My real learning came from the lost schoolmaster whom I must find. I spent the night sleeping in the open air, and I do not know where I will sleep tonight. I do know something about the vicissitudes of life." Just as I did not tell him about the dollar in my pocket, I would not inform him about my complicity in the disappearance of Ichabod Crane.

"You must look for the Free Bridge. You will know it when you see Hyatt's Tavern. You must stop there to eat and drink. Be careful of the hairy, red beast that warms itself by the fireplace within. It might be werecat or even a wolfman."

"I would imagine that there is nothing there but some hairy men, and perhaps, a red cat," I responded wondering why such thoughts filled up his head.

"Well, since you are Dutch, I thought you would expect, and require a legend or two." I shook my head and laughed. I could not shake off the headless Hessian so readily. There was no need to think me a superstitious person. I wanted to protest, yet I did not.

The man in the checked trousers said he could walk no more. Again, he reminded me to eat at the tavern.

A soon as I was alone again, thoughts of Josefien welled up. I did not know her half, as well as I, would like. Papa and Mama had arranged our union. Twas something touching, and a little funny, about the way she awkwardly tried to fit herself into our conversations at home. As I made my way down the Albany Post Road, my stomach began to rumble, and my head pounded. My heart was just breaking. I wish it would break and have done with it. I would never have to feel anything ever again. Bucking up, I told myself that New York City could not be too far off now. The end of the trek was coming into sight.

Chapter Seventeen

The Hayride

So Damen was about to arrive in New York City. Good luck with that. As for me, I was headed his way. Why had I allowed Bonnie and Brooke to rope me into that hayride? I didn't want to go, but the next Saturday proved so empty that I came to see that it wasn't so bad to have a place to go. The weekend broke cold and gray. That's the way the work week felt as well. There was no life at all after work. The temperature was in the fifties. There was nothing out there worth looking out, so I closed the light filtering drapes, then pushed them back again when Chester wanted to sit in the window. Mixture of sun and rain coming today, with the emphasis on the rain, Chet. Enjoy what you can. That's all you can do. After cleaning the apartment, I took some time to read finally read *The Legend of Sleepy Hollow* which proved quite entertaining. Irving sounds like a sophisticate who mocks people with mercy.

Around three I headed out for Grand Central Station. Halloween was less than a week away, but the city was cranking up for Christmas. There were all these portents of the upcoming holidays, and a few reminders, such as the huge flags at Grand Central, of 9/11. It was impossible to conceive of it, but the onslaught of Christmas visitors was soon to overwhelm the island which already tolerated some eight million people. We would survive. We always did. I wonder how many people were present when young Damen cross over the Farmer's Bridge. He could never have imagined this scene. For now, it was all pumpkins, witches, gourds, and monsters going to Halloween parties. A tall witch and warlock held hands as they swept down the ramp to the lower level. A werewolf in a St. Xavier's high school jacket, howled at his friends near the ticket booth.

Did it take this long to get up to the Hudson Valley? I thought the journey shorter. The towns started rolling by the window. I changed my seat on the train not once, but twice. The first time to avoid a group of chatty women. The second to get away from the tinny sounds coming out from a teenager's headphones. It must be hell up in that head. I buried my head in a newspaper someone had left on the seat. It seemed I would never get to my destination. I should have stayed home.

In Tarrytown, I made my way up Main Street once again. God, this hill is a killer. I made it to the top just in time to catch the tail end of the Ragamuffin Parade. The real Halloween Parade was scheduled for 7:30. Three Batmans, in assorted sizes, were being chased by a little bat. They were heading to the firehouse for a party. I walked up yet another hill to the Milepost with the leaves slipping beneath my feet. The weather couldn't make up its mind. It was raining now, but I was sure it would stop the minute I went inside. As I walked up to Hamilton Place, I could see Bonnie wrestling with her son Alastair next to a Honda Civic. When a burly man came running down the Croton Trail in their direction, the boy jumped into the car to hide. He almost broke his key to the outer door trying to get in. Bonnie plowed in after him. They weren't fast enough to shut the door. The crazy man, apparently Bonnie's husband, tried to pull Bonnie out but she and her son ran out the driver's side, into the building. Just as they got the lobby door open, the angry spouse put his foot in the door. They all ran up the stairs.

I rang Brooke's bell in the lobby. Bonnie appeared at the top of the stairway reddened with rage and out of breath. Her blouse had been ripped. "I'm sorry Richard. I should have held the door." Huffing and puffing, she went into her apartment to tick the buzzer. The British do remember their manners. The men in her life were shouting at the top of their lungs. At the sound f the buzzer, I pushed the lobby door open just as Brooke was coming out from her apartment on the ground floor.

"Richard, so good to see you. Please come in." Telling me to sit down at the kitchen table, she offered me a cup of tea which I declined. "I'm still unpacking, but I seem to be settling in. Make yourself at home." The buzzer started groaning nonstop. Shouts could be heard on the floor above us.

"I think that's Bonnie trying to buzz me in. Is she ok? What's going on? Who's that guy? Should we call the police?"

"Bonnie's husband. They're having a family argument. It's all about Alastair, of course. Would you mind if I went upstairs to see how she is?" I nodded my assent. The kitchen was cozy with red quarry tile on the floor and rough, whitewashed plaster on the walls. Everything was neat and tidy though a little bare. It takes time to move in. An excellent collection of Toby Mugs lined a large corner shelf. I looked out the kitchen window. Past the parking lot, there were glimpses of the Croton Trail made visible by an old fashioned, yes-quaint-street lamp near the building's parking lost. The rainy mist made it look a little spooky. Some fake spider webs adorned a bush. Some gossamer ghosts hung from a tree. I hadn't even wanted to come, and now there was all this fuss with Bonnie's husband and son.

I could hear Alastair and his father in a shouting match. They were stomping around so much, the ceiling shook. Bonnie had gone quiet. I heard the husband running down the stairs pounding the wall as he ran down. That's going to hurt later. I came out into the hallway. With his belly pushing out from under a thick, black turtleneck sweater, he rushed past me, unsteadying me. "Sorry, man!" he said in a Scottish accent. As he stomped outside, I could hear the car engine revving up.

When I went upstairs, I found Bonnie, Brooke, and Alastair standing in the kitchen with their hands at their sides. Battle shock. Pots, pans, newspapers and even cans of food were strewn all over the floor. The sofa and chair cushions had been flung about in the living room. Pictures on the wall were awry. Suddenly, Bonnie came to life.

"Alastair, straighten this stuff up. Your brother has friends coming over later." With his chest deflated, his stringy black hair falling over his face, the young man said, "Yes, Mom," like a little boy. Bonnie tottered a little bit, so Brooke steadied her. "Let's all go down to my place. I'll put the kettle on," Brooke offered. I didn't know if we were coming or going. Though all I was looking for was an exit, I followed the two women back down the stairs. As Brooke started to prepare tea, Bonnie slumped down at the kitchen table. She seemed very lethargic.

"I keep myself low when Donnie's around." Did he threaten her? What if he comes back? I thought I should just leave. Then again, they might think me afraid.

"Are you sure everything is OK. I mean, is Donnie, er, your husband alright with me joining you. Maybe we should invite him to the hayride or something. We don't need a jealous husband. He's not going to go all Brom Bones on me, is he?" Don't ask me if I was serious or going for comic relief. Bonnie and Brooke laughed.

"Certainly not. Hubby can feel the chemistry between the two of you. It's all about Alastair. I don't understand him myself. His brother Robin is the all-American boy. I used to think Alastair might be gay, but even that wouldn't matter that much these days. He cuts himself with razors. I find blood on the sheets. He also flirts with Wiccan, which doesn't help his course as all. Don't ask about the bullies at school. Then, there's all this Goth stuff. I'm sure he has a black, dragon tattoo somewhere on his body," said Bonnie.
Brooke was squinting at me looking for the chemistry which we both knew wasn't there.

"Black dragon tattoo?" said Brooke as poured hot water into our cups.

"Like, Gerald Gardner. Maybe Alastair is a throwback to my maternal grandfather who followed Gerald Gardner, the warlock. He had some club north of London. God knows what they all did there. Nudists, philosophers, warlocks. He doesn't take after Donnie, his father, at all. Who'd have thunk it." Robin is having some friends over to watch a scary movie, The Corpse Bride. Alastair would probably try to hold a séance. With bulging eyes, Bonnie rapped the wooden table. Brooke shook her head. "Maybe it's just a phase. He's only sixteen, right, Bonnie." Bonnie. Donnie. I almost chuckled when I thought that the Drummonds were Bonnie and Donnie. Such Scottish names.

"Of course, Alastair thinks we are the crazy ones. He says Britain didn't revoke the ban on witchcraft until 1995. He wants to take part in a Wiccan baptism in public, probably up at the lake where the pointy trees match his pointy head. My son thinks I should get a divorce and become liberated. What he needs in an exorcism. Too bad about Father Karas. Didn't he die at the end of The Exorcist movie? We sure could use him here. Woowoo. Voodoo or Hoodoo. What's he want me to be, a hoyden?" Probably just needs a witch girl to straighten him out."

"No, Bonnie," said Brooke with a sigh. "Not a witch girl." Bonnie headed to the bathroom.

"A hoyden? Where did she get that expression?" I asked.

"From her grandmother of course. She probably knew Alastair Crowley. Even that boy, Damien, who served time for killing those little boys in West Memphis, Tennessee, knew about Crowley. No, I'm wrong. It was Memphis, Arkansas."

"Well, that whole trial was a travesty. That's why the men were freed. That boy and his cronies were convicted for studying witchcraft in a so-called Christian town.

Someone else killed the little boys," I added.

"Maybe these young men just wanted to empower themselves. Alastair, I mean Drummond, not Crowley, doesn't play sports like his brother and often cuts classes. His father gets furious. They just can't get along. Bonnie has it out with him every other day or so." We hushed up quickly as Bonnie came back in.

"Let's go out and eat pizza or something. Did you have supper yet, Richard?" asked Bonnie. Her speech was slowing down as her pupils were dilating. Was she mixing alcohol and pills behind out backs? We agreed to walk down to Broadway since Bonnie's husband had taken the car. Parking near the shops was impossible ay, Brooke said. So, in a light rain, I followed the two women down the hill. There was a pizzeria on Broadway where the tables were covered with traditional, red-checkered cloths. We settled into a table by the window. The police were putting up barriers on the side streets in preparation for the Halloween Parade. Everything seemed OK again.

"I came up for the parade last year when I was seriously thinking of moving up here. The Headless Horseman, of course, leads off the parade," offered Brooke.

"The real one, Richard. The real thing, " laughed Bonnie. I laughed too.

"He's becoming a big part of my life. I got around to reading the legend this week. I also made some headway into Damen Willem's journal. I think that may be the real thing too," I said.

"Oh this is getting very Henry Jamesian, all this talk of the real thing," declared Brooke. The reference went over our heads. I got on with it.

"I think that Damen Willem was one of the Sleepy Hollow Boys and that his journal may very well be nonfiction. The uncle who edited it uses a humorous tone, not unlike Irving but, that doesn't mean that the characters and events are fake.

"It could be a hoax like *The Hitler Diaries* or *The Diary of Jack the Ripper*. You would have to look for an anachronism, something which does not belong in the late 1700's, the time of the legend," said Brooke. A waiter came over to take our order. The place was filling up. So was the parade route outside. People were setting up folding chairs along the sidewalk. Kids were sitting down on the curbs. I could see people sitting on *The Milepost's* stone walls. They had umbrellas and plastic rain slickers. Traffic had been cut off, and the rain was tapering off.

"Like Ichabod sits down under a tree and whips out a Nook. Or stops to text WTF on his smartphone?" asked Bonnie.

"Ha. Ha. Smartphone? Nook? Oh, that's all too obvious," laughed Brooke. "You remind me of the Richard IIII production on Broadway in which Al Pacino stood up to zip up his pants. Some people in the audience snickered."

"Well, I don't know if it's worth the trouble, but I might consult an expert somewhere down the line. I only got about half way through. As for Irving, he is kind of interesting. Things are not what we think. There are always things lurking in the shadows to shake us out of our complacency. We want them too. I came up to see Sunnyside and Philipsburg with my family when I was a kid just like you Brooke." I said. Brooke's eyebrows shot up. Bonnie looked amused.

"Yes, I should have shared that at the bank. There are black characters in the story though they only have minor roles. I was a little uncomfortable with the description of 'the negro' who delivers the invitation to the ball to Ichabod. It says something like he spoke with an important air and made an effort at fine talk on important occasions. Then he scampers off like a little animal. The black musician rolls his eyes, bows down to the floor as St. Vitus," I said hoping I remembered the details correctly. More and more children were coming to see the parade with their parents. Lots of Starwars characters including some adult Darth Vaders. The kids probably wanted to create laser mayhem and cut us all up.

"Everything was whitewashed. There is a black burying ground near the Old Dutch Church which was paved over. Kongolese slaves traveled from the coast of Barbados to Rye to Philipsburg where they built the upper mills. People described hearing their drumming at night. Frederick Phillips chased a runaway slave named Jack all the way to Stratford, Connecticut. That was around 1697. A black couple later built the dam to prevent flooding. I believe they are buried in the Old Dutch Burying Ground. I'd have to look that up. History left much of that out. Imagine hearing the African drums at night here," gushed Brooke.

"A slave said that if they didn't finish building the church, the river would flood. I heard something superstitious like that. Of course, I am just a late comer who spent her childhood over the waters listening to Tam O' Shanter," Bonnie chimed in.

"Now some attention is being paid. Philipsburg celebrates Pinkster every spring which includes African American dancing, singing, and drumming. Folks wait a long time for justice to come their way," said Brooke.

"But it's all about the Dutch. What is it about the Dutch? Wooden shoes and windmill cookies. Who are the Dutch? Skaters dressed in orange?" laughed Bonnie. Bonnie's Scottish accent made everything she said funny.

"The Roosevelts, Van Gogh, Vermeer, and Rembrandt. Ronald Reagan, or was 'Dutch' just a nickname?" said Brooke just bubbling over with knowledge.

"Tell me about some living person or contemporary contribution to my world," demanded Bonnie.

"Matt Lauer's wife and Dutch Boy paint. Do they still make Dutch Boy paint?" I added. A waiter finally came over with the coca colas. Sounds of drumming and shouts carried in from the street as the parade began making its way down Broadway. We had the best seats in the house.

"I think we can hold Irving accountable for our attraction to the Dutch. Someone, Hazlitt, the English critic, said he was just a tourist, a lightweight. In the edition I bought of the legend, a reviewer says Irving sentimentalized the Dutch, emphasizing their old world charm, their folklore, and quaintness. He called it the Windmill effect. There is something comforting about Dutch architecture, the steeply pitched roofs, and goblet-topped gables. Think of The Dairy in Central Park, Valkill Cottage, and Sunnyside," I mused.

"By the way, I hope we are going Dutch. Ha. Ha," Bonnie interjected.

"Yes. And Howard Johnson's. Now Ihop. What thoughts of food and comfort their familiar buildings conjured up in families crisscrossing the American highway. Then there was Gaslight Village in Lake George. Did you ever go there when you were a kid, Richard? The stuff of fairytales. When you throw in Hansel and Gretel, you get a frisson of horror in the bargain. Just the description of the architecture, spout-gabled, goblet-topped takes me away," said Brooke.

"Yes, I agree with you there. Goblet-topped roofs bring in lots of old world charm."

"What? Goblin-topped? Is that what you seek here, Richard. You leave big, bad New York City to become Thoreau in the woods? It's not a wood. It's a park, Douglas Park. It has a playground for tots. Do you get transported to another world there? Don't go all Alastair on me," snarled Bonnie.

Just as Bonnie, out of the blue, sunk those incisors into the jugular, a vampire appeared at the restaurant window. Just vote me most haunted. The pizza pies finally came. Something better to sink out teeth into than one another. Our coke glasses were almost empty. Where did that waiter go? As if it was written, that slim blond boy tapped at the window. He that was fleet of foot this time in new black, high tops. He placed both thumbs in his ears and mouthed, ya-ya. If there is magic in the air here, I call on it to make this kid disappear. Bonnie's phone rang. It was her spouse calling to tell her he was back so she could take the car. He was the thoughtful husband again. We ate in silence until Bonnie said she would go and get the car to drive us to Sleepy Hollow for the hayride. She paused to get in some last licks.

"He used to keep me in things. I mean when we were young. I used to love him. I don't know. I am not a fan of love right now. I was. Maybe someday I will be again. I am not a fan of life. Right here on Broadway, some doctor was molesting a young boy. Story breaks on the news disappear. I still see him strutting about our town. You know what the real horror is? Besides the doctor I mean. Someone like you Richard, a bill collector coming up through the floor like a Zombie to suck the money out just when the birds are singing, and the frogs are croaking, or Shrek is happy in his house or something," said Bonnie going off on me all over again.

Feeling the roof coming down, I went away somewhere in my thoughts. What had Bonnie said before? I keep myself low? When was the last time I felt something? It must have been last December. The snow had been falling through the barred windows of my apartment, Don Maclean's And I Love You So," was playing on the Ipod through the speakers, and I was about to call Diane. A tear fell from my eye which I wiped away with the sleeve of my hoody. Bonnie left abruptly to get the car.

"I'm very sorry Richard. I don't know what came over Bonnie. She's worried about Alastair, especially the cutting habit. I guess there are money troubles too. Still, she should not take it out on you," Brooke said in a soft voice.

"It's not what Bonnie said. I was thinking of someone who left me." When I went to grab my coffee cup, it slid off the table as it if had a life of its own. Maybe the spirit of Damen Willem had entered me to give me the Heebie-Jeebies or something.

"Brooke, in that vast literary cannon that resides in your head, I bet you do not have a story about a man who goes about his New York apartment haunting himself? Do you?" As I waited for Brooke to respond, I thought of Dave. I know what he would say. Richard, you just need a good lay. You want the lit chick or the bonnie lass?

"I do, Richard. *The Jolly Corner*. Not Irving, but Henry James. A lonely, middle-aged man wanders around his New York apartment wondering what he would have become if he had stayed in the city instead of living abroad for three decades. He pursues, and is pursued by, his doppelganger who is missing two fingers and has 'ruined sight.' He deliciously crapes about in crepuscular light, searching for the man he could have been."

Saying that I would look into that one; I tried to focus on the parade. It had everything from the large firetrucks I had admired on my first trip up, high school, marching bands, to floats with Zombies playing Heavy Metal, and a pick-up truck carrying banjoplaying hillbillies sitting on bales of hay. Brooke's phone pinged. It was Bonnie indicating that we should cut through the lower level of Mrs. Green's to meet her in the parking lot. Everything near Broadway was cordoned off.

We went through the lower level of a natural food store, to jump in Bonnie's car. A cold rain had started up again. Of course, it did. We were heading for the woods. Not too sure if Bonnie was fit to drive, I kept a close watch out. She seemed OK. As we drove through the side streets, Bonnie sounded that death-tolling bell that all tourists must endure. The hayride was okay now, but you should have been here one year ago.

"The Haunted Hayride started out as a lark with a hodgepodge of people's stuff strewn about the woods. A professional company took it over though they soon moved on to put on the show at Philipsburg, *Horseman's Hollow*. You would have thought that the expert presentation would have gotten by Brooke, but she was here last year as a tourist. Not to worry, though. The local folks have taken up the gambit. We might be in for quite a show," said Bonnie we headed to the firehouse in Sleepy Hollow where the Hayride began. The rain was starting to pour.

At Broadway and Beekman, a police car sat with the cherry whirling around. The streets glistened in the rain. The reflected cherry was a smudge of red against a sea of gray. It struck me to the heart that there would be no horror in the woods as ghastly as the molested child, the ragged edge, family violence that brought the police, and ambulances to your door on those days that always begin in such an ordinary way. We parked at the back of the firehouse, then went inside to take our place on the line.

It was a long wait. Without the rainy weather, the line would have been too much for me to bear. At last, our turn came. We went outside in the drizzle to take our seats on the hay. The truck slowly drove off the main artery to Douglas Park where a series of tableaus passed by our eyes: the workshop of an ax murderer, a gallows, a ghost looking out a window in a cruddy, cardboard house. Déjà vu all over again. Don't remind me. "Looks like Maddie does the cleaning there," a husband mocked. A little girl screamed. Mostly, we all laughed.

Above all, I was hoping I wouldn't be recognized as the nutcase who ran across the Hayride's path fleeing the woods a week ago. Of course, no one knew about that. I was just some middle-aged, nerd in glasses sitting on a bale of hay with my mouth gaping. I took off my glasses and wiped my eyes. Freak that I am, just give me a setup in the woods. See the fireproof man. I wear an asbestos suit, so the heat and flames don't lick me.

Soon the hanged man came into view. The thrills were over. Don't think the horror ended there. I am not that lucky. The crazy teens in the death masks jumped out to chase the hayride down New Broadway. As we jumped off the truck at the firehouse on Beekman, Bonnie had the bright idea to drive us down to Yonkers to visit Empire City Casino. Brooke seemed happy to comply, though I think gambling was against her better judgment. Oh, it would be okay. Bonnie would drive me to the train station there after we won a million or two.

We drove across the flatlands of Yonkers. Everything was so flat and run down, except for sporadic, apartment buildings, the city was flatlining. Apparently, the potholes hadn't been repaired for years because we bounced around so much my head hit the roof of the car more than once. About thirty minutes into our ride, the massive structure of Empire City Casino rose up not like the golden city on the hill, but the ones on the plains, Sodom and Gomorrah. It was just asking for the sky to come down. Brooke referred to it as "the art deco jewel of Westchester," but both of us remained unconvinced.

Once again, we got out into the rain to walk past all the smokers lingering outside the less than stunning architecture. We entered to loud music, shrill voices, and clinging, clanging, money-eating machines. The smell of whiskey hit my nose, making my throat swell. "Let's start out small with Double Diamond Free Spin Slots," cautioned Brooke. Bonnie looked dubious but went along. We followed her to the section under the skylights near the valet parking. Presumably, we would be close enough to the exit, to not abandon all hope. Let others be swallowed up by the vast, dark interior.

"Lord-a-mercy, I spend the drug money," cried out some wide-eyed, inebriated, lost soul while an elderly, no, the ancient woman watched over his shoulder. Was she a relative or a missionary come to save his soul or bank book from his addiction? At twentyfive dollars a spin, the drug money was spinning away fast. "Lord-a-mercy," he kept crying. Maybe there was a patron saint of gamblers to cover all losses. Did Saint Anthony cover that?

Apparently, Brooke had the magic touch. No sooner had she sat down at the penny, Double Diamond slot machine when three bright, yellow and purple free spin signs froze on the screen with resounding dings. Bonnie was amazed. "I wish I could do that. Every time those bright, yellow free spin signs slam down, my eyes light up," declared Bonnie as her eyes widened.

"Every time those bright yellow free spin signs slam down, my head explodes," shouted Brooke over the din. As she spoke, three more yellow, free spin signs clanged. She put her hands to her head, then pushed them high into the air indicating an exploding head.

Though Brooke was amused, Bonnie just bent her head down to study the screen with the intensity of a Talmudic scholar. I just shrugged. They may have been through this routine before. Brooke hopelessly demonstrated caution to the full-steam-ahead-nothingcan-stop me-now Bonnie. Having place twenty in the slot next to Bonnie, I sat there pushing the buttons as slowly as possible. I tried to take on Brooke's when-in-Rome attitude.

"Did you win anything, Richard?" Bonnie shouted. When I shook my head, she admonished me: "How you going to win anything with your hand in your lap. Spin it, Richard, spin it." Through the gap between the machines, I could see a small, Asian man playing the slots when a large Hispanic man grabbed him by the scruff of his neck. Next to them, two women fought over a hundred dollar win. "That voucher is mine. I do not like ugly. Give me that voucher." "Well, you like me because I am beautiful," the other argued.

"You are playing my machine with my money. I left my money in that machine. You know you are playing my money!" The smaller man wasn't waiting for security to appear. He jumped off the chair to run for the door. Down the row, a man was slapping and kicking the Fireball machine, screaming, "Bitch, you take all my money. I slap you again, bitch." He high kicked the slot. I could have stayed home and listened to my neighbors if I wanted this. A woman tottering on high heels, wearing a fur coat, stumbled by our row. "Does anyone know how I get to Georgia, please? I just came in from Westchester Airport. Help please."

Then I recognized them all. These gamblers were our clients, the one who threw the money out so they could not pay their bills, the ones who magically believed that every cent they ever irresponsibly threw into the fire would come back bigger and brighter than ever. You know, the ones who defaulted when the bucks didn't come back. They threw the money away. Not only were they just dumping it into the slots, but they were also drinking it up, and outside, since this was a New York regulated, no smoking casino, they were smoking it up. "Let's go get some drinks," said Bonnie when her machine registered zero. I could stand no more.

Chapter Eighteen

It's All Over

I am a human, and none of this makes any sense at all to me. I didn't think Bonnie was fit to drive, but I wasn't ready to suggest that I should take the wheel. Brooke didn't drive. After a few drinks, Bonnie got me to the station, and Brooke safely home. No needy Queen came to my door. No beseeching brother called on the phone. Chester took one look at me, then disappeared under the daybed. Taking off my clothes, but not bothering to put them away, I fell into a deep sleep with shifting dreams. I woke up with dark images disappearing into a dark tunnel. My chest was wracked with coughing.

Seconds later, Bonnie's hurtful words came back to me. Who are you, Thoreau in the woods? That is Thoreau in the woods that were a park. Who are you? What wrong with me? A forest wouldn't heal me. Maybe I should have to go to Lourdes. No, I was an able body man. In Lourdes, I would be a brancardier who carries the sick to the grotto. No, that would mean being of use to someone else. I would be nothing at all so I wouldn't go to Lourdes at all.

That is what I did all day. Nothing. I didn't even bother to check to see if the junkies were still lurking down in the street. I didn't care if the one with the gray/blond one was looking up at my window or not. There is something dreadful about a Sunday morning coming down or however the song goes. It was something like that. I went downstairs to get the Times but didn't bother to read it. The TV played football games all day long but don't ask me for the scores. If the landline or cell phone, rang, I didn't pick up. Now it was just me and the void.

I kept sinking. Next morning, I didn't go to work. After taking care of Chester, pulling the plug on the landline and turning off the cell phone, I went back to bed. Dave will think I had a hell of a weekend. No one else will miss me. Remembering that I had turned rather sullen when with the ladies on Saturday night, I thought I might have said something ugly. Probably not. Did I drink too much at the casino? I couldn't remember. What did it matter?

I stopped drinking coffee and relied on whatever what in the fridge and cupboard. Mostly I lived off dry toast. I could hold out like this for quite a while. Soon I experienced a metallic taste in my mouth which was drying out. Sometimes my hands shook. When I glanced down at my foot, it seemed unreal. It didn't belong to me. That is irrational, but that is the way it was.

It would have been nice to wander endlessly about devoid of feeling and desire, but something was haunting me. I caught an image of myself in the mirror. I didn't see a man with shot-out fingers or ruined sight, facing back at me. I saw a worn out Richard with his cat sitting at his feet, or someone else's feet because I still wasn't convinced they were mine. I put out extra food for Chester in case I forgot to fill the bowl up for supper. He could hold out far longer than I could. There were packs of cat food on top of the fridge. This void go on forever, though it felt as if it would.

Somehow Monday became Tuesday. It was all the same to me. Around three o'clock there was a knock on the door. Chester jumped down from the bed and ran to the door to investigate. I lay on the daybed stock still. If I stay quiet, enough they will just go away. They had too. There was no choice. I had to be left alone. Chester sat down before the door with his tail switching back and forth.

"Richard! Richard! Are you in there? Are you OK? Open up the door." It was Dave. Couldn't he get it? If I wanted to talk to him, I would be at the office or on the phone. He had some nerve coming here. He started pounding on the door

"Richard, if you're in there, come to the door now. I'll call 911. I'll break the door down if I have too." He kicked the bottom of the door. Chester jumped back as some dust popped up in the air. I pushed myself up into a sitting position. "Go away, Dave. I'm OK, but I want to be alone. I need to work some things out," I called out.

"Richard? Thank God. I thought something terrible had happened to you." The genuine sense of relief in Dave's voice took me by surprise. Relief turned to anger in a New York minute.

"What? What did you say? You have to work things out? How about work? You had me worried sick, and all you can say is you have to work things out? Give me a break. You want to come help work out some overdue bills or something?"

"Not today, Dave. Not tomorrow either. I don't know when. Sue me if you feel a need to, but I need to be alone to work things out. Is that too much to ask?" I kept myself in a sitting position to project my voice, but it took every ounce of strength left in me to do so. All I wanted to do was sink."

"Open the door, Richard. Just open the door."

"I cannot open the door, Dave." I knew what I was doing. I didn't know what I was doing. Why wouldn't Dave just go away?

"Go away, Dave. Go now. If not, I will call the police on you. Who let you in anyway?

"I followed the Chinese restaurant delivery man inside the lobby door. Let me tell you he smiled and held the door for me. He gave me for more decency than you. What's going on? If you don't talk now, just tell me you need a few days off, and that you'll be back next Monday. Say it, Richard."

"I won't say it. I don't want to come back, Dave. Just go. Is that too much to ask?" I heard an apartment door open above. We were probably disturbing David Poole.

"You're not dissolving our partnership are you, Rich? Because that's what it sounds like to me."

"I am dissolving, or maybe absolving, our partnership, Dave." Talk of my quitting the company made him sputter.

"In that case, you will be hearing from me, or from my attorney, that is, Rich. Oh, and Rich you are a Dick." Dave punched the door, then left. I heard him running down the stairs. The door upstairs closed. I had pissed him off. He may have threatened legal action, but at least he didn't use his creepy voice on me. I should be grateful that at least some vestiges of humor remain in me, if not in him. I slumped down on the bed. Without caffeine, I was sinking fast. If this kept up, I wouldn't have the energy to plug in the cell phone to transfers money to pay the bills which would mean that I would become one of those deadbeats, the bane of my existence. Yes, that was it. I was the bane of my existence.

When later that night, the downstairs neighbors started arguing, I upped the volume on the TV played on. I drifted off but the sounds of the neighbors' loud shouting, woke me. I lay flat on my back with my hands curled at my sides. Sweat was pouring off me. A swirl of dust rose in the corner. It shaped itself into my dead fiancee. Images of the emergency room flooded my mind. Putting the pillow over my head, I slept and slept with Chester curled up next to me.

I woke up hard. Whatever brought that on? In any case, it didn't last. It was morning or maybe afternoon. I didn't want to know. The TV was still blaring. How did I sleep through that? I must have dreamed of Diane but, this time, no images came back to me. It must be Wednesday I thought. My newspapers would be lying down in the lobby. Oh, why worry. Someone probably helped themselves to them. What could there be in the news to interest me? I dragged myself over to the card table only to find the painting of the Hudson Valley mocking me. Did I think I would find something there? What was I even looking for up there? Chester leaped up into the window. Nothing out there Chester. You're barking up the wrong tree. I hit the daybed. There was not grand checkbook of the world to balance. All that remained was a man and endless, space. I started floating.

The doorbell rang. And rang. Grabbing the pillow away from Chester, I put it over my head. Wanting it back, Chester walked across my back, turn his body around, then plumped down on the pillow. Good, the sound is even more muffled now. All things pass. The ringing stopped. I went back to sleep. Sleep was my only friend. Craping about, (was that the word Brooke used to describe the man in the story, in what, crepuscular light?) At one point, I awoke with a start to catch another glimpse of myself in the mirror. I put my hands to my eyes, but they weren't there. Just some ribbons of pink flesh. I screamed. How could I see if my eyes were gone? They must be there. I looked again only to find I was missing my head. Sleep mercifully overcame me.

Things went aground when Chester woke me up with loud meowing. The litter box needed changing, and there was no fresh litter. I didn't want to go on living, and something this insignificant was vexing me to action. It wasn't trivial to Chester. I might go down, but Chester shouldn't have to go down with me. Looking into his owl-like amber eyes, as he peered intently into mine, I said, "There is no one home in here, is there Chester, no one. Mindless. There was a blackness at the center of my head. The top and sides were

pressing down on it so much, the black hole ached. There was all that in my head about what I should do, but it was overridden by the fact that I couldn't do it. Everything should just go away.

It wouldn't. Chester wouldn't go away. The meowing escalated. He needed a clean box. Then a thought hit me. I could go downstairs to pick up the newspapers, if they were still there, to fill up the box. That is if I could get out of bed and go downstairs, which I couldn't.

Chester meowed louder and louder. OK. I went down the stairs to the lobby. Three days' worth of the Wall Street Journal and Daily News lay on the floor in the vestibule with other people's newspapers were strewn about the stoop. The sun was shining, but what of it. I saw a man with a scruffy beard looking back at me in the lobby mirror. I knew it was me but thought that just couldn't be. It was quite cold outside. Winter must be moving in. I let the door slam behind me. Some shadows moved behind me. Did someone slip in behind me? I wasn't convinced they had, but it would be alright. Just take me. Put me out of my misery.

The radiator near the outside door gave a little hiss. At least my upstairs dungeon would not be too cold. I was so dehydrated and worn out that I broke my rule about the elevator. I took it back up. As I stepped inside, I heard some people run to the stairwell. Had I let in some robbers? Or worse? Maybe the junkies were moving up in the world. Maybe they would move in with me. Well, I didn't care. They might make themselves useful by looking after the cat. I put my hand on my doorknob. Some shadows seem to move behind me.

As I entered my apartment, a woman rushed up behind me, pushing her way inside. Another pushed in behind her. They both tumbled to the floor. It was Brooke and Bonnie. "Richard!" they both cried in unison. Bonnie sized up the situation. "So you are alive, and well. Well, you don't look so well, but you're alive. I think we overreacted. Mania is what happens when you live with Alistair. You think everything's a crisis." She walked to the window, pushed back the drapes to look down to the street through the bars. Looking contrite, like a girl called up to the principal's office, Brooke seated herself upon a kitchen chair. I sat down on the daybed. I had no words.

"It's okay to sit down, right, Richard?" she began looking as if she had done something terribly wrong. "We're so sorry to barge in on you like this, and I do mean literally barge in on you. I kept calling because you left your wallet in Bonnie's car. When you didn't answer your phone for three days, I called your business number. It was on the card you gave me. Your partner David was worried. He said you had gone off the charts. He thought you had lost your mind quitting the partnership without a word of warning. He told me you wouldn't even open up the door for him, so I decided to come over on my lunch break." Chester jumped up into the window to join Bonnie who petted his big head. He pressed his face against the bars. Keep talking Brooke, I thought. Keep talking, so I don't have to. There were dirty dishes in the sink, newspapers strewn all over the floor and clothes that needed to be put away. I felt a deep sense of shame. So I could still feel but what was the use of it?

"You know, Richard, I didn't know what to do. I came over earlier at lunchtime to ring your bell. There is a church I pass along the way as I make my way up to Grand Central, I mean when the weather cooperates, and I decide to walk. It's a Dutch Reform Church. The titles of the sermons on the placard seem interesting, but I have never gone inside. When you wouldn't answer the buzzer, I walked over there. The senior minister had made himself available to me as a walk-in. He's a very kind, down-to-earth man, in a posh office. I told him how worried I was. He said that if I got you to respond, we could go over together to talk to you. He also gave me the number for their helpline but cautioned me, that I might have to call 911. Oh, Richard. I know you are a private man. I went back to work after calling Bonnie who was in Bronxville for a medical appointment. She drove down and came over with me. I am so happy that we did."

Bonnie spoke up. "Bonnie to the rescue. Call me anytime but not right now because I need a smoke. You gave us quite a scare. My highlander's second sight was just spinning this way and that as bad as that slot machine. You know it's never wrong. Was that a McDonald's over on Twenty-Third? Maybe a Burger King. I'm going out to have a cigarette, then grab a burger. I will leave you too alone. Bye-bye." With that, Bonnie carried Chester over to dump him in my arms. "Watch out for his leg!" I pleaded which got me a hard look. Brooke looked relaxed.

"We wouldn't have snuck in on you if Dave hadn't told us you had barred the door to him. We figured if you wouldn't let him in, we did not stand a chance. I guess we should have spoken to you downstairs, but I was afraid you would shut the door in our faces. Didn't you miss your wallet? Are you Okay? What happened?" said Brooke. I said nothing. The landscape painting caught her eye.

"I am looking at you. Richard, against the backdrop of the magnificent Hudson Valley like a solitary, Romantic figure in a landscape. Your Hudson Valley School painting becomes you.

I thought of the phrase, "Death becomes her," but death did not become Diane at all. As Diane became death, all the color is her skin and eyes was sucked out, the movement and flow of blood through her lovely limbs were sucked out down to the marrow. I looked at Bonnie who was standing in front of the painting my mother bought. I didn't want to tell her about Diane.

"And I am looking at you Bonnie against the backdrop of the tasteful still life my mother picked out, and I don't know what to say. You look lovely? Well, you do, but I feel as if I owe you something, and I am not in a position to pay." Bonnie raised up her hand to protest.

I won't do myself in. I can say that. I thought I heard intruders as I started to open my door, but since the intruders here are two decent women wasting their time over some lonely, half-baked man, no harm will come to me today. You should go home to Tarrytown. You must have had a long day. I am very sorry that I caused you to worry. Your train will be leaving Grand Central soon." I wanted her to leave. The bathroom door was open, the electric curlers just visible on the top of the medicine chest. Her gaze seemed to follow mine. She saw the curlers.

"Do you live here with someone, Richard? Don't worry about my train. Bonnie will give me a ride back."

"No. It's just the cat and me. Some milk, Hershey Bars, and almonds to keep me alive. I ate up all the staples, but kept the best for last." I looked down to my feet which were clad in yesterday's socks. Or the day before yesterday. Or the day before that. How could I get her out the door? Though neither of us had moved, the curlers seem to wobble.

"Do you crape about the apartment Richard in the crepuscular light? Do you see the Richard you could have been? I apologize. Your breakdown is the real thing, and I am stuck in books. Henry James is famous for saying, 'the real thing.' Oh, no. There, I'm doing it again,' said Brooke shaking her head. The corners of her mouth went down. She looked disappointed in herself and her literary bent. I should offer her some tea, but that would only prolong her visit. I wanted the phone to ring, or the doorbell to buzz. Maybe Bonnie would return, saying that's enough foolishness, Brooke. Let's move on.

And, yet Brooke sat. "I can feel my heart beating, Richard, like a kind of Telltale heart. It must mean that there is a tale to tell." Not body beneath the floor? Look it up. It was in her chest, and it was pulling on my own.

"I did think of the story about the man craping about in the crepuscular light. I remembered what you said. But it was all those dead things in the Sleepy Hollow Cemetery and Douglas Park, both the real ones and the fake. Maybe it started when Bonnie mentioned *The Corpse Bride* movie. I had one, you know. That is, I had a fiancée. I was to be married, but she died. If you can believe that.

I wasn't always alone. Diane and I laughed and loved and fought. We fussed over things, like where to take our honeymoon and what to name our children. She wanted awaii. It was exotic, expensive and unforgettable. I wanted Ireland, the country of her European roots. We would have a boy named Paddy Padraic but call him Finn. A girl she said, name of Sutton Hoo. Oh, how ridiculous that sounds."

"No, Richard. Fall, a kid with that name will probably turn up in my class. Children these days have all sort of odd monikers. Please go on. May I put on the kettle for some tea or coffee?" Bonnie poured some water into the teapot, then topped off Chester's dish. He rubbed her leg with gratitude.

"Yes, sure. Why not? You are in for the duration. I hope Bonnie likes hamburgers. My fiancée's name was Diane, but I didn't enshrine her memory like your beloved Washington Irving. No one will say in hushed tones; Poor Richard has lost his lady love. I did my best to shut her out, to forget her. I just got on with it. And it worked quite well. Up in the Hudson Valley, there were graves, and skeletons and even Corpse Brides prancing all about the cemetery and Douglas Park. No one cared. It was just a hoot. I walked through Douglas Park on my first tourist visit and found the back way into the cemetery

was open. Someone was beckoning, but they could not get beyond the broken gate. They cannot live on in a dead brain which will not have them in.

"The hayride drove through the cemetery. The dead just lie there. Corpses should have got up out of their graves to protest. A graveyard is a sacred place. 'Soft and holy are the fens.'" I was going off.

132

"You sound guilty Richard. But I am sure you have no cause to feel like that. How did she die?'

"No cause? No. What I did was horrible enough. No, there is not heart beating between under the prewar floor slats. I did something. It was nothing. What I did was nothing. If I did find my doppelganger in a mirror staring back at me, he wasn't missing two fingers. He didn't have a head. His sight wasn't ruined. He didn't have any eyes. Or, head for that matter.

"And, that is just it. I was mindless, clueless, and acting as if I didn't have a head. I know nothing about her. I don't even know how she died. An overdose of painkillers she was taking for a back injury sustained in a car accident in Brooklyn when she was a teenager. Did I know she was addicted to painkillers? Maybe. I think I forgot. This overdose. Was it deliberate? She didn't drink, but she did have a drink or two the night she died. Maybe she didn't know what she was doing. She didn't drink at all much of the time which may indicate that she had a drinking problem. Who would know? Her sister and mother argued about this in the emergency room. Maybe that was a century ago. They yelled at each other in the emergency room. It didn't matter that I was there. They shut me out. I am happy that they did because I walked out the door. I guess they were happy then."

"No, Richard. I am sure they were not happy that you did," Brooke insisted. As I sat there motionless on the bed, the tea kettle started to whistle. Chester ran off to the kitchen to check it out. I thought of the day the snow was falling, and I was sitting in the chair where Brooke now sat with the radio playing. Don McClain was singing about how much he loved someone, and they loved him too and how I'm happy that you do. Brooke got up to make the tea. As she passed me, she laid a hand on my shoulder. After turning the burner off, she bent down to remove my glasses from my face. I sunk lower into the daybed's mattress.

"I don't know if you are growing a beard or if you are just to take up your razor," she remarked with a sigh.

"I didn't bother to shave, and I hadn't noticed the growth until I got a look at myself in the lobby mirror."

"Tell me I was right to come, Richard."

"You were right to come. And, you should come again under better circumstances. What would a poet say, 'Before the snow flies?'"

"You will be alright, Richard, won't you? Please call me tomorrow."

"Well, I won't go back to work. But with my do-nothing life, I had enough put by to be OK. I do not know what I will do, but I will be OK." I still wanted her to go. I had said far too much. Brooke had mercy. Saying she would go down to look for Bonnie in the fast-food place, Brooke left. Chester ran to me. I gently shook his big orange head. I pulled off my pants. I peeled off my putrid socks. A gentleman is a gentleman even in his shorts. All I wanted was to be alone. I had no use for brazen spiky headed Scottish lasses coming down from their highs to go off on me. I should have such highs. I don't need goodhearted school marms worrying about their kooky friends or me. No brothers, sisters-in-law, or nephews to visit or call me are required.

I thought of all my deadbeat clients. All those Noggins Heads and Pumpkin heads. Twenty years of excuses rattled my brain. Why couldn't they pay the bills? You know. They lost their jobs; they had a kid in the hospital. They were sick themselves. They had a hysterectomy. They had to provide for elderly parents. The constant refrain, "I was in the hospital." Some of them didn't even speak English or didn't want to speak English when they found out who was on the line. Oh, no you didn't, I wanted to shout.

But maybe some of them did. You could not look into the hearts of deadbeats. You wouldn't want to know what was in their hearts. It was our job to strain the money out and get the bill paid. I wanted to line them all up and float them up the river so I would never have to consider them again. Now their hearts were beating beneath the floor. I wouldn't go down on my knees to start scraping them up. You wouldn't want to look into their hearts, but maybe some of them did have a hysterectomy. Maybe they had been in a hospital or were supporting their dying parents. You didn't know their backstory. Most of them were crap, but here and there, for all you knew or cared to know, you might be harassing someone with a good heart but bad luck.

I got out of bed. I would never go back to that job again. I would write a memo to call Brooke to let her know I was OK even though I knew I would remember without it. The fog had lifted a bit. It was five o'clock, and it was getting dark already. I wouldn't want to do much right away. There wasn't anything I cared to do. As I lay back in bed, I grabbed the Damen Willem book and read on to the end.

Chapter Nineteen

Prayers and Rest

December 1, 1789

At last, in the distance, the city stood before me. I do not know if this is how the city on the hill is supposed to look, but I doubt it. I started picking up colorful shells and pebbles which sparked in the cold sunlight. I fantasized about collecting enough of these beauties, to purchase Manhattan Island from the Wilden and give it back to the Dutch. Father would be proud. I saw buildings two, even three stories high. I thought that if I blinked, the city might magically disappear at any moment. I felt like a kid of the morn of St. Nicholas with my head all filled up with wonder. The river, which could flow north or south, was moving downtown. Shoving the pebbles and shells into my pockets, I pushed on with vigor.

The island was long but not too broad. So many blocks. So many people. It would take an act of God to find one man in this vast crowd. It may be my hunger, but I thought of the harbor where Hobnail said all those delicious foods from 'round the world come in. Hoping I would not have to walk on into the darkness, I walked until I thought I could walk no more. The lower end of the island may have been twenty miles or more, but I trudged through the city as I had trudged through the country. After many a mile, I stopped to catch my breath and rest my feet.

By twilight, the grand dockside stood before my wondering eyes. How I wished my ship would come in. The water rushed by into the sea. The harbor smells the bulging warehouse where goods were taken in from all over the world to feed the appetites of the city dwellers filled up my senses though I had not a morsel left to eat. A thousand masts of the tall ships matched a thousand points of light and a thousand footfalls that echoed down the crooked streets. It was a magnificent sight. I wished that Josefien was standing here with me to witness this.

But besides my silly shells and pebbles, all I had was a dollar to my name. What a foolish man I must appear. My apples all consumed. As for the business at hand, a thousand footfalls to follow and not one of them may prove to be that of Ichabod Crane. I went into The Holly Man Tavern to see what my dollar might get me. I soon had some cold meat and a mug of beer before me. Just as I was about to take my first bite, I noticed a man sitting across from me. He thought me a curiosity of sort. When he asked me my business, so I told him straight out that I was looking for a man named Ichabod Crane.

"Oh, that is a different kind of name for you. No such man here. I think I have heard of such a one lying in the grave on the muddy island that sits across the river. Or, was it an Elias Stork I have in mind?" A man lying in a grave on a muddy isle made my heart shiver. I moved over to the fire to warm myself up. The fire was big and crackling, but it did not prevent me from shaking. A man sitting on a small stool in the corner asked me if I wanted to walk on "holy ground." Seeing the confusion cross my face, he clarified his words. "Do you need a woman to warm you up?" I refused his offer and made my way outside where the wind was blowing, and the snow was starting to fly.

Time was winging away. The hanging sign of the inn creaked above my head. Right here will be my starting point. I will walk in ever widening circles returning here to eat and rest. No matter how long it takes, I will search the faces of all who walk about the city and make my inquiries. My feet began making light tracks in the thin, but crunchy, layer of snow that was forming on the city streets. I was creating a labyrinth in sugar snow. Round and round I went. My head formed circles for my feet to walk but my feet fed my brain more circles whirled faster and faster about my head. My feet might have danced me into eternity had I not collapsed. There may have been a thousand points of light at the New York Harbor, but they all went out.

December 15

I begin each day with a prayer. I do my work at the Garden Street Church. I walk the streets selling songs sheets and posters to bring more people in for Sunday service.

Gerrit is the minister. He, and Rupert, the voorleezer (reader), are young men who find laughter in all they do. Ludolf, an old minister who should be ministering Uptown, is often here complaining and denouncing up a storm. No one or nothing that can please him. I did not give up my search for Ichabod, but I take a systematical approach by going to libraries and churches, places he might be expected to visit. Dominie Gerrit thinks that I might have a vocation for the church, but I do not know about that. It felt strange today to pick up my pen to write in my journal again.

Often I am immersed in a world of frenzied violence. The sound of Yankee Doodle fills the air as the clocks fight, the horses race, and the Negroes get flogged. It is a sad sight to see a man treated like a dog. I cannot bear to look into their eyes. I consider myself a lucky man to be up on my feet moving all about town.

I awoke in the dominie's bed two weeks ago. I overheard old Ludolf harp that, "Someone who was scraped off the sidewalk should not occupy the dominie's bed." Gerrit laughed, and said, "We may be entertaining an angel unawares." "Humpf!" was all Ludolf had to say.

Ichabod came for me in my dreams again. On my second day, I awoke in the middle of the night not knowing where I was. The schoolmaster and the Horseman were circling about the room. There was no way to lay my head. Ichabod hovered in a dark corner of the chamber crying out for his thwarted life and love. Gerrit, hearing me moan, cried out, "All is well." He got up in the dark to fetch a glass of water for me. He lit a candle and poured some sugar and water in a cup. "Drink this to put your fever out." I believe he sat on the bed watching over me until I slept.

December 16

This afternoon, as I shivered in the bed, a woman with her hair parted down the center with lovely ringlets circling her head came to me to feed me gruel. She had such a beatific smile I cannot tell if I imagined her or not. By the end of the day, I was embarrassed to be taking up this space in the dominie's bed. When I tried to get up, my head started swimming again. Every day I regained more vigor, so I came to sleep on the floor. It is a good thing to be inside.

December 17

Gerrit is outside raking the coals. Somewhere a bell is tolling though not in this church. Rupert is sitting at the table pen in hand. He is translating a book from French to English as I write my journal.

Gerrit came in blowing on his hands. He was happy to see Rupert writing away at lightning speed. "He saves me again and again. Rupert talks me out of my unbelief to bring me back to faith. He is a young, but very learned man, Damen. You could learn a lot from him. You might even become a man of God."

"How would I learn to be a minister? I have more questions than answers when it comes to faith."

"We have questions too, but we have books from Holland to answer them. I tutor Rupert, and he tutors me. Our church here in the new world was not too long ago but a little church in the wilderness. The Church of St. Nicholas Church, was no more than a stable, pieces of wood wishing to be stone. It was in Fort Amsterdam, but now this island is the center of the world, we keep moving uptown. Look at us. Our church has the steep roof of all those country churches in Europe with all the bells and whistles. Coats of arms of cloth and stain glass and lead decorate our sanctuary. Our ministering angel, that woman with the angelic smile entered the room to serve us water, cold chicken and thick slabs of bread.

"I can envision a church uptown as grand as a cathedral with towering bell towers," I cried.

Ludolf scowled. He was having none of it. Spearing a slice of chicken on his fork, he sneered.

"We are not a rock. We are laboring in a city, not unlike Sodom and Gomorrah. We are heading back to smoke and mirrors. Popery. You know what happens when you grow to grand? We will not live to see your church, Damen. All will fall!"

"Damen might live to see it," said Gerrit with kindness. Rupert joined in.

"A church like the one you imagine may appear uptown someday. From the start, we have been a reforming people. The new world made us more innovative. Our people came here with no documents. So much had been lost at sea. It was hard for an orderly organization to dispense with them, but we took people at their word and began again. Someday uptown a gothic building of strong stone as grand as Notre Dame will stand for all we know. On this rock I build . . . "

"If the whole city moves uptown, we should not," said Ludolf raising his voice. "We admitted families to church without records of baptism out of necessity, not innovation. We should stay put." There was thumping outside. Ludolf shuffled to the door.

"Heavens to Holland, man! They are stealing our coal. Go out and chase them away boy. Make yourself useful. Children, black men, and Wilden taking the coal! Probably the ones black as coal themselves. Get them away!" ordered Ludolf. He waved a large slab of bread at them. I stumbled outside in my shirt to find some raggedy children scooping up the hot coals in their hands. I had hardly the heart to give them a yell, so I flapped my arms about and off they ran. It sure was cold out there. I came back to the table to resume our conversation.

"We do the work of God. We are blazing a new path. We cross oceans. The whole world is watching. The sea will part for us. We even prevent evil, by scaring off freezing youngsters from stealing our coal," said Gerrit.

"Here, here," said Rupert approving, slapping him on the back. I laughed.

"We are not Moses. As for the children, they should knock on the door and ask for coal. Not that I would give it to them, but they could ask." cautioned Ludolf. "I do get carried away," said Gerrit with a sheepish look. Rupert put his arm around him. Ludolf stared at me.

"Gerrit you are as empty headed as that Megaplensis minister. He had eight wilden sleeping on his floor. You gave up your bed to this Dame here. If we did not keep a watch out, there would be a whole tribe inside the small room. We must start with the church. There are as many depraved souls within our churches as there are outside in the debauched city streets. We have preachers who are evil incarnate. One is no better than a buck goat in a barn filled with nannies. I say they must not sit down in the presence of the Lord."

"No place at the communion table, Ludolf? If every man looked within there would be no man without sin, and therefore by your logic, no man to sit at the communion table at all," challenged Gerrit.

Gerrit and Rupert were righteous men. Even Ludolf for all his dark views carefully collected the Sunday offerings and distributed them to the poor. They visited the sick to comfort them including prisoners down by the river. They were learned. They studied books. I do not know how they found time to pray. What would they think if they knew that a murderer was sleeping next to the dominie on the floor? They took me in not knowing who I was. I I was low, and I trust, not too weak in the head.

December 18

I was well enough to go out. It felt like months had gone by me. The crystal, crisp air stung my face. My gray skin scared people off, so they gave me a wide birth. I was still unsteady on my feet. As I stepped into the street to cross the road, I was almost run over by a cart. A man reached out to pull me back, then moved away from me as if he was afraid to touch me.

The sun hurt my eyes. The sound of a blacksmith pounding his hammer, the neighing of a horse, the screaming of a black man as he ran down an alley, shattered my ears. I was determined to make myself of use. With my song sheets and sermon posters tucked up under my arm, I set about to distribute them all over the city and to look for Ichabod as well. And so the days passed.

As I walked crossed Orchard Street where the trees had all withered, burnt and bent in the war, I heard a man spreading the news that a body had surfaced near Hell Gate. A man threw the contents of the chamber pot down from the window as I ducked into a doorway. I kept moving. On Mulberry Street, there was a grove. I could imagine the sweet fragrance Spring would bring. Flowers just for the asking. What was I thinking? Nothing was free in the city. Flowers would not come cheap. There was a burnt out mansion on Delancey Street but, as I later learned, no Mr. Delancy. Washington Square was swampy, but Fraunces Tavern stood proudly.

When I grew too cold to distribute my posters, I stopped at the Tall Cedar Tavern. I was hoping people inside might have some news about the body. What I discovered was hardened men talking of war. Like my father, they were living in the past. I willed myself not to look back. If I thought of my family now, the tears would flow. The men stopped their talk to take a gander at me.

"Have you been sleeping rough or something boy?" one asked. I did not think I looked too bad though I might have lost some weight and my eyes some luster. "Not since Valley Forge have we seen such a sorry sight. At least you are wearing some shoes." He unsteadied me. Looking down at my feet to check out if I was wearing shoes, I brushed myself off and smoothed back my hair. I did not look half as bad as they claimed.

"Do not forget yourself, Jacob. We may have been poorly clothed and barefoot as any orphan, but we fought with Geroge Washington. We did do not hold our manhood cheap as the bard says. You should show respect. Were you there man? No, you were not there. I did not think so." When he winked at me, my shoulders relaxed. Another fellow had a go at me saying I should go to the church where the Reverend Holy Mother would take care of me. "Mother looks after the body, but not so much the soul." I took it that they meant a bawdy house.

"That's more meant for a whoreson caterpillar such as yourself than a fine young man like this," said his companion. "Look here at Diebold who says he fought with George Washington. He must have been eight years old back in 1776."

"Might have been a drummer boy, though," another man allowed. A man with a large sheet of paper sat in a dark corner smoking a pipe. It seemed that every ugly sentiment had a benevolent one to counter it. With a piece of broken charcoal, he looked at me then began sketching. "Do not draw me," I protested.

It seemed that every man in the tavern looked up at me. I took a big gulp of ale. "Does anyone here know about the body found in the river," I ask emboldened. I did not want to answer questions about myself.

"You have something to do with that boy," asked the man in the corner. "Is that why you do not wish for me to draw your face?" A man at the back said nobody knows who drowned, but said he had witnessed the body come up. "All I can say is he sure was a tall man."

At that, I went a little bit off my head. "Take me to the Sheriff!" I heard lots of laughter. The tavern keeper came over. Discerning by my posters that I might have something to do with the Garden Street Church, he called upon an urchin to take me back there. As the tavern door slammed, the man who witnessed the fished up body, cried out, "He was a tall man but as fat as a hog. Hope that helps you, man.."

I was embarrassed to return to the church in such a state. A man can never be too sure of success in this world. Just when I had become a fit man on an earnest mission, I became a lost soul all over again. Gerrit felt my forehead to see if my fever had come back. "Something's burning up your head, Damen. Tell me. Have you a woman in your life?" He took me by the hand and led me to the table in the parlor.

"Yes, Gerrit. I am, or I was to be married this year."

"I am to be wed soon, myself. Oh, you should see the comely woman God has picked out for me. Rupert thinks I am bewitched because I have fallen hopelessly under her spell." Gerrit laughed.

"Do you expect to do well and prosper in your mission to serve NY?" I asked.

"I do not expect much. I would like a rent-free house, and a salary paid out I money, not in chickens or firewood. When the times comes to depart this world, I hope to have something to leave my wife and any children I might have. Do you expect to appear before your maker as a wealthy man Damen?"

"I have not thought much about that. I am content to work on my father's farm. There is a portion of land reserved for me where I am to live with my Josefien. My little brother Enoch will have a share too I reckon. I do not know how far I can go with that."

"So you do have a family. It seemed that you dropped out of heaven onto the streets of New York. Your family must miss you very much. Your absence may press on their spirits more than they can bear. A man must leave his mother to marry, but you have left the whole homestead to come up to New York. That is quite another matter. You must miss them very much. Your heart has not grown that rocky now."

"Stand up my soul and shake off thy fens," said Ludolf who was preparing tea. "It is a commandment that we love one another." As usual, he was listening in on our conversation.

"It is a commitment of the heart," added Gerrit.

"It is a commandment to love your neighbor as yourself. I think that Damen has love in his heart but that he is on a mission," said Rupert who entered the room bearing a stack of books.

Damen is not making much headway with the farm. I do not know what mission a farm boy has here in the city," Ludolf scoffed wrinkling up his brow.

I looked away. What does a man do to make things right again? I am the one who maintained that forgiveness could not be bought. I was the man who swore he could save his own soul, but I was making no more progress with my salvation than the farm. I had to ask for help.

"I come from a respectable family, but I am not a good man. In this land of liberty, it might be good to lock such a one away. There was a decent man up in Tarrytown; a Yankee schoolmaster come down to us from Connecticut. He was an itinerant teacher who only wanted a good meal to eat and a pretty woman to keep him happy. He came to the Van Tassel frolic hoping for a jolly old time. We went at him so hard; there was nothing left of him but his hat and –" Rupert interrupted me. His eyes were glowing. He could not wait to tell his tale of his own. Ludolf left the table to sweep the floor.

"Nothing left but a hat? We had a case like that right here in New York City. Oh! He was a big man, a bookkeeper, banker, a businessman, an emissary, even an attorney general. Tienhoven. Cornelius Van Tienhoven. He was a thief too who got himself indicted for embezzlement. His hat and cane turned up in the river. Though he owed so much money, they wrote him off the books as a dead man. Nobody was fooled, though."

"Oh, speak not to me of the dead." Rupert's words receded in the distance. As I reached out of a glass of water, I saw blood pouring off my hand. I shook it in the air.

"I said nobody was fooled. He wanted people to think he was dead to avoid his debts, Damen," said Rupert raising his voice.

"You speak of one case, but I speak of another, Rupert. My case may be the real thing. You might have a murderer sitting here at your table, and you do not know it."

"Our Lord had a killer sitting at the table with him. 'Have I not chosen you and one of you has a devil inside him.'" Rupert started to say, but Gerrit cut him off.

Ludolf stopped sweeping the doorway to listen in. Dead leaves were swirling in through the open door. "Oh, I hope his body does not turn up here because in that case, we will have to bury him. I have allotted out all our cash. Cost money to bury a body you know." The old man pulled at his pockets to assure me they were empty. He took up the broom to sweep as hard as he could.

"Not sure if I am following this. A man unlucky in love might have moved on to court another. As an itinerant schoolmaster, he might have moved on anyway. Tell me more about that night," said Gerrit shaking his head.

"Brom Bones, I mean Abraham Van Brunt, said we should ride out after midnight to chase the schoolmaster down as the festivities came to a close. Usually, it was Ichabod who held us spellbound with tales of the supernatural. In fact, I have one of his books about witchcraft in my satchel. That night Brom turned the tables by telling the legend of the Headless Horseman, a local Tarrytown spirit."

"Who is 'we'?" asked Rupert.

"Brom, Caleb, Hobnail and me. Brom told us to follow up behind him on foot rustling up the leaves and making moaning sounds. Brom's horse Daredevil just flew through the trees, but Ichabod's old farm horse, Gunpowder, got confused. A better animal might have gotten spooked, but Gunpowder started going around in mindless circles in a thicket of closely spaced trees. Ichabod's eyes bugged out of his head as he switched at him with his hand. Brom pulled his horse up behind a willow tree. He was stymied because he did not want Ichabod to get a close look at him. I cannot tell you how much he longed for the chase.

Riding back to me, he told me to take a branch and smack Gunpowder sharply on the rump to get him going. "As soon as the dumb brute moves, run to the bridge, then make yourself scarce," Brom hissed under his breath. I picked up a branch as large as a man's leg. I did not mean to throw it, but the limb flew out of my hand striking Gunpowder on his big behind. "Boo!" I hollered.

As horse and rider plunged through the trees to the road, I saw Brom throw a cape with a high collar over his shoulders. Something on his saddle was on fire. Keeping out of sight, I came upon Caleb who was chasing Hobnail with a large switch. 'I am the ghost of the schoolmaster Ichabod Crane coming to punish you for sins. If I spare the rod, I, er, well, you will never have any brains," he intoned in spectral tones. They ran off down the Post Road. 'Wait for me,' I called out, but they did not hear. Out of breath, I sat down on a tree stump near the Burying Ground.

"There was not a sound to be heard. Green gasses started to arise all around me. I half expected the dead to rise. Brom dismounted his horse round the back of the church. A shovel scraped the earth. I put my hands over my ears. My body shivered. A sudden wind came up. The large willow tree started swaying in the wind. Suddenly, Brom appeared on his horse. "Jump up, Damen!" he cried patting Daredevil's backside. Away we flew like the wind.

"I snuck back in my house in the middle of the night. I had hardly slept a wink when I heard Mama telling me it was time to get up. I was anxious to see Ichabod, but he did not come to school or church service. A crowd of people gathered where Gunpowder's saddle and Ichabod's hat, and the smashed pumpkin that had been found. There was no sign of the schoolmaster, himself, but folks did not seem overly concerned. "He will turn up," said the dominie. "Now come to church."

Oh, what have we done? I thought. My brain pressed in. If the schoolmaster lies unmourned in an unhallowed and unmarked grave somewhere, just hang me up on a tree like Judas of old."

Rupert's mouth was open in amazement. Ludolf sneered while Gerrit looked at a loss for words. Just then there was a loud knock on the door.

Chapter Twenty

Pink Footsteps in the Snow

Gerrit opened the door to reveal a man with a look of abject terror on his face. He or someone had torn up his clothes. His hair was standing on end, and his foot was scraping up the floor. The stranger slammed the door shut with all his might. "He is coming for me. He is right outside the door. I call upon you to call down the wrath of God upon his Godforsaken head," he pleaded. Wringing his hands, he threw himself to the floor. Rupert and Gerrit raised him up and sat him down in a chair. Ludolf took the candle from the table to light up his countenance. Black hair was clotted in strands of sweat, and his face, though youthful, was scored with deep lines in his forehead. I thought the sheriff had come to the door to capture me, but now I was caught up in this man's struggle.

"Who is at the door? Who is coming for you?" asked Gerrit. With rattling breath, the man stood up to grab hold of Gerrit's collar. "He's right there. He's pounding down the door. He is evil incarnate, and he has come to pollute your church." Ludolf and Rupert pulled him back down to the chair. He started ringing his hands again. "Act now!"

"Rupert, go see who is outside," said Gerrit kneeling down to hold the man's hand. As Rupert opened up the door, the man screamed, "For God's sake man. Do not let him in. Think what you are doing." I stepped outside with Rupert. There was no one there. Even the ones Ludolf always complained about, the street urchins, blacks, and wilden had gone home. Still, he found something to groused. "Close the door. You're letting the leaves inside."

"God has driven him back. The holiness of this place that has pushed the evil doer away. Do not be fooled. He lies in wait. Evil cannot be dispensed with so readily. If I step outside this door, he will dash me down to the flames of perdition," declared the Wildman going eyeball to eyeball with Ludolf to make his point.

"What is your name and where are you from?" asked Gerrit. The man said nothing. "Whatever you are called, I will see you home. No harm will come to you this night," said Gerrit as tenderly as if he was speaking to a child. Either the man was collapsing out of exhaustion, or he was absorbing Gerrit's deep sense of calm, but he was deflating in front of my eyes. It was a shell of a man who slumped to the floor.

"My name is Thomas Raeburn and I stay at Mulraney's boarding house on Broadway and Beaver Street," said the fallen man in a quiet voice. As Gerrit guided him to the door, he glanced around the parlor. "This is not a Catholic Church, is it?" he asked with a look of disappointment.

"No. It is God's house all the same," said Gerrit with a look of amusement. As Gerrit pulled on his coat, I said, "I will go with you." The temperature was dropping, and the snow was beginning to fall. We turned down Beaver Street just as a tavern brawl sprawled out into the street. Gerrit flinched as if to say, what has God gotten me into now? There was a lot of pushing and shoving. As the dominie tried to make peace, a man brutally heaved a small fellow into a brick wall. As my friend attempted to pull the man off, another started pulling on Gerrit, so I pulled on him. Then it all happened so quickly. A rotund man barreled out of the tavern to tear through the mob. I witnessed a small thrusting movement as he moved toward the man who was up against the wall. I saw a sharp blade plunge into the thick material of the coat. The man fell to the sidewalk gushing blood. The crowd stepped back.

A man bent down to cradle him in his arms. I saw a tear fall from his eye. Only the dead lies so still. The dominie knelt down in the snow to pray. Tom Raeburn seemed preternaturally calm. "Let us take him to the church," cried Gerrit.

"He is my brother. I will fetch up the cart to take him home," said the man who held him. The blood looked startlingly red against the white snow. Putting his hand upon the man's shoulder, Gerrit said, "Stay strong. I will come with you." The fellow shook him off. With that, we walked away. Tom Raeburn, walking with his head down, said in a quiet voice, "That was not the one." I took it that he meant his potential assailant. "I am just glad Ludolf will not complain about having to bury him," said Gerrit with a sheepish look. I wished that he had not said that, but I was happy that he did. Maybe he said it so Tom and I would not worry too much about the dead man. We walked Tom to the boarding house. A fat woman in a mob cap opened the door. It was Mrs. Mulraney who was happy to have Tom back. "Did you object to the cooking, Tom? You did not have to leave to make your point. Come inside to warm up," she brayed.

Then I saw him. As we doubled back, we saw that the brawling had started up again. The body had just been removed; the blood was mixing with the snow. Two men were squaring off with their fists raised up in the air. A circle of watchers gathered. A man's head was moving back and forth like a shuttlecock so as not to miss one bit of the action. He was standing on tippy toes. "Tis him, tis him!" I cried just as the mob started to surge. Gerrit pulled me halfway down the street away from the scene.

Breaking away from him, I ran back only to find the tall man who was Ichabod Crane, or who I had taken for Ichabod Crane, was nowhere in sight. All the men were fighting now. Teeth flew out into the snow as one man struck another on the chin. A bone crunching sound was made by a thug kicking someone in the shin. Blood flooded from a nose. "Come away Damen. There is nothing we can do." Grabbing the cloth of my sleeve with unnatural strength, Gerrit ran me down the street just as the mob broke into a frenzy. I pulled with all my strength to get loose.

"It was him. I just know it. Convincing Gerrit to walk back with me to the scene of the brawl, we turned on our heels yet again. The wind had died down The streets were silent. The fighting had ceased. Men were licking their wounds. But, the one I wanted to see was not there. I cannot figure out how Ichabod could have disappeared into thin, or I should say, snowy air like that. As the snow started coming down more heavily, the crowd dispersed. Soon there no one on Beaver Street. Just some footprints in the pink snow. It was time to go home. Gerrit tried to cheer me up.

"Let's walk to Cherry Street to see the president's mansion. It will be colder down by the river, but the mansion will be aglow with bright lights. They say the president is having a family portrait done by a renowned painter. "The dominie's infectious love of all things could not be denied. We headed toward the river.

We were let down. The mansion was dark. Everyone had gone to bed. There was a group of men gamboling about the street singing a Christmas tune. But that was about it. Thick snow flakes were covering their hats and coats, but they were too drunk to care. Gerrit brushed some snow off my jacket. I did the same for him. Back to the church we went.

Rupert and Ludolf were asleep. We lit a fire to thaw out our limbs. Gerrit was at peace. "The kingdom of Heaven is within you. You know Damen, we came to America to find God each one in our own way. We figured many of us could do without the indulgences, pilgrimages, and relics just the way we gave up burnt offerings at the altar. Have you heard how Ben Franklin keeps a self-improvement journal? Can you imagine him ticking off all the righteous things he does, and the evil he avoids, sitting at his desk in a bearskin cap? Oh, I seem to have lost you. Where ever did you go?"

"I am seeing a little boy at a pine table with his head bent to say grace, keeping one eye open to spy on his family. The wood is painted dark gray, but there are panels of orange. His father is saying grave things while his mother and siblings listen with patient care. Now his father is pouring thick buttermilk into a hole in the middle of the corn porridge. There is a vacant chair where a runaway boy who may never come home again waits."

"I knew your heart was not so rocky as to forget your family, Damen. Life itself is the pilgrimage, and you are running the wrong way." Brushing his hair off his forehead, Gerrit raised the candle to my face.

"It is a sad, broken world, Dominie where bad things happen to good people, where just when you are trying to mind your own business and do some good, you get swept up by the devil into mischief you cannot undo," I protested raising, then, lowering my voice.

"Gerrit rose up from the table candle in hand to trace a line with his foot across the floor. "On this side, the world is redeemed," he declared looking down at his feet. "But America is a big forest, Damen, and you might easily lose your way."

"The forest? What about the city? You could shout out for help at the top of your voice, and no one would hear. The throngs would press you down to a paste," I declared.

"No amount of congestion can crowd out God. God will hear. Yes, the devil desires us but God puts mileposts all along the way. If you think you are in the devil's hands, then you missed a few. Take this faith back to the woods with you, Damen. Do not leave it in the pew. Do not let howling sermons of belching smoke and forked flame stay in your mind and heart. Fill your heart with the love of others to do some good along your way. There is nothing more than that."

So we talked into the night.

December 19

This morning I took up my sermon posters and song sheets and hit the streets. I continued my search for Ichabod Crane. It was not as if no one had seen him. People were always saying he was just around the corner. There was no shortage of tall, thin men with bobbing heads and cloths that would rest still.

In following up their leads, I discovered a man at a school near Cherry Street who loved to wield the birch. In the library on Wall Street, I found a scholar studying Cotton Mather. In a tavern on Hester Street, a famed storyteller entertained crowds with tales of a man who fought on in the Revolutionary War even after he lost his head. None of the clues panned out. No of the men were Ichabod.

Or were they? Maybe Ichabod was an everyman. He could be every man who desired a woman and a sumptuous meal who would not settle for a small farm but wanted to be lord of the manor. As for the man in the crowd the night of the brawl, I never saw him again. One day as I neared the East River, it struck me that I would have to give up the search and accept the uncertainty. It may be that that is what it means to be a man. I sat down to watch the river. Ice was starting to form. Soon it might freeze. I reckoned that I would tell the dominie that I would be leaving before the new year began.

Tonight at dinner, I wanted to express how grateful I was for all the help I received at church. I wanted to include Rupert, even Ludolf. When Abigail served our meat, I remembered thinking her an angel. I suppose in some ways she is. I was not sure what to say, so it all came out a little awkwardly.

"When first I came, I was no better than a Wilden, Gerrit."

"A wiilden. Do not speak to me of wilden. Give them a Bible they go off to sell it for whiskey. They are bad as bears; they fornicate like bears. They gamble away my salary. A little knowledge for them makes for ruin. Garden snakes!" sneered Ludolf tamping down my gratitude toward him.

"Now, they do not fornicate with bears. It is true though that we do not handle them very well. They listen better to the Jesuits because they understand ritual," Rupert suggested.

Gerrit added, pointing to his chest, "There is something deep within. The wilden feel it. Hearing the holy word astounds them mostly because they measure it against the way we act. We preach that God loves us, that sin will cast us into everlasting flame, and then we murder, cheat, lie, and commit adultery. Sometimes I wish I was as good as a Wilden. Well, we are all no better than the native people.

When you consider a wilden whooping it up, brandishing a tomahawk above your head with the intent to scalp, your blood runs cold. You might think you have run into the

146

devil himself, but many a native has sat listening with utmost patience to our explanations of why we worship our Savior. They can be very curious about particulars. We bring Bibles, guns, and crucifixes, preach love and make war. They struggle, in earnest, to understand.

"I struggle to understand you Damen. I guess you will never find out what happened to your schoolmaster. You could back to the woods to dig where your big man wielded his shovel."

"I told Brom of my concerns about that spot. By now he may have removed whatever he buried to put me off the trail. I might give up the search, content to be a better man."

Rupert gave me a big smile. "I do believe you really do have a predilection for the cloth. You should study with us." Gerrit was not too keen on that.

"Damen must get back to his family. All roads lead not to Rome but God. He saw a headless monster walking like a man but Christ walked like a man, and as a man, he will go back. In the country, city and the town, God is a rare commodity, though his mercy is always at hand. We will miss you though Damen."

Growing embarrassed by all the attention, I shook each man's hand wishing them to prosper in their ministry to save men's souls in New York City. Ludolf added that "New York City which should be New Amsterdam." At that, I longed to be with Father. To Gerrit, I pleaded, "Remember me."

"I will remember you. Friendship does not fade," Gerrit assured me. Never was there such a church with a burning heart like this.

December 31

I waited for the stagecoach. Ludolf warned me not to pay more than four pence a mile, and I did not. I wanted to give some of the money I had earned to the church, but Gerrit said it was honest wages and that I should bring it home. Some folks complain that stage coach travel is hard what with all that jostling around the rough road but to me it was heaven. In passing all the places, I had tramped on wet foot and dry, I felt myself to be a privileged person. When I was but a few miles from my home, a rider bounded up to the coach to peer at me. It was Caleb.

"Damen! Tis you. Damen oh Damen, where have you been. You have returned. Have you heard that Mahalalel has gone missing! I thank God you have returned," he shouted while trying to reign in his plunging horse. My hand flew to my forehead. I groaned as I asked the driver to set me down.

"Do not worry Damen. He only got as far as the tavern near Milestone 27. He was wobbling a bit over the side of his horse, so the Hessian, Karlheinz Bach rode up to steady him. He was determined to get down to Manhattan, but Bach persuaded him to take rest in the Hobgoblin Inn. He has been crying in his beer over missing you for the last three hours. "I had a wife and three children, but now there are only two." When I left them, the Hessian had just about convinced Mahalalel to go home with him. Your father said he would if he could just have a little more ale to liven him up. You better watch out Damen. Karlheinz is tall handsome with bright blue eyes though his mouth looks cruel. You should not leave your sister or Josefien alone with him," hooted Caleb. I mounted onto the back of Caleb's horse.

Soon I stood before my door. It was just after midnight. The air was crisp and clear. There was The top of the door swung open. Mama with her mouth wide open in amazement to see me standing there. The tears turned to mirth.

"Bless the mark! You are the first foot, Damen," Mama said pulling me to her breast. "The Scotch say the first person over the threshold is called, 'first foot,' and that they must carry a gift to bring good luck." She was laughing and crying. Margreet and Nochie came out of their beds to see what the fuss was.

"I do not have a gift, but I do have a book about witches."

"I think that witchery book may bring back luck, Mama," cried Nochie.

"I have already found my luck. Damen is home."

Mama may have been overwhelmed to see me. Margreet was too, but she did not want her joy to show. Enoch had many complaints. As I took my place at Mama's table, Nochie moaned about how they almost did not celebrate St. Nicholas Day.

"'There will be no Sinterklass coming here when Damen is missing,'" Mama declared.

"I shouted 'Nooooooooooo,' so Mama made cookies in the shape of SinterKlass and windmills, and sugar candy horses, cows, pigs just to quiet me down."

"Did she make lemon-flavored white bread to give to the poor?"

"Yes, and we put carrots and hay in the wooden shoes and placed them near the hearth for St. Nicholas and his horse." Nochi's eyes were dancing with joy. "I did miss you Damen. I did. It is just that St. Nicholas brings such joy, I had to have some fun. He came over to give me a big hug. Margreet held my hand. I was gone for two months but embraced as if for twenty. Sleigh bells were ringing outside.

"I know that you did, and I did miss you too," I swore leaning over to kiss the top of his head. Just then the form of the tall Hessian, Karlheinz Bach filled the doorway. Father came safely home.

January 3

Today we had a party. The rag rug was rolled up. A fiddler. Hot coffee and gingerbread. We decorated with holly and ivy, bobbing for apples. Little Cuz came. "Everyone from apple-john to the Lord of Creation should come to see Damen who has come home," she teased. What she wanted most was to play blind man's' bluff. Father said the church should sound the bells and the cannon should boom for me as if I was George Washington

"I was very sad when you left Damen. I told Mama to make doot coekjes (cookies for the dead) big as silver dollars," said Father. Mother stood near the hearth laughing at him. "Damen, Father told everyone, 'I've got a wife and only two kids because one left with his head filled up bursting with goblin law. He would stamp his foot and lower his head.'" "Damen, I did stamp my foot and lower my head. I should not have said a gill of rum for everyman if my son returns because the men at the tavern will hold me to it now. Pointing to the painting of the four seasons on the wall, Father swore, "I told Mam you would be back before nature spins these seasons around. Tis by a Dutch artist of course, because you know the English cannot paint. Mama was always speaking of spring, with its skunk weed, pussy willows, and spring flowers."

Father seemed okay to me now. Scholar or fool was I to want to look up to a better man than Mahalalel. Caleb and Hobnail came in to sample the punch and join the dance. A large, burly man appeared at the door in a cape with a high collar. It looked like he did not have a head. Poking his big head up through the collar, rearing his broad shoulders back, he brushed his thick hair back to let out a roar. But it this was Brom, who was that other headless figure in the cape heading out the door? I was back where I belonged.

Extract from a letter dated October 22, 1809, from Damen Willem to Roos Steen (Little Cuz)

Today in Tarrytown we had a visitor who brought to mind memories of the past. Dominie Gerrit Michaelius stopped by en route to Kingston where he is to minister to a new church. He did not say why he left the one in New York City. I sincerely hope you recall the stories I told you about him many years ago long before you married Johannes Steen.

He joshed me in that familiar way saying he had heard so much about the great farm of one Damen Willem that he had to see for himself. He admired Josefien and our two superexcellent children, Anouk and Malkiel. I told him that Malkiel wants to become a man of God. Gerrit seemed pleased to hear that. Saying he had a wife and four children who would be joining him after he settled into his new parish, he declared himself a lucky man. Seating himself between Josefien and Anouk, who looks more like her mother every day, Gerrit announced, "I am a thorn amongst the roses." When Josefien brought him a mug of beer, he declared that it was drawn down from heaven by little angel brewers.

Then, as is his way, he grew serious. "I have thought of you from time to time throughout the years Damen. I always thought that the church, not God, mind you, had failed you, and that it was the words of the minister more than anything else that precipitated your flight. You did seem a good man, a kind of Adam expelled from Eden, your warm, loving home, to make your way in the world."

"The world rattled me, but some folks steadied me."

"There are some folks present in this world with no purpose than to upset the apple cart. Though it took arduous picking and tender care of trees to fill it up, folks who do little sowing come to reap. Your dominie may not have meant to tumble your apples off the cart and scat them down the road. Rather, he may have desired to smash and mash them into a sauce," said Gerrit.

I hope that you will think of this Roos when things in life do go as smoothly as you expect them to go. Gerrit inquired if Dominie Hunthum was still with us. I told him he had gone to his Redeemer. He was more curious about Ichabod than our latest Dominie. "Did you ever hear anything about your lost schoolmaster or the headless Hessian?"

"Yes," I said. All the time. There are so many stories abounding regarding the fate of Ichabod Crane that they could fill a book."

"Don't believe the half of it," admonished Gerrit. I told him had how good it felt to see him again.

Epilog

I, Richard Post, will have the last word. Reader, I did not marry her. I do continue to visit the Sleepy Hollow area where I visit with Brooke and Bonnie and an ever-widening circle of friends. I was not yet fit for romance though someday soon something may go into bloom. I suppose Brooke would come up with something about a warm June, but I am not sure of how that quote goes. The Hudson River Valley is a nice place to visit, but I prefer to live in New York City.

I did visit with my family in Florida that Christmas and was as avuncular as I could be. On a more somber note, I made a visit to Rosedale to talk to Teresa Sullivan, Diane's mother on a cold day in the new year. Though I was determined to stay calm, I no sooner got inside the door when I started to throw the blame around. I went on about feeling shut out of the emergency room the night that Diane overdosed, that I never understood about her addiction to painkillers which began after the car accident that injured her back, and that the whole Sullivan clan was in denial. I carried on about all the phone calls I made that no one returned but then I came to a sudden stop.

I owned up to being the one who shut the world down that terrible night. I admitted my phone calls stopped way too soon. I didn't try hard enough. Now, I said that if Teresa had not opened the door, I would have knocked it down. I regretted not calling in advance but was glad to be there. I said I loved Diane, though I could have known her better, and that due to whatever happened, that night, accidental overdose, or suicide, I would never get the chance. There was more anger in my voice than I intended and Teresa did turn away from me. I noticed she winced at the word "suicide."

I pushed harder. "Do you think Diane overdosed accidentally or on purpose?" Teresa's face went as rigid as the theater mask of sorrow. I know my words were hurting her, but I knew all too well the pain shutting people out could cause; that I would not allow.

In a crescendo of emotion, I shouted, "Do you think that this is easy for me to say? If Diane took her life, that I may be the one to blame? Do you realize that?"

"No daughter of mine would take her life, Richard. You sure did not know her if you think that. She was Catholic." Her eyes wandered to the Christmas tree which was still up. It was drying out. The branches were sagging. Going up behind her, I put my hand on her shoulder. She lowered her head. Turning to me with a tear in her eye which would not fall, Teresa said she the truth is she just did not know, and, perhaps, she never would. There wasn't much to say to that, so we held each other. A picture of Diane in a hand-colored frame made probably when she about five in kindergarten or first grade, rested on a frosted branch of the Christmas tree. We cried.

Made in the USA
Middletown, DE
04 July 2017